STEEL 7

A BODYGUARD REVERSE HAREM ROMANCE

STEPHANIE BROTHER

STEEL 7 Copyright © 2022 STEPHANIE BROTHER

All Rights Reserved. This book or any portion thereof may not be reproduced or used in any manner whatsoever without the express permission of the publisher except for the use of brief quotations in a book review.

This book is a work of fiction. Any resemblance to persons, living or dead, or places, events or locations is purely coincidental. The characters are all productions of the author's imagination.

Please note that this work is intended only for adults over the age of 18 and all characters represented as 18 or over.

ISBN: 9798796441411

# 1

LUNA

My hands shake as I fasten my seatbelt across my lap. Air travel is something relatively new to me, so everything from the odd smell of the air conditioning to the strange rushing sound of the engines fills me with unease. This isn't a normal commercial airliner. It's an extremely luxurious private jet that will be taking me to the city where I'll be kicking off the international leg of my world tour.

Berlin.

Since I signed with Blueday Records, my life has been unrecognizable. My story is a fairy-tale one. A girl who grew up in the care system gets spotted singing for money on a street corner. It's the kind of story that's featured in movies, but no one believes actually happens in real life.

I pinch the soft fleshy part of my hand between my thumb and forefinger, needing the little bite of pain to ground myself. Is it stupid that, after nine months of living this dream, I still need to pinch myself to make sure I'm not really asleep?

My head throbs from the stress that has swamped me today. Just packing my suitcase felt completely overwhelming. My stylist has handled all the gear I require for the shows, but I had to figure out what clothes I would need for all the parts in between: twenty countries, forty shows, and at least five different climates. I rub my temple and try to remember if I packed any nail clippers.

Ugh.

I'm pretty sure someone could go out and buy me some if I've forgotten.

My chest feels strangely hollow as my lack of freedom settles like a weighted blanket around my lungs. Gone are the days I could throw on my hoodie and head down to Walgreens to pick up cosmetics. Now I need a whole security operation to even walk from a limo to my hotel room. I need a suite that can accommodate seven burly ex-military bodyguards because my record company doesn't trust that I'm safe to sleep alone.

This is what fame has done to my life. It's taken a bundle of my old worries and replaced them with a bouquet of completely new ones.

Suddenly, money is no problem, but my safety is.

My phone lights up in my hand, and I swipe at the security screen to find a message from my brother Tyler. **Keep safe, baby girl**, he says. **Message when you get there**.

It's been a long time since he called me the pet name from our childhood. Things between us have been strained since Jake died, but maybe they can get better.

As the plane's engines growl louder, I feel lonelier than I have in years. Or maybe lonely is the wrong word. Alone would be better. I am surrounded by people, but no one touches me, not my body or my heart.

I'm like a queen bee, surrounded by workers. I'm the

reason all these men have jobs.

Connor is the last to take a seat, having completed whatever checks he felt needed to be done. Who knows what he sees and what he knows? As the boss of the security company assigned to take care of me, all the responsibility for my safety ultimately rests on his broad, muscular shoulders.

Yes, he has the backing of his team. The other Steel 7 bodyguards are all as fierce as he is, but Connor is the one who reports to the senior executives at Blueday. He's the one whose head would roll if I got hurt, or worse.

He secures his belt around his narrow waist, tugging at the sleeves of his impeccably cut black suit jacket. Everything about him is precise, from the brisk way he checks the time on his large silver-faced watch to the shine on his shoes. I wonder if he makes his bed with military corners, the sheets tucked so tightly you can bounce a coin.

I wonder if he ever makes a mess and doesn't bother to clean it up.

His piercing green eyes choose that moment to flick to mine, and a rush of heat floods my cheeks.

Connor is gorgeous because of his meticulousness. The comb lines are still visible in his hair, and his strong jaw is shaven so closely I bet it'd feel totally smooth to the touch.

And those eyes are as clear as the marbles that Jake and I used to play with as kids. Clear and bright but somehow deep as sinkholes.

I have no idea what he thinks of me.

Brat, probably. I'm twenty-one, but I'm the size of an eleven-year-old. There's definitely over a foot of height separating us, and however much of a woman I might be in my curves, being so petite definitely puts me at a disadvantage.

But sitting down, we're almost eye to eye.

"Is everything okay, Miss Evans?" The deep gravel of his voice vibrates between my legs as real as if he moaned against my skin.

Biting the inside of my cheek, I nod curtly. I need to stop having sex thoughts about the men assigned to keep me safe. They are professionals first and foremost. They're all at least ten years older than me and have seen the world already. Even if they weren't employed to watch over me, there's no way they'd be interested in someone like me.

I gaze around the plane, taking in Elijah's messy brown curls and Jax's perfectly crooked nose. Asher and Hudson are deep in conversation. Hudson's the taller of the two, with long legs that stretch into the space in front of him. Asher's blond hair reflects glints of the sunshine from the window, giving him an ethereal air that doesn't fit with the thick biceps straining at the fabric of his shirt. Ben shifts the leg that I've worked out is only part his own, as though the prosthetic he's wearing is causing him pain. Lastly, my eyes trail to Mo, the most mysterious of the Steel 7 bodyguards, only to find that he's looking directly at me. His obsidian black eyes send a jolt of something through me that feels slick like fear but tickles like arousal. In my chest, my heart skitters like a mouse, and I suck in a quick breath, shivering.

Either the pilot has turned up the air-conditioning, or my body temperature is affected by my nerves.

Without a word, Connor unfastens his belt and reaches to open a cupboard to his right side, retrieving a soft gray blanket that he passes to me. That's Connor all over. Observant to a fault.

"Thanks," I whisper, pulling its warmth over myself. The fabric rasps against my gooseflesh, and I close my eyes as a sense of safety washes over me.

The intercom clicks and crackles, then the voice of the pilot rings out. "We'll be heading on over to the runway in a minute or so. The weather in Berlin is rainy, so I hope you brought your umbrellas."

Shit. That's another thing I forgot to pack.

My phone buzzes on my lap under the blanket, and I reach into the warm space to retrieve it.

I'm expecting it to be Tyler again. Or maybe Jordy, my best friend from high school, whom I have somehow managed to cling onto through everything crazy that has happened in my life.

Except it isn't Tyler or Jordy.

It's another psycho piece of shit sending me an image that I wish I could immediately erase from my mind. The phone slips from my hand and clatters onto the floor, attracting the immediate attention of everyone on the plane. Connor has scooped it up before I can say anything, staring down at the still-visible image of a piece of a stalker's anatomy that should never be revealed to another soul.

"For fuck's sake," he growls. His eyes close as though he's trying to trap his bubbling fury inside himself.

"They just don't stop," I say, the tears burning behind my eyes and constricting my throat.

"They will," he says, his forest eyes dark and cold with fury. "They will because we'll make them."

2

CONNOR

The plane touches down in Berlin during a rainstorm, which isn't ideal. Luna isn't a seasoned flier, so the additional turbulence has her grasping the seat arms until her knuckles are white and her long red nails almost pierce the fabric.

Airport security is tight, but I'm still worried about getting her out of here in one piece. I wish I knew why she has attracted so many crazies in such a short time but trying to work out the darker side of the world is pointless.

It exists, so we do too. The good guys. The men who put their lives on the line to protect the innocent and make the world a better place.

My crew is all connected by earpieces that are tiny enough not to cause us issues or draw too much attention. I press the button hidden behind my lapel and murmur the instructions I want them to follow so Luna doesn't have to hear all the details. She's stressed out enough as it is and keeping the boring security plans as far away from her as possible is all I can do to try and help her relax.

Luna needs to know that we've got her back, but she doesn't need to know how much effort we're putting in to keep her safe.

One of the reasons that Blueday Records chose us for this tour is that we have a reputation for security that seems effortless to the client. They know how volatile Luna can be. She's a tiny thing, but her personality is fiery. I've seen how quick she is to anger, but also how vulnerable she is underneath the surface.

She has that rare quality of a woman who seems so much larger than she actually is, as though her aura casts a wide glow around her petite frame.

Maybe it's her aura, her special quality, that has all the psychos across the world drawn to her like moths to a flame.

Or maybe it's just the way she looks.

I try not to notice her soft skin or her eyes that switch between shining like bright, hard emeralds and glowing softly like spring growth on the most delicate plant. I try not to let my eyes scan the curves that her clothes do nothing to conceal. I know that's part of the record company's plan. They play up her innocence but lace it with sex too.

I have to keep my mind away from her delicate collarbone and the narrowness of her waist, even though when I'm alone in the dark my hand and my cock have other ideas.

I shake my head as I stand, glancing at the girl I'm being paid to care for as she unclips her seatbelt and reaches for her purse.

"Just give us a moment," I say softly. Luna nods, her long lashes lowering as though she's growing tired of never being able to do anything in a straightforward way.

The perils of celebrity.

Some people get used to it, and others just can't take it.

The airline staff are in contact with personnel on the ground. Somewhere out there the limousine for Luna and the accompanying vehicles are waiting. All we have to do is get her safely from point A to point B.

It should be easy, but I never underestimate a single part of my job. I never underestimate how bad people can be because I know the truth from my own life. When a person experiences violence as a child, there can never be any innocence for them about the horrors of the world. I rub my hand over my shoulder, where my scars are the worst. Those fuckers left me with damage, but no one has gotten close since.

Pain can provide us with valuable lessons.

I use my lessons so that no one in my care ever experiences the kind of pain that scarred me.

Mo is the first by the door. His jet-black eyes find mine and a quick nod tells me he's ready. Instinct drives him to check his firearm, but local law prevents us from carrying any weapons while we are here. None of us will have anything other than our extensive physical combat training.

It's not our first time traveling to Berlin or being in an environment where we don't have guns at our disposal. It will be Luna's first time being anywhere without firearms protection since her fame has drawn the wrong kind of attention. I hope it doesn't worry her. I've been careful not to mention it in front of her.

I grab the large umbrella that I carry everywhere. It ensures that my client is always dry and that I have a weapon hidden in plain sight. I know it sounds very James Bond, but I have had this particular umbrella crafted with an exceptionally strong steel pole and a very pointed tip.

Half of my team leaves the plane first, then Luna and

me, then the rest. We make quick work of the VIP security area and then hustle her into the waiting limousine. Ben does all the vehicle checks. I know he's the most meticulous because of what happened to him in Iraq. Pain left its mark on him too.

Elijah and I ride with Luna. Mo sits next to the driver. The rest of the crew ride in an SUV behind our vehicle.

As we take our seats, Luna reaches for a crystal glass from the bar and pours herself two inches of whisky. My eyebrow shoots up, but I don't say anything. It's not my place to question the client, no matter how much I want to.

As she raises the glass to her lips, her green eyes meet mine.

There's a challenge there in their emerald depths.

She wants me to tell her that she shouldn't. She wants me to question her judgment so she can push back.

I know this girl.

"You want some?" she asks, knowing full well that I won't drink on the job.

"I'm Irish," I say. "We drink that for breakfast. But not while I'm working."

"Alcohol is the work of the devil," Mo says from the front.

"Hell must be one big party." Luna takes a long swig of the amber-colored liquid but can't quite swallow it all.

"If you keep knocking on the devil's door, at some point he's going to open up." Elijah is staring out of the window, his arm resting along the window ledge as though he's relaxed, but I can tell from the way his fingers are twitching that he's not. When he starts delving into bible stuff, things aren't good. He joined the military to escape the cult he grew up in. The thing is, you can leave your past behind, but it's still curled up inside you in one way or another.

"Isn't that the point of knocking on any door?" Luna says, finishing her drink and slamming the glass down a little too loudly. "You know you guys aren't exactly making this limo ride fun."

"Fun is Connor's middle name," Mo says.

"No, it's not, it's Patrick," Luna says.

Elijah's head whips around, and he raises an eyebrow. "How'd you know that?"

"I've read your profiles." Luna shifts, crossing her leg and leaning back so that her arm is resting across the top of the seat. "You don't think I'd agree to travel the world with men I knew nothing about."

"Very thorough," I say, nodding. Most celebrities aren't interested in their staff. They leave the boring stuff to people they employ. But not Luna.

"What did our profiles tell you?" Mo asks.

"That you're qualified," Luna says.

"Qualified?" Elijah shifts a little, turning his body, so he's perfectly aligned with the girl trying to push all our buttons. "Qualified for what?"

"To keep me safe. To keep each other safe. Maybe to make this tour less boring for me."

"Why do you think it's going to be boring?" I ask.

Luna shrugs, crossing her legs and sliding her hand over her thigh. My mind drifts to follow her actions, distracting me from what I should actually be doing—looking around. Making sure I'm fully focused on the job at hand. "Everything's boring if you don't have someone to share it with," she says. "I grew up with two brothers…I'm used to the company of men."

I met her brother Tyler when she visited to say goodbye. Her other brother Jake died four years ago. They argued about that in front of me, and I felt sorry for Tyler. He seemed broken by Luna's blame, but I think they figured things out. I hope they did. We all need family if they're good people.

"Well, now you have seven brothers," Mo says from the front.

"Seven brothers." Luna's eyes drift over Elijah and me, and then she turns to take in what she can see of Mo's profile. Something about her languid movements makes me think she's not on board with the brother idea. "How did your girlfriends take the news that you're going to be away for so long?"

"None of us are dating," Elijah says. "It's easier that way. No distractions. No ties to home."

"No sex," Luna says.

"No trouble," Mo adds from the front.

"No fun," Luna quips. Her fingers trail over her long hair, hair that I've imagined sliding my own hand through or gripping firmly at the nape.

"We're not here to have fun." Elijah nods just once to punctuate his statement. "We're here to stop you from getting kidnapped or hurt by one of these fucking crazy pieces of shit."

I hold my hand up to stop him. He's said enough.

Keeping the crazies from the door is our job. Keeping it all away from Luna is also our job.

Luna's pretty complexion seems to pale a shade. "All work and no play…" she says, but I can tell from her tone that Elijah has rattled her confidence.

When we arrive at the hotel, I'm relieved to see that Luna's location hasn't been compromised. There aren't any screaming fans outside or hotel security trying their best to maintain the flow of guests through the revolving door. It won't stay that way for long, but for now, we can enjoy the unusual peace.

Luna's prepared, and she pulls her sunglasses from her purse, sliding them on to obscure her beautiful face. They're tinted enough to make it hard for her to see in the dark, but she has us to steer her.

Mo and the rest of the team are on the sidewalk first, and when they're content that everything's safe, Mo opens the door. I let Elijah exit first, then Luna, and lastly me. We crowd around her so that not an inch of her small frame is visible. By the time we're inside, Ben has the keycard to the penthouse suite, where we'll be staying for three nights.

Luna has a day to acclimatize and practice and then two days of shows.

The elevator speeds to the top floor, and my ears pop as the doors open. The hotel's VIP manager is waiting at the door. She's expecting to show Luna around, but my team stroll past, taking time to scan the room for anything untoward. Ben uses the black box I call his magic machine to scan for cameras and listening equipment. This is a good hotel, but who knows who's stayed in this room before us. Even good hotels can have staff who'll accept bribes for access.

"This looks great," Luna says vaguely, placing her purse on the console by the door. The suite has four bedrooms and an open-plan seating and dining area at the center—enough space for us all to keep close.

The hotel VIP manager begins her spiel about the room and all of its facilities, but Luna isn't listening. She's drifting across to the floor-to-ceiling windows, gazing out at the city beneath.

I know this is the first time she's seen a place that isn't home. Berlin is so different from the small town where Luna grew up. I wish we had time to look around. I could show her some cool places and open her eyes to this new world she's being thrust into. But that isn't my job.

"Just let me know if you need anything at all. I'll leave

my card by the door."

"Thank you," I say, showing the disappointed manager out.

As soon as the door clicks shut, Luna throws her coat over the nearest couch. "So what do people eat in this place?" she asks, flopping into a bottle-green velvet armchair.

"You ever tried a German sausage?" Jax asks.

"Not that I know of." Luna winks, and Jax snorts.

"Well, now's the time," he says.

Goodness knows what room service thinks of our order: eight German sausage hotdogs and eight pints of German beer. While we're waiting, the porter appears with our luggage, and Luna disappears into her room.

I'm staying with Mo and Jax, Asher and Ben are together, and Hudson and Elijah will take the last room. We remove our jackets, loosen our ties, and unbutton our shirts. By the time the food arrives, Luna has reappeared, dressed in a Snoopy shirt and shorts set with her long brown hair hanging loose around her shoulders.

I know I'm not the only one who stares for a little too long. We've been protecting Luna for a few weeks but never like this.

It's like she peeled away the armor she wears for the world and revealed the person she really is underneath. Dressed like this she seems cute and soft, vulnerable even. Her green eyes meet mine, and I can feel the heat of blood across my cheeks. She caught me staring. Big mistake.

"Connor, get over here," Jax says, as a server arriving with our food pushes a huge cart into the room. Behind him, two other servers are carrying heavy trays of drinks. Everything is set up on the huge walnut dining table, plates covered by silver cloches placed at each setting.

We all take seats, leaving space for Luna at the head of the table. I take the other end, so we're facing each other like husband and wife in a British palace, about to tuck into a banquet. The whole setup seems very upscale until we lift the cloches and reveal our ridiculous-looking hot dogs. Luna leans over, inhaling the scent of cured meat.

"It smells good," she says, picking it up tentatively. We all watch as she lifts the hot dog to her lips, wrapping them around the thick sausage. My dick stirs between my legs like a creature waking from a long sleep. Damn, Luna has a pretty mouth. I know it would feel hot and smooth wrapped around my cock.

When she bites, Jax clears his throat. Our eyes meet, and he winks, letting me know that I'm not the only pervert sitting at this expensive walnut dining table.

"Mmmm..." she moans, chewing slowly and rolling her eyes.

Mo has taken a bite of his vegetarian hotdog, nodding his head in appreciation. The rest of us follow, mostly out of hunger, but I'm pretty sure that all the men at this table are having impure thoughts about Luna right now and are hunting for distraction.

She rests the hotdog on her plate and takes a long drink of the cold German beer. She's only just legal back home, but in Germany, the legal drinking age is much lower. "Is this the kind of meal you treat your girlfriends to?" she asks. There's a glint in her pretty eyes and, as she dabs her lips, I catch a hint of a smile that she seems to want to conceal.

"Yep," Jax says. "If I girl can tackle a hotdog or a burger, she's my kind of girl."

"No one likes a salad eater," Hudson says. "Always picking at leaves and looking hungrily at my real food."

"A woman should eat," Mo murmurs. "She needs to be strong to make a family."

"Women aren't just breeding machines," Luna says.

"That isn't what I meant." Mo glances at me as though

he's seeking permission to talk openly. I give a nod, trusting that he'll keep things appropriate. "What I meant is that it's important that a woman looks after herself so that life doesn't take too much from her. It's the same as for men. If we don't eat enough and we don't train, our muscles waste away."

"Well, that is something we definitely don't want. I'm trusting all those big, bulging muscles to keep me in one piece," she says, her eyes drifting over the bodies of all the men at the table. There isn't a man among us that hasn't trained long and hard for our physiques. It's not just about appearance. In our roles, we have to be fit and strong enough to take on anyone who might pose a threat. We've all seen combat in one form or another. It's left its mark on more than one of us, but that doesn't mean we've lost our power, more that we've learned our limitations.

"You don't need to worry about that," Asher says. His blond hair flops down as he keeps his eyes low. He's a good-looking kid who should have more confidence around women. "We've got you, and while we do, nothing is going to touch you."

Touch.

My hands tingle at just the thought of the silkiness of Luna's chestnut hair running across them, or the softness of her skin. But it can't happen. I curl my hands into fists as if to send a message to my brain that there can be no tenderness with this woman. My job is protection, and that's where it ends.

We all eat and talk about our experiences of being in Germany. I'm not the only one who's spent time here, and listening to tales of German nightclubs, sightseeing, and women has Luna laughing and me relaxing.

And when we're done, we all head to our beds to rest so we're ready for an early start.

As Luna passes through the doorway to her room, she turns, her eyes finding mine as she slowly closes the door, and damn if I don't want to follow her to her bed more than I've ever wanted anything in my whole goddamned life.

3

JAX

This bedroom was designed to fit two queen-size beds, but the hotel has accommodated a third one without any trouble.

In fact, I'm sure that this room has the square footage of my whole apartment back home. The finishes are luxurious, and as I slump onto my bed, I moan with approval. It's like resting on a cloud.

I was the last to shower, so Mo and Connor are already in bed. I was expecting them to be asleep, but they're both staring at their phones.

"This place is something else, isn't it?"

Mo's eyes sweep the room as though he's taking it in for the first time. "I don't like that there are places like this in the world when so many people don't have a safe place to sleep."

"The world is fucked up, man, but that doesn't mean I'm not going to enjoy every minute of sleeping in this bed."

"It's definitely more comfortable than a bunk," Connor says without looking up.

"It'd be even more comfortable with a woman next to me." I turn onto my side, letting the soft pillow cradle my head. Connor's lamp is still on, casting the room in a muted yellow glow, highlighting the wall paneling and extravagant walnut furniture and gilded picture frames.

Mo snorts, placing his phone on the nightstand. "Always with the women."

"Women make the world go round, my friend."

He purses his lips and nods. "This job – being a bodyguard – isn't good for relationships. We're away too much. Always in a different time zone."

"Too much other temptation," I say.

"Temptation?" Connor lowers his phone and cocks his head.

"Don't play the innocent with me. I've seen the way you look at Luna. You'd break that girl in two if you ever got her where you want her."

"Fuck off," he says. "Don't talk crazy."

"I know what I see." I place my hands behind my head, staring up at the blemish-free white ceiling. I wish mine back home was as perfect, but rented accommodation is always far from perfect. "I know what I think."

"You think about Luna?" Mo straightens, his pebble black eyes narrowing at me. He's a good guy, but I keep trying to tell him he doesn't have to take everything so seriously. But what the fuck do I know? He's grown up in a place so different and lived through things that even I would struggle to imagine.

"And you don't?"

"You shouldn't," Mo says. "You start thinking about her that way, and your mind won't be on the job."

"Amen," Connor says.

"Don't go getting all religious on me. Out of all of us, you definitely have the biggest hard-on for her."

Connor stares at me, his green eyes narrowing, then he exhales, and I can immediately see how much my insinuations are burdening him. "Regardless of what I might be thinking, this stays professional."

"Of course. We have a job to do. I know that."

"But?" Connor knows me so well.

"There'll come a time where we won't be her bodyguards. This tour won't go on forever, and maybe the crazies will calm down once she's more established."

"Sounds like you have it all planned out." Mo nods knowingly, reminding me of a wise owl.

"NO!" Connor says abruptly, louder than I think he intended. He glances at the door, his brow furrowed. Is he worrying that Luna might have heard?

"No, none of us should be thinking that way, or no, I shouldn't be thinking that way?" I ask.

"None of us," Connor says more calmly.

"But you are…aren't you?"

Connor's nostrils flare he expels a rush of air like a pissed-off bull. He blinks slowly, seeming weary of this conversation, or maybe the burden of having to keep everyone around him in check. "What I think is my business. All you have to know is that Luna is off-limits. That's it. Keep your head in the game, and if you have to get her out of your system, then jerk off in the shower."

"If you're going to do that, make sure you clean the shower after," Mo says, his face screwing up with disgust.

"What? You don't jerk off in the shower?" I ask him.

"This isn't a conversation I'm going to have with you, Jax." He slides down the bed and rolls onto his side so that his back is toward me.

"Mo's right. We need to get some sleep. Hudson's

keeping watch tonight, so we'll be one down tomorrow. Just focus on the job, Jax."

"I always do," I say as Connor flicks off the light.

I'm the last to fall asleep. I've never found it easy to rest. Maybe it's because when I was a kid, I always had to keep one ear open to potential dangers. Not all foster care is shitty; I had a few nice homes over the years, but in between those, I had some that shouldn't have been allowed to care for dogs, let alone children. I'm not alone in having a difficult past. Connor's mom was an alcoholic, and her boyfriends were a long string of assholes with fiery tempers and fists that liked to rain down on a kid who couldn't fight back. Mo probably had the best upbringing of us all. A loving family. A father who's a doctor and a mother who spent all her time doling out affection and caring for her family. His hardships came from outside the four walls of his home.

Maybe they've both just found a way to bottle up all their demons, where mine seem to come to the fore the minute I lay my head on the pillow.

I toss and turn for around thirty minutes, feeling the building frustration of insomnia. Usually, when I'm at home, I get up and wander around my apartment. I put on the TV and make myself a cup of cocoa like an old man who needs to warm his bones. I wait until I'm exhausted, and then I try to sleep again. Sometimes it works. Sometimes it doesn't. I guess over the years I've gotten better at managing on a few hours than most people.

Sliding out of bed, I creep to the door and open it as quietly as I can. In the huge open lounge area, Hudson is sitting in the corner of the large white couch; his eyes are focused on the widescreen television playing softly. He's up and alert as soon as I come into view. At six-foot-four, he's an imposing figure.

"Fuck, Jax. What the hell are you doing wandering

around?" He slumps back on the couch, running his hands through his messy brown hair.

"Sleep is a fickle bitch," I say.

"I could sleep for a week." His light-brown eyes are rimmed with red, a sure sign that he's tired.

"We could swap shifts," I say.

Hudson shakes his head. "You know what Connor's like about us deviating from his plans. It's not worth the aggravation.

"True."

"You got something on your mind?"

I flop onto the couch next to him, grabbing one of the fancy pillows and hugging it against me. "Angels and demons," I say, winking and grinning. I try never to dwell anywhere too serious for too long. It's easy for negativity to drag me down, and down is a place I never want to go back to.

Hudson's hand drifts to his heart, and I know immediately where his thoughts have gone. Ever since he had the tattoo of his twin's name inked there, he touches it whenever he remembers him. "Fuck the demons," he growls.

"Fuck the demons," I repeat.

"But tell me more about the angel."

I wiggle my eyebrows and run my hands across the rough beard I've recently grown. "She looks like an angel and sings like an angel, but I'm pretty sure she's got a darker side too."

"Luna?"

"Bingo."

"She's fire and ice, that girl," Hudson says.

"That's a good description."

"Those eyes."

"Those lips."

"Those tits."

Hudson snorts. "You craving pussy?"

"Like a fucking addict." I shake my head as my cock stirs between my legs.

"I hear you."

"I just hope that this tour flies by and we get moved off this contract."

"And then what? You're going to ask a superstar out for a date at that dive bar you love to hang out at."

"Nothing wrong with Hannagan's. They serve good beer and great food."

"Your standards for both need raising." Hudson snorts, probably remembering the last time we hung out together there. He picked at his burger like it contained rat meat.

"Who wants a girl who can't rough it every now and again?"

"Does Luna look like she's used to roughing it?" Hudson lowers the audio on the TV and shuffles in his seat until he's facing me. I guess the conversation's drawn his full attention.

"Oh, she's used to roughing it. Didn't you read that article about her? She has more foster homes in her past than I have in mine. And parents who are fucking useless too."

"Oh, so you're going to be kindred spirits…"

"That's not what I'm saying. I'm saying she knows. She gets it. There won't need to be any explaining. And she's hotter than hell."

Hudson nods, his brow raising as he casts his mind across the mental images of Luna that he's gathered. "What makes you think she wants to slum it again, Jax? Now she's climbed to the top of the pile, she could have the pick of any man. Shit, most celebrities end up marrying another celebrity. She might have grown up in your world, but she's so far out of it now."

"I don't think she's that kind of girl," I say. "I think she's got her feet firmly on the ground."

"Regardless, she's off-limits, okay?"

"Now you're starting to sound like Connor."

Hudson tosses a pillow at me, accompanied by a grin. "Connor's my brother by another mother, but there's no way I'm as serious as that dude."

"It's okay. I get what you guys are saying, but…"

"No buts, Jax."

"Do you remember when we took Luna to visit her brother's house?"

"Yeah. I didn't go inside, though. What was it like?"

"Cool. There were six dudes living together and one girl."

"I saw that girl. The one in the skimpy pajamas."

"You know that they're all living together. Six dudes and one girl?"

"Living together like housemates?" I shake my head, and Hudson's eyes bulge. "Shit…is that even a thing? I mean, I know there are men out there who want multiple wives. It's a cultural thing. But are there dudes who want just one wife?"

"I guess there are. I overheard Connor discussing it with the label. They're worried it might get out and cause Luna publicity issues."

Hudson rubs his stubbly chin, nodding his head. "That could be bad."

I throw my arms along the back of the couch, watching on the silent TV as police arrest a wanted felon. Damn, the news never shows anything positive. "You ever thought about what it will be like when we all get girlfriends, and those girlfriends turn into wives?"

"And those wives breed spawn." He grins, showing his pearly white teeth.

"Exactly. I mean, can you imagine us with families? Will we meet up at the weekend for barbecues? How will it work?"

"How the fuck should I know? To be honest, I don't hold out much hope. Maybe we're all too battered in one way or another to find the perfect relationship. All of us have made our fair share of terrible decisions when it comes to life and women."

I nod, my mind trawling through all the bad experiences we've had. There have been more than a few manipulators, and they are the worst. Constantly trying to isolate you from your family and friends and always trying to turn you to their way of thinking or using sex as a weapon.

"We need to get better at those decisions," I say. "There is no way I want to end these years I've spent with you guys falling out over some chick."

"I hate the phrase, but bros before hos." Hudson grimaces, but I totally get what he's saying. The problem is that men are so driven by their physical urges that bros often get left behind. It's not until you're deep in the shit that you realize what you've lost.

"You think Luna would be up for the same kind of lifestyle as her brother?"

Hudson begins to laugh, the effort to suppress the volume forcing him to curl over and bite his fist. I shake my head and roll my eyes, pissed that he's not taking me more seriously. I guess I'm asking for too much, bearing in mind I spend most of my time trying to be humorous. "Fuck, no," he eventually mutters, then starts laughing all over again.

"Why the hell not? It's in her family."

"There's a lot that's in all of our families that none of us want to replicate," he says.

"It would give her the ultimate level of security."

"And the ultimate negative exposure when it comes to the press. There's no way she would keep her success living that kind of alternative lifestyle."

Maybe he's right. Maybe I'm mentally stumbling down a path that has thorny bushes on both sides. The thing is, I want her. I want her as much as I wanted the red remote-control car that Santa never brought me when I was a kid. I want her as much as I wanted to escape from my life when I joined the military. I want her as much as I wanted to survive the battles I've endured overseas.

If Hudson's right, I don't stand a chance.

But I learned early on that having a positive frame of mind can open doors.

I just hope that Luna's door is one of them.

4

LUNA

This hotel room is ridiculous. It's so large that when I forget my phone in the bathroom, it feels like too much effort to go get it. It's only when I hear another message vibrating against the counter that I drag my lazy ass out of the princess-worthy bed so I can see who wants my attention.

The familiar dread rises inside me. Whenever I get an unsolicited message, I block the number, but these assholes keep finding new phones or switching SIM cards because it doesn't seem to stop them from getting through again. I swipe to open the screen, and a whoosh of breath passes through my lips when I see Jordy's name; my best friend whose been with me through the best of times and the worst. Mainly the worst. Thank God it's not another gross dick pic.

Are you there? What's it like?

She has a copy of my itinerary, mostly, so she understands the different time zones and when I'm performing. I don't want her to think I'm ignoring her when I'm probably on a plane or shaking my ass on a stage somewhere.

I'm here, and it's ridiculous.

I take a picture of the marble bathroom, complete with a freestanding tub, a walk-in shower that could accommodate the seven men sharing this suite and me, and a double vanity with brushed bronze taps, and what looks like an antique mirror.

She replies with the shocked emoji head, and I can imagine that expression overlaid on her real face.

Are you nervous about tomorrow?

I leave the bathroom, replying as I walk.

Nah. I'm ready for it.

I'm not really. I'm fucking terrified that I'm going to fall over, or my voice is going to sound terrible. Maybe they'll get the sound wrong, and I won't be able to hear myself over the band. I've seen many musicians fall foul to that one. But I won't admit that to Jordy. Showing confidence, even when it's a mask, helps me convince myself that I can do it.

You're going to be awesome. She finishes the message with a clapping hands, and a star eyes emoji, and I slide into bed, flicking off the light before I reply.

I really hope so. Night J. I'll call you when I can.

As I'm plugging in my phone to charge overnight, I hear laughter from beyond my room. Intrigued, I slide back out of bed and pad quickly across the hardwood floor until I've pressed my head against the door. What I hear is a conversation about me between Jax and Hudson that blows my mind.

Jax is interested in me. I guess I knew that. I've seen his warm brown eyes lingering on parts of me that should be off limits. I've seen the way his gaze drifts to my lips when I'm talking, as though he's imagining kissing them, or maybe having them wrapped around parts of his body that I shouldn't be thinking about.

A shiver of arousal passes up my spine and over my scalp. It's almost like I can feel his fingers trailing my skin.

I ache for physical touch. It's been so long since I rested in the arms of someone that loved me.

To be honest, my brothers are the only ones who ever gave me that kind of pure affection. Any guy I've been with since hasn't had the right connection outside of the sex, and I gave up looking when I realized that real love is hard to find.

I don't have it in me to give more of myself. There isn't enough to go around as it is.

But the way Jax talks is with intention. It's with thoughts about the kind of future that he wants. The kind of connection he wants.

He's always such a joker that it surprises me to hear him be so serious. It surprises me, even more, when he talks about Tyler's poly relationship with Sandy and his friends as though it's something he can see the merits in.

I can see them too, but I'm a woman who's desperate for stability, love, and affection. I want to make the kind of home that I never had as a kid. It seems like Jax does too, but it would take a lot of convincing for seven men to want to share one woman. I find myself shaking my head at the very thought.

Playing with the silver chain at my neck, I picture Sandy at the center of six good men who love her, and my throat aches with longing for the same thing.

Stupid thoughts.

I could never be enough for seven men. If my own mom and dad couldn't give me love, how could I expect seven men who are effectively strangers to go there?

Love might not be on the cards, but I'm sure of one thing. If I offered sex, they'd be tempted. Their lingering eyes tell me as much.

When I was just Luna Evans who sang on street corners, I would never have considered pushing for what I want or need. I let the world drag me around by the collar and I waited for other people to offer what they thought was important to me.

Now I'm a headline act, on a huge tour, with crazy perverted stalkers trying to infiltrate my life, and as fucked up as it sounds in my head, somehow now, I want to start taking the bull by the horns. I want to push forward to fulfill some of my dreams and indulge in some of my cravings.

And those cravings mainly center around the seven men of steel who surround me.

I'm not little Luna Evans anymore. I'm powerful and I'm strong. I'm a superstar who should expect everything I want.

I wait until Hudson orders Jax back to bed, and then I make my way to my four-poster bed to try to get some sleep. As I sink into the deliciously soft mattress, surrounded by luxury bedding, I tell myself that this is where I deserve to be. I've paid my dues. I've slept on enough grubby mattresses, on floors that were sticky with grime. I've shivered my way through enough nights. I've gone hungry more days than I can count.

This is my life now, and best of all, my bodyguards have got my back.

By the time I'm showered and dressed in the morning, my bodyguards have already ordered breakfast. Since my first assistant was caught trying to steal my clothes, my bodyguards have taken on many of her duties. The tour manager, Angelica, has also arrived and has pages of information for me to take in.

"Is this the kind of food you think Luna needs to be

consuming?" she says to Connor, poking her finger at the pile of pancakes and Danish pastries that rests in the middle of the table. With her hair scraped back into a messy bun, and her baggy jeans, she looks more like a mom than a woman in control of a world tour, but all power to her for climbing the ladder.

"She's going to be dancing all day. The girl needs to eat," Connor says in a way that sounds protective.

"I've been told to make sure she sticks to the diet plan arranged by Blueday's nutritionist." Angelica riffles through her stack of papers and pulls out a sheet that must contain all of the recommended foods I should be consuming. "Here."

Connor scans the paper. "This all sounds great, but it's not going to get her through a tour like this. She's going to burn out."

Angelica huffs. "You know what this industry is like. Stars need to stay in shape."

"She's in shape," Jax says.

"Look…" Angelica throws her hands up, palms facing out. "I'm not asking. I'm telling. Okay?" I guess she didn't get to her position without breaking a few balls.

I can almost hear Connor's internal voice telling her to fuck off, but as I round the corner, coming into view, he's gritting his jaw hard enough to make it tick. Damn, he looks good with his dirty-blond hair still damp from the shower and his suit pressed to perfection. In contrast, I'm wearing high-waisted leggings and a cropped sweatshirt. The trainers on my feet are comfortable for dancing, but none of it is classy-sexy attire.

Angelica smiles and strides toward me. "Morning, Luna. I have everything organized for today. You'll be traveling with the rest of the crew by bus to the venue. We'll spend the morning running through the routines and doing the soundcheck. Then you can rest for a couple of hours before we'll need to get you into hair and makeup."

"Sounds good," I say. "Where's the coffee?"

"Coffee's not on the list," Angelica says. "Warm water and lemon are good for your voice. It's going to be under a lot of strain over the next couple of months. You need to stick to the plan."

"But I feel like death," I say. "The jetlag is messing with my mojo."

"Tea, then," she concedes. "It has caffeine too."

Ugh, the prospect of going without my morning coffee is set to put me in a bad mood for the day. Connor is holding a mug of what looks like frothy cappuccino, but as soon as he sees my disgruntled expression, he puts it on the table.

"These pancakes look awesome," I say, flopping into a chair and forking them onto my plate before Angelica can object.

"I guess it's okay just for today," she says. More like she can tell from my expression that if she pushes me any harder, I'm going to unleash the dragon of my wrath.

As we eat, Angelica talks nonstop about everything that she's working on. Unlike Connor, she seems to think that I want to know all of the behind-the-scenes details, but I really don't. Just tell me where I need to be and help me get there on time. That's it. The rest just blows my mind, and not in a good way.

I stay quiet, taking my time to chew my food well so that there is no risk to my throat. My vocal coach has drummed into me how important it is to maintain my voice health to see this tour through to completion, and that is a plan that I am going to stick to.

Elijah is sitting next to me, and halfway through breakfast, I feel his eyes on me. When I look up, his fair brows are drawn together over his pretty sky-blue eyes. The almost transparent lashes that give him an innocent look lower as he blinks. "Are you okay?" he mouths as Connor and Angelica butt heads again over the surety arrangements.

I nod, but my shoulders rise and then fall in an almost imperceptible shrug of uncertainty.

"It'll be okay," he whispers and then smiles in a way that encircles my heart with warmth.

It'll be okay.

I don't remember anyone ever saying that to me before. It's the kind of thing that a mom and dad should say when you fall over or fail a test or get picked on by the class bully. It's the reassurance that lets you know that you're not traveling through life alone.

Elijah has shown more care in that one sentence than my father ever has, and I glance around the table at the seven men who make up my security detail. They are seven friends who've been through the toughest times together and still find ways to focus on others.

Last night, Jax spoke about how worried he is that life will pull them apart in the future, and maybe it will.

Maybe there's another way, my internal voice whispers.

But I stuff that thought back down because everything Hudson said is true. An alternative lifestyle might work for Tyler and his friends, but they're not in the public eye. They don't have the press hounding them at every turn. They don't have the weight of contractual expectations resting on their shoulders. A relationship isn't on the cards for me.

As the men of Steel 7 Security hustle me onto the bus and travel with me on a journey to the biggest stadium I've ever played, I let my mind wander over what it might be like to be the center of their world because it's only reality that can be damaging.

Fantasies can't hurt anybody.

At least, that's what I hope.

5

ELIJAH

Luna has been practicing the entire dance routine for the past two hours. Her tank top is damp with sweat, and her hair, which is pulled into a messy bun, is cascading around her face in wet tendrils. Her chest is rising and falling with exertion, and I've never seen a woman look fiercer.

"Again," Lucas, the choreographer, shouts. The music is paused, the four female dancers revert to their starting positions, and Luna stops, putting her hands on her hips, the picture of frustration.

"We've got this," she yells.

"You're missing that last beat," Lucas yells back. "This is the first night. It has to be perfect."

"It will be perfect," she hisses. "At least, it will be if I'm not totally fucking exhausted."

Lucas's fists ball at his sides, and instinctively I take a step forward. On the other side of the stage, Jax does the same. "This guy is pissing me off," I say onto our comms channel.

"He's just doing his job," Jax mutters. "But I know what you mean. I hate the way he's riding her."

"She can hold her own, but if he goes any further, he's getting a warning."

"I need a break," Luna says, then without waiting for Lucas's approval, strides across the stage toward me. There's a table holding all the things on Luna's rider; the brand of water she prefers at room temperature, dark chocolate, apples, date bars, nuts, and her nutritionist's approved salad pot that seems to contain chicken, rice, and avocado in addition to enough greens to feed a hutch of rabbits. I don't understand it, same as Connor. She must have burned off two thousand calories this morning. She needs more than this healthy regime. She needs steak and mashed potatoes or meatloaf with gravy. The girl needs more meat on her bones.

She gulps down a whole bottle of water, tossing the empty plastic container in the trash. "Did you ever kill anyone?" she asks, completely out of the blue. Before I can shrug of my shock, she carries on. "Because I always thought that it was something beyond my capabilities but now, I'm starting to seriously think that I could snap that asshole's neck with my bare hands and not break a sweat or prick my conscience."

"He definitely has a death wish," I chuckle, relieved she's not really inquiring about my military service. There are things I barely ever talk about, even to the men who know everything that happened during combat. I certainly wouldn't feel comfortable talking about it backstage with Luna.

Forgive me. The words that follow any thoughts of my active service whisper in the back of my mind.

"You should eat something," I say to block out my conscience as Luna flops into a chair. She reaches for the salad and begins to shovel it into her mouth like a hungry animal.

"This is good, but I could murder a cheeseburger."

"Me too," I say. "With curly fries and slaw. And some chicken wings on the side."

"Mmmmmm." The sound she makes vibrates in her throat, and her bottom lip is drawn into her mouth as though she's physically savoring our imagined meal.

"Luna, we need to get the dances wrapped up," Angelica shouts from behind the huge speakers at the side of the stage. "Lucas might be busting your balls, but it's for a good reason. We're on the clock."

"I need to eat," Luna yells. "I'm not a machine."

There's a long moment of silence while Angelica gathers all of her patience.

"Okay, everyone, take ten, and then we'll get back to it."

The dancers who had been fixed to their spots, waiting to see what was going to happen, drift to the other side of the stage. I smile as Jax grins in their direction. He's always had a way with the ladies that isn't sleazy or creepy. He just loves women and loves life and is happy to show his appreciation for both.

"You can do this, Luna. This part's the grind, but later, when you're on stage, and the crowd is shouting your name, you're going to forget all the hard work and just bask in the glory."

"You're right," she says. "I know you're right. It's just, I know I can do it. Even if we're getting it wrong now, I know what needs to be done. I just wish Lucas had more confidence."

"This is his job. He's only got this far because he demands perfection."

"I guess."

"Just trust that everyone around you is working to

deliver the best possible experience for everybody buying a ticket."

"And what about me. Should I trust that they have my best interests at heart too?"

"You can trust that I do."

I leave my words to hang between us so that she feels the full weight of them. If there's one thing I've learned in my life, it's that talking too much smells like weakness. There is a reason that the strong-silent-type description exists and is so appealing to women.

Luna places the salad back on the table and gracefully stands. She's so little that I'm looking down, and she's gazing up, her eyes wide and searching. I guess she must find what she was looking for in my expression because she blinks slowly and whispers, "Thank you." Then she's jogging across the stage.

"I'm ready. Let's kick the living shit out of this routine."

"Yeah," the dance team shouts in unison, bounding onto the stage.

Lucas starts the music again, and, in a flash, Luna is dancing, her body lithe, her movements perfectly in time. She hits every beat and masters every move, and even though she's disheveled and sweaty, she still exudes superstar from every pore.

As the music draws to a close, Lucas begins clapping, and his tanned face is lit up by a mouthful of exceptionally white teeth. "That's it. Perfect. Perfect," he shouts, and I want to call out that he shouldn't doubt the girl whose talent has brought us all to this place.

She's got this.

She was made for this.

And maybe I was too.

There isn't much for me back home. My family doesn't

want to know me. I've stepped too far outside the fold for them to ever accept me back. I knew, when I left home and the church behind, that I would never be a part of that life. Sometimes, I regret it. In the middle of the night, when I lie awake, I feel the loss of my parents and my brothers more keenly. When things are going wrong, my instinct is always to find the right piece of scripture to fit the circumstance, and I have to push back in case I drag myself back into a place where I never felt truly comfortable.

But when I'm with my Steel 7 brothers, I know I've found the kind of home that counts. A home without judgment or expectation. A home where I can expand to become the self I couldn't be when I was surrounded by so many rules.

And looking after Luna has given me a sense of purpose that I haven't felt in a while.

She's like a shining diamond, set into a priceless crown.

After Luna's soaked up the appreciation, she surprises me by bounding over and throwing her arms around me. For a second, my chest feels like the wind has been knocked out of it, and I can't find a thing to say that fits with this moment. Then Luna's off to hug all the dancers that are going to contribute to making tonight's performance spectacular.

When I look over, I find Jax with a knowing smile on his face. I have no idea what he's thinking, but I doubt that it's the same as me.

I want this girl.

Stupid as it might seem to crave the person I'm being paid to protect; I can't help myself.

Her safety is in my hands, but I wish it was her heart.

6

LUNA

The rumble of so many people seated in such a large venue is something that I'm not sure I'll ever get used to. In a way, the crowd feels like a huge animal. Before a show, I'm worried that the animal will be angry, but during a show, I feed off the animal's appreciation. It's electric, hearing my name shouted by thousands of people. It's addictive knowing that they are all there just to experience my talent and creativity.

Backstage, there is a buzz of anticipation. It's the first night of the tour, so everyone is feeling uncertain. We've practiced hard, but things can still go wrong. Adella, my makeup artist, puts the finishing touches on my scarlet lipstick. With dark smoky eyes, the look is strong and intense, which it needs to be to create an impact all the way to the back of the stadium. I'm laced into a corset that feels too tight. I've raised concerns about it but the costume designer for the tour assures me that it's going to be fine for me to sing and dance in. Apparently it fits with the whole tour aesthetic.

And who am I to question their judgment?

Only the poor woman who has to struggle to wear it.

My eyes find Elijah's in the mirror. He's standing close by as though he can feel my nerves and wants to provide me with some reassurance. His strong presence is enough to settle the butterflies a little, and his pretty blue eyes are soft and encouraging. I can still remember what it felt like to have my arms around him, to breathe in his scent. It was instinct to rush over to him when I got the dance right. Instinct to share my happiness and success, and it felt right to be in his arms.

I felt protected and cared for.

But I'm stupid because the way he is with me isn't personal. It's not about him being my friend. It's certainly not about more. He is my bodyguard. Protecting me is his job.

"You're done," Adella says, lowering her brush. "Break a leg." Her smile is broad, her own fuchsia pink lipstick perfectly in place.

Rising from the chair, I smooth the tiny, ruffled skirt over my red net tights. The look is punky and alternative, which suits me and fits with the image that Blueday Records have been cultivating for me.

Innocent with a sexy edge.

It's kind of gross, but who am I to question them when they've propelled me so high, so fast.

"I need to warm up my voice," I tell Elijah. "Can you clear the room?"

"Sure."

As I make my way to the corner of my dressing room, I can hear his low, husky voice urging everyone to leave.

When it's quiet, I shake out my arms, facing the wall while I loosen my lips and jaw muscles. None of this is attractive: not the sticking out of my tongue as far as it goes or the rhythmic blowing of breath through my O-shaped mouth.

I never knew that any of this was important until my vocal coach walked me through a routine. Nurturing and preserving my voice takes priority over appearance. These exercises are a must. I begin to sigh, allowing my voice to gradually build, letting it wander up and down the full range of notes that I can sing. When I'm confident that I've hit the highest and lowest notes, I begin to hum and finish with some gentle lip roles and tongue trills.

When I've finished and shaken my arms and legs out some more, I'm feeling looser and ready for the exertion tonight's performance is going to take.

The door to my dressing room opens, and Angelica yells, "Ten minutes!" before disappearing as quickly as she arrives. My eyes meet Elijah's, and he smiles softly.

"You have such a pretty voice," he tells me. "Like a friggin' angel."

"An angel dressed as a devil," I say, glancing down at the lace-up leather boots that complete my outfit.

"Don't you like the clothes?" he asks.

"They're not really me. Just the fantasy of some sick fuck at the record company."

Elijah's smile drops from his face. Maybe he thought I chose all this. Maybe he thought that this is who I am. From the frown playing between his brows, the thought that I've been dressed up this way doesn't sit well with him. "Can you choose to wear something else?" he asks.

"No one is interested in my choices." I shrug, feeling the weight of my own statement. I thought becoming famous would give me more power but that definitely isn't the case. All that fame has brought is higher stakes to everything I do. It's all just a greater weight on my shoulders.

"You're going to blow them away," he says. "You could

do that in a potato sack. Just remember what it is about doing this that you love. The rest doesn't count for shit."

"That sounds like really good advice," I say. "If I could actually breathe properly, maybe I could." Grabbing the top of the corset, I try and tug it up, but it's tighter than a second skin.

"You can't breathe?" Elijah steps forward.

"I can't get a full breath in. I told them that I'm worried that I'm not going to be able to dance and sing in this thing, but nobody will listen."

"Can I rest my hand on your back? I want to check something."

He's so close to me now that I can smell his cologne. It's something gorgeously fresh that tickles my nose and momentarily transports me to an alpine field in a country I've only ever seen on Christmas cards.

"Sure."

When he rests his big warm palm against my back, half is on the corset and the other half on my bare skin. A shiver runs up my spine, cresting over my scalp and making me gasp.

In the background, the crowd roars as the support act sings their biggest hit.

"Breathe in as deep as you can," Elijah says. I try my hardest to inhale as much air as possible, but it's not enough. "Shit," he mutters, glancing at his watch. Then he's striding into the corridor. I can hear a rushed conversation with Connor and Mo, who are outside the door, then the rustle of the walkie-talkie. Angelica's voice sounds through the static. "Can you get down here? We've got a problem with Luna."

"What is it?" she shouts, and even though her voice is reaching me from a distance, I can hear her frustration and disapproval.

Elijah returns to the room. "Luna, do you have another

top you can wear instead of that corset?"

"Only my black tube top," I say.

"Will it go with the skirt?" He eyes the rest of my costume as though he's totally out of his depth in a conversation about women's fashion.

"Yeah, but it isn't what the costume designer wants."

"Fuck the costume designer."

It's at that moment that Angelica appears, her cheeks reddened with exertion and her nostrils flaring. "What's wrong?" She eyes me, waiting to hear what petty thing I'm going to complain about. I know that other artists have ridiculous ridders that include things like bowls of red M&M's, but I'm not like that.

"Luna can't breathe in this costume. It's dangerous for her to go on stage like this to perform if she can't breathe." Elijah moves to stand closer to me as though he wants to show that he's supporting me.

"Costumes aren't my department." Angelica glances at her watch, her exasperation obvious.

"No, but an unconscious artist who fails to perform a full set will be."

That gets her attention. "Why didn't you bring this up with Laurence?" she spits.

"I did, but he wouldn't listen."

"You really need to get better at advocating for yourself," she says. "Rather than leaving this shit to the last minute and risking a late performance. If you don't wear that, what the hell are you going to wear?"

"She has another black top," Elijah says, taking another step closer. I swear, if he could put himself between Angelica and me, he would.

"Well, you'd better get that on quickly. You're on in five minutes."

"Can you help me unlace?" I ask Elijah, turning so my

back is to him and glancing at his wide-eyed face over my shoulder.

He stares at the laces as though they're a trigonometry paper he hasn't prepared for. "What am I supposed to do?"

"Just undo the bow at the top and unlace."

"Shit," he mutters, looking for a second at his hands, contemplating their capabilities.

Angelica huffs and then leaves as Elijah tries to use his thick fingers to disentangle me from the torture device I'm strapped into. They brush my skin, causing more shivers, fumbling with the bow, and then testing each string to gradually loosen the top. I'm not wearing a bra, so I hold the front of the corset close to my chest, breathing deeply as the strings are loosened enough to allow me to fully expand my chest.

"That's better," he says as he reaches the bottom. His finger brushes the skin at the base of my spine. "You have red marks," he says gently. "I don't get why women wear this shit. No kind of fashion is worth hurting yourself." Then he takes a step back and turns to face the wall. "You'd better get that stupid thing off, and your tube top on before Angelica has a shit fit."

Dashing over to my bag, I rummage around for a bra and my tube top, finding both folded neatly where I left them earlier. I push the corset down, allowing it to hit the floor. It doesn't take me long to fasten my strapless bra and tug the top over my head. It leaves an inch of skin bare between the hem and the waistband of my skirt, an inch that is marked with corset welts. When I turn, Elijah is still facing the wall, his hands flexing, and shoulders bunched high.

"I'm ready," I say. When he turns, those baby blues of his scan my outfit.

"That's better," he says. "You don't need that stupid

contraption. You need to be able to use your body." His words settle over me, sending my mind to darker ways I could use my body, ways that would give us both pleasure.

"Thank you...you know. For advocating for me. I should have done better at it myself."

"Hey...don't even think about it. You tried. I get why it's hard to stand up to these industry douchebags. They want to do what they want to do. There's no consideration of the person being affected by their choices."

"Except you," I say. "You've been considerate beyond your job role."

He shakes his head, shooting me with a smile that makes my heart skip a beat. "You're forgetting something, Luna. My job is to protect you. Whether it's from psycho stalkers or rabid costume designers or raging tour managers, that's my job."

I grin back and bounce on my toes, hearing the roar of the crowd as the support act finish their final track.

It's time.

And I'm ready. All thanks to Elijah, the bodyguard who goes the extra mile.

7

BEN

I finish the backstage check just as the MC is announcing that it's time for the main event. Touching my lapel, I call in confirmation that my side is clear. Asher comes into view, confirming the same. Mo and Jax are upfront, and Connor and Elijah are waiting to escort Luna safely onto the stage.

The lights begin to flash, a deep beat pulsing from the huge speakers, and I hear Connor confirm that Luna is on the move.

My heart is in my throat as I gaze into the almost black expanse of the stadium. There are people out there. Thousands of people screaming Luna's name. Thousands of ordinary people worked into a frenzy by their love of the way she sings or the way she looks. Among them there will be the fans who are obsessed. The ones with the unhealthy psychologies who invent stories about how close they are to Luna. Maybe they think they should be dating her. Maybe they want to touch her in real life because of the words of a song that some middle-aged music executive came up with.

Scientists estimate that one percent of the population are psychopaths, but in my life experience, I'd put that number higher. Yes, there are probably one percent who are the real terrifying fuckers, but there must be at least another five percent who are the ones who function in day-to-day life without slaughtering animals, who fly under the radar, but exist with no conscience. They're the ones who worry me more.

I don't know how Luna has the confidence to exist in the public eye. She'll go out there and stand in front of all of those people, singing and dancing as though it's the easiest thing in the world. I'd rather somebody emptied a Glock into my temple.

The beat begins to rise, the lights flashing so rapidly that it's hard to see. I stand, braced for anything, knowing that my team are doing the same. The men of Steel 7 are my brothers.

Just thinking about them that way makes my throat burn. We should have been Steel 8 and we would have been if Hudson's twin, Hartley, hadn't caught the worst of an IED.

Seven is supposed to be a lucky number, but for us it's just a reminder of how dangerous the world is, and how unfair.

For the companies that hire us, seven is always justifiable because we share a flat fee and are willing to take on the work that a personal assistant can do. There's always a way to encourage a company to take us all on. Working apart just wouldn't be an option.

"Five seconds." Connor is a little out of breath in my ear.

And then there she is, bounding onto the stage. Luna's dancers follow and they start the first number, a rousing tune about Luna getting over her ex. It's stupid, but every time I hear her sing about the douchebag who broke her heart, I want to punch the fictional asshole in the mouth.

The crowd go crazy, almost obliterating her voice with their cheers, and then they quieten to listen to Luna's crystal-clear melody. They hold up their phones to capture her perfect performance.

My eyes scan the section of backstage that I can see. At the front, Mo grabs hold of an overenthusiastic fan who's desperately trying to scale the barriers onto the stage. He puts the girl down as gently as possible and holds his finger up in warning. I scan the stage, finding Luna hitting every beat with a dance routine that seems too taxing to manage while singing at the same time. Backstage, I spot Marcus, one of the lighting techs, watching Luna as though he's in a trance-like state. There's a smirk on his lips. At least, it looks like a smirk rather than a smile.

My eyes flick back to Luna, checking that all is okay. When I glance back, Marcus has moved on.

The song comes to an end and Luna stands, her chest rising and falling, gazing out into the sea of shadowed faces. "How are you doing BERLIN?" she yells the last part and the crowd go crazy again. "This next one is my favorite from the album. I hope you enjoy it."

The band starts to play a track about first love, and Luna begins to dance slowly, her male dancers coming one by one to grind with her suggestively. My eyes meet Elijah's across the stage, and he grimaces. I'm not sure what's driving the response. This music isn't exactly his style so it could be that. Or it could be Luna's hand trailing over the muscular chest of yet another man with perfect rhythm.

That's how I feel.

Jealousy is a fucked-up emotion. It's fucked up at the best of times, eating through perfectly healthy relationships, but it's even worse when you feel it and have no right to.

Luna's not my girl. She can touch any man anyway she wants and feeling anything about it is way outside of my remit, but I can't help it.

The girl is just too pretty, too funny, too sassy, and too perfect.

She's everything that lights me on fire and more, wrapped up in a ball of dynamite.

And I'm her bodyguard.

Could this be more cliched?

I feel like I'm replicating a nineties movie, except my feelings aren't replicated.

"You okay, Ben?" Connor asks, his voice raspy through our equipment.

"All good," I say, but he must have noticed my mind wandering, my concentration lapsing. And that's why thinking about Luna is dangerous. I need to keep my mind clear.

She wouldn't want me, anyway. If she was going to break the rules with any of the Steel 7, it would be with one who still had all their own limbs.

As if my stump can feel me thinking about it, it begins to ache where it rests in my prosthetic. Things have come a long way with technology, but even with all the gel covers and ergonomically shaped equipment, there is still discomfort.

Luna continues her performance, and I manage to keep my eyes on her and all the places in the stadium that I'm responsible for keeping clear. She's sweating and out of breath but killing every song and the crowd are lapping it up.

As the final song comes to an end, Connor tells me to make my way around. I guess things must be getting busy on his side and he wants extra backup to escort Luna back to her dressing room.

"Thank you, Berlin. You've been awesome," Luna shouts, kissing her palms and blowing it into the crowd. She bends at the waist, her cute little skirt rising high enough to see her panties through her red fishnet stockings. My cock stirs in my pants, an image of her bending to rest her palms on the dining table in our suite flooding my mind. I'd love to show her how deep I could fuck her; how good it could be. In that position, she'd never have to see the place my leg used to be. She'd never have to see that I'm not whole.

I'm almost around as Luna jogs off stage, pulling the fabric of her tube top a little higher. Damn, doesn't she know that adjusting boobs in front of men just gets us thinking about boobs.

"On the move," Connor says, just as I take position next to Luna, holding her arm at the elbow.

There are people everywhere, standing around drinking and laughing. Most have lanyards around their necks, official backstage passes. We don't have far to go but it's tight in the hallways. I keep a watch behind us, swiveling every so often to check we're not being tailed. By the time we get to Luna's dressing room, I'm sweating and out of breath.

Asher throws the door open, scanning the room before he allows Luna to enter. Connor follows, and so do I, leaving Elijah to stand outside.

"Dressing room," Connor mutters into the intercom, confirming to Mo and Jax that Luna's safely back.

Luna slumps onto a couch, resting her arms along the back, pulling in deep breaths. "That was crazy," she says. "Fucking crazy."

"You did good," Connor says reassuringly.

I clear my throat. "It was awesome. The perfect way to start a tour."

"It'll be all over the news sites tomorrow," Asher says.

"And I'll have to do it all over again tomorrow." Luna runs a hand over her face, the body language of a person who feels worn down. But this is night one. There's a whole tour to finish. She's going to be doing this show so many times that we'll all know the words and dance moves by the time we're heading home.

With a huff, she heads over to the chair where her bag rests, pulling out a bottle of water. She needs to keep those vocal cords nice and wet. "What the fuck?" Bending over, she pulls the corner of her bag to open it wider, gazing inside. "What the fuck is that?"

Asher's there in a flash, nudging her behind him, so that he can investigate the bag. "Fuck," he growls. Pulling out plastic gloves from his pocket, he reaches in to find whatever has Luna spooked. A pair of white panties has been slashed up and splattered with scarlet. Attached is a note but I'm not close enough to read what it says.

"WHAT IS IT?" Luna shouts.

"Nothing," Asher says, turning his back to her so she can't see the full extent of what he's dealing with. I can see he wants to shove it in his pocket, but he knows that would destroy evidence.

"Luna, come over here," I say, reaching out for her elbow.

"Don't fucking touch me," she yells. "Don't try and hide this shit from me...to treat me like I'm a child who can't deal with the world. I've dealt with bigger and uglier shit than this when I was ten years old, so can you just show me?"

Asher's eyes seek out Connor's. There's a tense moment when both men try to debate what's best to do with just eye contact. In the end, Connor nods and Asher turns, holding the panties out to Luna. "Don't touch anything," he says. "We need to give this to the police as clean as possible."

Luna squints trying to read the scrawled words. "I would tear you up so you wouldn't be able to walk for a month." Her voice is so flat that it hurts my heart.

"Fuck," I mutter under my breath, just as Luna turns to look at me. Her eyes are glassy and unfocused. I'm expecting her to rage again, to tell us what a fucking asshole the man is who's done this, but she doesn't. Her hand raises and hovers over her chest and then her knees seem to go out from under her. I'm close enough to catch her before she falls, pulling her against me tightly. "Luna!" I tip her face up to mine and her eyes roll and then close.

"Get her onto the couch," Connor says as I scoop her into my arms and carry her to lay her down. Chestnut hair fans across the dark leather and Luna's lips part as her head lolls.

One minute, she's the strongest one in the room and then next she's passing out.

It can't be a coincidence. As strenuous as her performance was, she's practiced enough to deal with that. No, it's not dancing that's the problem, it's knowing the truth of what's out there and getting closer.

Too fucking close.

"Luna…" I pat her face gently then fan my hand back and forth, trying to create a cooling breeze that might rouse her. Asher and Connor crowd behind me.

"Undo her bra," Asher says. "She needs to be able to breathe without the fucking underwire constricting her chest."

He's right but that doesn't make this feel any less wrong. She's fucking out of it and I'm fumbling her out of her underwear. If she wakes up while I'm doing it, she's going to think the worst for sure.

But she doesn't.

"Get me a wet cloth," I shout. "And a glass of water for when she comes around. And get that shit out of here."

Asher heads to the doorway, calling for Elijah, Mo, and Jax. Connor is at the sink, wetting a towel. When he returns, I press it gently to Luna's forehead and then dab it around her neck and over the top of her breasts.

A little gasp leaves her lips and then her eyes flutter open, the green of her irises so vivid it's like looking into a priceless jewel. "What…"

Luna goes to sit up, but I rest my hand on her shoulder. "You passed out, sweetie. Just rest for a moment so it doesn't happen again."

"Shit." Her hand flies to her head as she groans.

"Are you in pain?" Giving me a closed-eyed nod, she draws her feet up until her knees are bent at right angles.

"It felt like a flash," she says, "but it's getting better."

"You gave us a scare," Connor says, taking a seat at the end of the couch. "We should get a medic to check you out."

Luna puts her hand up, palm facing in his direction. "No medic. I'm fine. I just need a minute."

"We shouldn't take any chances," Connor urges.

"Maybe you should have thought of that before you let a fucking freak rifle through my stuff and defile my underwear."

Connor flinches backward, Luna's words cutting close, but instead of reacting angrily to her assertions, he seems to deflate. "You're right. I'm sorry. I thought we had it covered by keeping track of who was around the stage area. Anyone back here has to have been checked in and given a pass. But it won't happen again. From tomorrow, one of us will remain stationed at the door for security.

"You think they'll come back tomorrow?" The smallness of Luna's voice is heart-breaking. For all her raging and sharp words, she's actually so vulnerable and soft. It's like she holds a toughened forcefield around herself for as long as she can, but once it crumbles, she has nothing to shield her from the world.

Nothing except us.

Connor rests his hand on Luna's boot; a gesture that should feel too familiar but somehow doesn't under the circumstances. "There's a reason why Asher didn't want you to see what was there. It's our job to keep you safe and our job to deal with whatever is a threat. Your job is to perform and keep your fans happy. To do that, you don't need to be thinking about this stuff…just forget it all, okay? And trust us. We won't let anything bad happen to you."

Luna's lids lower and she exhales long and low as if the breath she's expelling can carry with it all the stress she's holding inside.

I do the exact same thing when I'm under pressure.

When her eyes open, they flick from Connor, to me, to Elijah who's standing behind me.

"No medic," she says softly. "And from now on, I'll leave you to deal with everything."

"Deal," I say, before Connor has a chance to disagree. If there's one thing that I'm sure of, it's that Luna needs to know she can trust us, and part of that is us having some faith in the fact that she knows what's good for her.

We're all exhausted by the time we get back to the hotel and Luna disappears to shower off the exertion of the day. By the time we're ready to eat, it's late. Luna's ravenous though, and she polishes off a huge bowl of a delicious German stew with a name that I can't pronounce. I have the same, but the others all go for different options. Conversation is subdued and even Jax can't raise much more than a fleeting smile from the group.

Hudson probes for stories from the day, but Luna isn't

up for sharing. She leaves the table first, heading to her room and closing the door.

When she's out of earshot, Asher updates Hudson on the post-concert drama. He's going to be working the stadium tomorrow, so he needs to be in the know.

"This shit is escalating," he says. "What did the police say?"

"They were going to dust it all for prints. They'll let us know if they come up with anything. One of Luna's bras is missing too. It's like they wanted to freak her out and take a memento."

"Do you think this is a German psycho or one that's traveled from home?" Elijah asks.

Connor shrugs. "Who the fuck knows? What we do know is that they got through into the secure backstage areas unchallenged. It doesn't fit with an inexperienced super fan with a fixation. It feels more deliberate…more skillful."

Mo shakes he head. "When someone really wants something, they will move a mountain to get it."

Connor nods thoughtfully. "Maybe. We need to get some sleep. Jax is taking tonight's shift. Better drink some coffee."

Jax grins and nods. "Don't worry about me. I've heard the German pay-per-view porn is worth staying up all night for."

"Now, I know you're joking, right?" Connor's eyebrows practically disappear beneath his hairline.

"Of course I'm joking."

As we're heading to bed, Luna's door clicks, the handle turning slowly. She doesn't appear, but instead pads back to her bed, switching off the light. My eyes meet Connor's, a knowing look passing between us. She feels safer with her door ajar.

STEEL 7

Now that's trust, for sure.

8

HUDSON

Luna sleeps late into the morning, and we're careful not to wake her. She must be shattered from her first performance, and, as she's not required to do much before the show today, we figure she should make the most of it. Jax retires to sleep as soon as I emerge from the bathroom dressed in a neatly-pressed white shirt and gray slacks. I'm making coffee when Luna appears, fully dressed in tight leather-look leggings and a black shirt emblazoned with Girls in a pink neon font. Her hair is scraped into a messy bun, and shiny chestnut tendrils surround her pretty fresh face. If she's wearing makeup, it's so natural that I can't tell, but then what do I know about women's things?

"Please tell me that's something with caffeine," she says. "I feel like I need it injected into my veins this morning."

"It's good strong coffee," I tell her, pouring a cup and handing it to her carefully. Angelica can take a hike if I'm supporting the no caffeine policy when Luna has so much on her plate.

She sips it tentatively, her eyes rolling when it makes contact with her tongue. "Now that is the drink of the gods," she says.

"Didn't you sleep well?" I ask.

She shakes her head. "Nah…I tossed and turned a lot, thinking in that horrible way where everything seems overwhelming and extreme."

"You know that there is always one of us awake. It was Jax last night. He would have cheered you up."

"I didn't want to disturb him."

"He would have been grateful. It's boring being the only one awake while everyone else is dreaming."

"I'll bear that mind." Luna smiles in a way that doesn't quite meet her eyes, then she wanders to the window, gazing at the city spread beneath our feet. "I want to go see some stuff today," she says. "What's the point of traveling the world if all you get to see is the inside of generic hotel rooms?"

Gazing around the room, she straightens her shoulders, taking another sip of hot coffee. "I shouldn't say this place is generic. It's so nice. Nicer than I need."

"Why nicer than you need?" I ask. "There's nothing wrong with some comfort when you're working so hard."

"I just can't get over the amount of money that something like this costs a night. That would have kept my family housed for a few months back home."

"Things are different for you now, though," I say, hoping I can make her feel better. "And you need space to house us too." The wink I give her aims to lighten the conversation, but Luna lowers her gaze to the floor.

"Things are different from the outside, but not that different on the inside." She blows a breath through her pursed lips, glancing back at the view. "How many people out there are sleeping on the streets, and I'm up here bathing in a huge marble bathroom like a modern-day

Cleopatra. It just feels wrong."

"It's the change," I say. "I think, with time, you'll get used to it."

"You think I'll forget my roots?"

"I think you'll feel less like you don't deserve your success."

As the words leave my mouth, I fear that I've said too much. She could easily take it personally. Instead, she frowns a little.

"Maybe it's better that I keep feeling like I don't deserve it. That way, if this all disappears, I'll just go back home as though I was an imposter all along."

"You're not an imposter, Luna. You're made to do this! It's your purpose."

"You think?"

"Of course. Your voice is…like an angel…and you can dance and entertain."

"And I look the part. Isn't that the main thing?" Her tone is sharp, believing maybe that her looks are the reason she's popular, and maybe she's right. How many ordinary-looking people end up becoming famous because they have a talent? Most of the celebrities you see on television are good-looking.

"You're the whole package, Luna. That's why you've sold out stadiums across the world."

"The whole package?" She puts her hand on her waist, cocking her hip. "You've seen me in my pajamas. Without all the warpaint, I'm nothing special."

"Without all the warpaint, you're even more special," I say. When she blushes, her eyelashes flutter with the surprise of my compliment. My cheeks heat too, and then someone clears their throat across the room. Connor and Mo are there, Mo eyeing me with a strange half-smile on his face and Connor's expression like thunder on a gray wintery day.

"Luna wants to go sightseeing today," I say, hoping that I can distract Connor enough for him to forget my overfamiliarity.

"I don't think that's a good idea," Connor says, shooting me another look that tells me I shouldn't be encouraging this kind of thing.

"Why not?" Luna pivots gracefully on one foot to face the man blocking her plans.

"Because it's not safe. It'll be harder to protect you out in the open. A clip of your show was on an entertainment program here last night. If people didn't know you yesterday, they know you today. And we have no idea who left that shit last night. There are just too many variables."

"You're saying I have to stay trapped in a hotel room for the whole tour? Seriously?"

"Maybe not the whole tour. I just think, after yesterday, that we need to be more cautious about today. We're out of here tomorrow. In the next city, we can have a little more freedom."

"This is bullshit." Luna makes a growling voice in her throat, and she stomps back to her room, slamming the door behind her.

Mo clears his throat again, raising his dark eyebrows. "That could have gone better."

"She was never going to like hearing no. She's that kind of girl," Connor says. "But if Hudson hadn't gone and got her hopes raised, then maybe she wouldn't have reacted so badly."

"Protecting her is our job," I say. "Obviously, it would be safer for all of us if we just stayed in this room. But protecting her isn't just about her physical wellbeing. It's about her emotional wellbeing too. If she's angry and stressed or feeling claustrophobic being trapped up here, she's not going to do well in her performance later. We have to find a way to balance both."

Connor's shoulders rise and then fall as he draws in and expels a deep breath. He takes his bottom lips between his teeth, eyes focused on the middle distance. "Maybe we can bring some of Berlin to Luna."

"What do you mean?"

"I don't know yet but let me think on it."

We sit down for breakfast, but Luna doesn't come back out of her room. When we're done, I gather some pastries and fresh fruit and a large glass of orange juice on a tray and knock gently on her door.

"What?" she shouts, sounding more like a petulant thirteen-year-old than a fully grown woman.

"I've got you some breakfast. You need to eat."

When Luna doesn't answer, I twist the doorknob slowly, allowing her time to object, but she doesn't.

The room is dark, the curtains still drawn, and Luna is curled up on a couch, staring into space.

"Hey." Placing the tray onto the small table nearest to her, I take a seat by her feet. "Look, I know you're frustrated. I know that this life has some pros and cons, and it's tough to get used to the extreme sides of everything. Just remember that Berlin isn't going anywhere. You'll be able to come back sometime in the future."

"When in the future am I not going to need a whole troop of burly men surrounding me, Hudson? When in the future am I going to be able to mooch around a little store and enjoy coffee sitting in front of a small café? When am I going to be able to go for a run outside or just choose to have an afternoon at the beach without getting hounded or worse?"

"I don't know, Luna. I don't know if there is ever going to be a time like that. You'll probably always need someone to look out for you. The world is a messed-up place at the best of times. But what will happen is that you'll get used to it."

"Maybe," she says softly. "Will you do something for me?" Luna's eyes meet mine, and even in the dark, they're the prettiest shade of green; unearthly, and enticing.

"Sure."

"Will you find a website about Berlin and read to me? Tell me about all the places that I'm not going to get to see. Describe the buildings and the art galleries, the people, and the music scene. Tell me quirky things that will stay in my mind. It's not what I want, but I guess it'll have to do."

"Of course."

As I pull out my phone and start searching, Luna swings her legs off the sofa, dragging the table closer so she can reach the food.

When I start to read about the history of Berlin, Luna's shoulders drop, and her eyes close. Maybe she's letting her imagination conjure as many images as it can to replace the ones that she's missing out on because of the crazy fucker who broke into her dressing room.

Halfway through Luna's breakfast, Connor's head appears around the door. He watches for a few moments, his expression confused at first and then holding a sadness that I didn't expect. I guess he feels for her as much as I do. He nods, telling me silently that he approves, and disappears again. When Luna's finished her breakfast, she lies back on the sofa, her feet with their pretty pink toenails resting against my thigh, and damn if I don't need every ounce of restraint not to rest my hand against her skin.

Jax, for all his crazy talk, isn't alone in being drawn to this girl. She's got a quality that settles on me like a picnic blanket shaken high and allowed to fall slowly to the lush green grass below. Whatever she needs, I want to find a way to give it to her.

A little later, I hear Angelica arrive, but Connor must manage to keep her away from Luna's bedroom because she doesn't disturb us. Even later, when I've almost exhausted every tourist website there is, there's a knock at the door.

"There's a surprise out here for Luna," Asher says.

"A surprise?" Luna pushes her palms against the couch, straightening herself into an upright position.

"Yeah. If Luna can't go to Berlin, Berlin will come to Luna." Asher holds his hand out like a gameshow girl displaying prizes, a broad smile splitting his face. I have no idea what they've arranged, but this better be good.

Luna stands first, smoothing her shirt and shooting me a quizzical look, and I follow her into the living area, finding that the furniture has been rearranged. The dining table is now against the wall, and chairs have been set up facing away from the window. Standing in the newly cleared space are six men dressed in Lederhosen and traditional German attire.

Luna's hand flies to her mouth. I'm uncertain whether it's shock or because she's trying to cover a smile. Connor and Mo urge Luna to take a seat, and we all follow. The largest guy at the back, with a huge bushy brown beard, starts some music. It's a fast and rousing piano accordion, and the men begin to dance in traditional German style, patting their thighs and kick their legs. I glance at Luna out of the corner of my eye and catch the expression of pure pleasure that passes over her face. Her hands begin to clap loudly in time to the beat, and we all join in, relieved that she's enjoying herself. After a while, the man nearest to Luna holds out his hand and tugs her to join in. She doesn't resist, taking a place next to him and concentrating on learning the steps. She has a natural talent for dance and is replicating his moves in seconds, much to his pleasure.

"Wooohooo, Luna!" Jax shouts, rising to his feet to clap along.

Asher jumps up to join in, picking up the dance moves as quickly as Luna, and soon, we're all up dancing. Somehow, Connor seems to be blending in some Irish dancing and Mo some Middle Eastern. Me? Well, I'm just trying my best to stay on two feet.

The sound of Luna's laughter fills my chest as my heart pounds a beat beneath the tattoo of my brother's name that I have carved into my skin. Hartley would have loved everything about this.

Later, when Luna's on stage at the monstrous stadium in Berlin, there's a natural break between songs. She tells the audience she's been soaking up German culture and begins to replicate the moves she learned trapped in a hotel room with seven bodyguards and six dancers-for-hire. And you know what? The crowd eat it up, cheering and joining in.

Luna's life may have changed, but maybe we can help her see that it's not all bad.

I look around at my friends, who are currently trying to maintain professional straight faces, and see a shared lightness in their expressions. Maybe it's me imagining things, but could they all be thinking the same?

9

ASHER

We land in Athens at lunchtime, so by the time we reach the hotel, we're all famished. Connor is still feeling awful for preventing Luna from going out in Berlin and has secretly arranged for us to take a quick guided tour of the Parthenon Temple and museum after an authentic Greek lunch. He might always seem like a hard-ass, but underneath the tough exterior, he has a heart of gold.

Luna barely gets time to freshen up before Connor tells her the plans. To say she's excited is an understatement.

"What is traditional Greek food?" Ben asks as we pull up outside a gorgeous taverna, painted white with blue shutters and lined with planters of pink and red flowers. The tables and chairs outside are crafted from smooth wood with woven straw seats. Grapes hang from the vine that shades half of the space.

The owners have sectioned off part of the outside at our request, pulling our table next to a wall so that we have some privacy. Luna is wearing sunglasses, like practically every other woman in Athens, so there's a chance she won't be spotted. In fact, today, it's us bodyguards who are standing out; Seven huge men out with one tiny woman. It's certainly a sight to behold.

When we take our seats, I find myself at one end with Luna on one side and Hudson on the other. The owner of the restaurant, a short man with a broad black mustache, comes over to welcome us to his restaurant. He obviously has the customer service skills perfected because he immediately tells Luna she looks like a Greek goddess, which seems to please her immensely.

"What would you recommend?" Connor asks, his finger trailing a long and complex menu.

"How about a meze?" he says.

"It's a mixture of lots of small dishes," Mo explains. "It's perfect if you want to try lots of different things."

At least, that's what it's supposed to be. When the food arrives, there is nothing small about it. The whole table is swamped, and our group is left wide-eyed at the amount of food we have available to consume. Dips made of yogurt and eggplant, soft salty cheese baked in tomato, salad with black olives, and squid fried in batter. It's all delicious. The bread that accompanies the meal is soft and perfect for enjoying with the dips. The final platter contains meat cooked on the grill and is served with home-cooked fries that are sprinkled with oregano.

"Try this," I say, holding out a plate of strange-looking tentacles.

"What the hell is that?" Luna asks.

"Octopus," Mo says. "Most likely cooked in red wine."

Her expression is so comical that Hudson starts laughing. "Octopus?"

"Yeah…you know, the thing with eight legs."

"Ugh," she says, screwing up her face. "I can't eat that! That documentary on Netflix about the octopus… they're so intelligent."

"You'd be fine to eat Ben then," Connor quips.

Ben tosses a piece of bread at Connor's head, but Connor manages to catch it before it makes contact.

"Manners, children," I shout, enjoying how light-hearted everyone is today. It's a rare occasion for us all to feel relaxed enough to step out of our professional roles, just for a time.

I finish eating first, mostly because I'm distracted. The food is awesome, but the setting is what really deserves my concentration. Pulling a pencil from my pocket, I begin to sketch on the back of a paper menu, my eyes flicking across everything in my view, picking out the things that spark my interest. The restaurant is set on a pretty stone square. Old buildings with intricate balconies and blue wooden doors frame the lively area. I try to capture passers-by with lines of movement to show the bustle of the place, but in the foreground, Luna is still and serene. From the side, her profile is almost doll-like, with a high forehead, button nose, and pointed chin. From this angle, I can't reflect the intensity of her soulful eyes, and so in a way, the woman I've drawn doesn't seem to fully reflect the woman she is.

Hudson leans to look at the drawing, his eyes meeting mine with a question. Is it obvious that I think of her more than I should? Maybe. It's certainly obvious to me that Hudson has a crush on Luna. And Connor. And Jax.

It might be all of us, for all I know.

Stupid men, the lot of us.

She's too young for sure. All of us have at least a decade on her and a whole lot of life experience, much of which we'd like to forget. It's an indulgence to think about her as anything other than a client.

But we're away from home, and I haven't fucked anything except my own palm in three months. I can forgive myself for some inappropriate thoughts.

But inappropriate actions are something else.

When Luna finishes her conversation with Connor about the tour, she turns to me, spotting the folded paper of the menu in my hand.

"What are you drawing, Asher?"

"Nothing," I say, turning it over so she can't see and stuffing it into my pocket. "It's no good," I add, hoping she'll accept that as the reason I don't feel comfortable sharing it.

"Let me see." Luna holds out her hand expectantly. When I don't move to retrieve the drawing, she launches off her chair, throwing her arm around my neck and rifling in my pocket. My instinct screams at me to restrain her like I would a threat. In a second, I have my arm around her like a vice, hand gripping her wrist. Her mouth forms a stunned O, and as quickly as I grab hold of her, I drop my arms like the very touch of her skin has scalded me. Seconds tick past, her green eyes staring into my wide-open blue ones. I hope she can see how much I regret shocking her. I hope she knows that sometimes when you're trained in an action, the reflex overrides any other thought process you might have.

Most of all, I hope I didn't hurt her.

As she pulls back, I hold my hands up. "Sorry…Sorry, Luna. You just…you came at me."

"It's okay," she says, flopping back into her chair. I scan the soft skin of her wrist, searching for any sign of a bruise, but there's nothing visible yet. We're both breathing hard, her shoulders rising with each breath in the same rhythm as mine. Around us, the group is silent.

"Asher," Connor warns, but I shoot him a look that tells him I can handle my own shit. I know my mistake. I'm not trying to cover it up or make excuses for it.

"Did I hurt you?"

Luna shakes her head, gazing back at me. "You really are a machine," she says. "Reflexes like a ninja. I'll have to remember that." A smile tugs at her lips, and then, from her clenched fist, she pulls out the drawing, holding it up high so I can't get to it as she quickly unfolds it.

I'm still too shaken to react. Instead, I'm left to watch her open the drawing I did of just her. There's no one else at the table in my sketch. I ignored all of my friends and zoned in on Luna, picturing her alone and serene with a backdrop of busy Athens behind her.

Bringing it close so she can study the scribbled image, her lips part. They look so soft and sweet, and mentally, I wish away everything that surrounds us. I imagine a movie special-effect that could pull us out of this scene into our very own private space. I could tell her that she's beautiful and not have my six friends chastise or ridicule me. I could tug Luna into my arms, and we could dance to soft music played by the unusual-looking Greek guitar, sliding into another time, over two thousand years ago, when this place was filled with art and philosophy. Luna could be my muse, and I could sculpt her beauty into marble that would be preserved in a museum. Years later, people would speculate over which goddess she was – Aphrodite, goddess of love, or maybe Nike, goddess of victory. They'd never guess she was just a flesh-and-blood woman or that I was just a man with a crush on a girl so far out of his league that it's a joke.

"It's beautiful," she says, smoothing it more firmly against the table. "I'm so sorry I crushed it. I didn't know."

I don't fucking know what to tell her. All eyes are on me, waiting.

Standing, I shove my chair backward. "I need to use the bathroom."

At the mirror, I reach to scoop water into my palms so that I can cool my face.

STEEL 7

Stupid. Stupid. Stupid.

Why the fuck did I draw Luna that way?

Why?

Because my heart never lies. What's inside of me always has to pour out through my drawings or my body. I can't hold in my feelings. I can't resist what inspires me.

I suppressed it all when I was serving in the military. In those days, I could focus on everything but the crazy desire I had to indulge in my art. My dad used to tell me that scribbling on a page would never work as a career. I wasn't talented enough or confident enough. He pushed me into signing up because he wanted me to follow in his footsteps. Now I'm left with memories that I can never wipe away, and the urge to be creative is still in me. But how can I be when I'm part of this group? They need me to be part of Steel 7, and I wouldn't want to be apart from them. Returning home for anything other than the holidays would push me over the edge. My dad is still the same cantankerous asshole that he was when I was growing up. Drying my hands and face on a paper towel, I take a deep breath, readying myself to face the music.

When I finally return to the table, the drawing is no longer visible, the plates have been cleared, and it seems that the check has been paid. Everyone rises, ready to move on to the next part of the day, and I follow, grateful not to return to questioning looks or worse.

It's as though everyone knows that mentioning what happened could push me over the edge.

The cars take us to a steep road that runs next to the Acropolis, and all the way, I'm taking mental pictures of a city I would love to return to at another time when I can meander and drift through the mix of ancient and modern. Where I can sit and find ways to capture the sights through my own fingers. The sun's intensity has reduced as we make the slow climb to one of the world's wonders, a magnificent ancient temple set atop the highest point of

STEEL 7

Athens.

It's spectacular.

Luna stays close, always making sure to position herself between us, never leaving, or allowing herself to become exposed. It makes it easier for us to keep her safe, but something about the timid way she walks and her slightly curved shoulders fills me with unease. For all her anger yesterday, Luna's been changed by the incident in Berlin.

The tour guide talks to us with great speed and animation about the people who built the temple, the artistry, and the craftsmanship. We stand before sculptures that I wish I could sit and sketch, and take in views of the city that blow my mind.

"This is so beautiful," Luna says, pointing to the statues that form pillars to a building. Her eyes meet mine in a silent acknowledgment of my interest in art. "I bet you could draw an amazing picture of these."

Shrugging, I try to brush off her comment, not wanting her to think about the drawing again. "I'm a bodyguard, not an artist."

"You can be both," she tells me. "I'm a dancer and a singer."

"And a woman," Mo says. "A sister and a daughter."

"I'm better at being a singer and a dancer," she says, stepping closer to stare up at the carved women's faces. "Do you think these are based on real women?"

"Who knows." Mo rubs his beard thoughtfully.

"Maybe they were. Maybe they were entertainers just like me."

"Maybe they were the wives of the sculptors?" I say.

"More likely to be their mistresses." Jax grins, and the Greek tour guide laughs.

"I'm so happy we came to see this today," Luna says, pivoting gracefully on one foot to take in the whole sight in a turn that feels as though it's part of a dance. "It's made me want to properly travel the world one day and take in all the sights. When this tour is over, there is no way I'm just going back home. I want to spread my wings." She holds her arms in the air, the warm breeze that drifts across us disturbing the strands of hair around her face.

"You look like a goddess," the guide says. "Like Nike herself."

"Aphrodite," Mo mumbles.

The guide pats him on the shoulder, nodding knowingly. "The goddess of love, huh?"

Luna rolls her eyes. "There's not much in the way of love in my life."

Making a tutting noise in his throat, the tour guide steps closer, pressing his hands to Luna's cheeks like you would a child. "My darling, you are so young. Love comes to all of us. Maybe it doesn't stay forever, but it comes. Don't you worry about that."

When he lets go, there's a glassiness to Luna's eyes that hurts my heart.

The tour continues, but even when we're home, and Luna is asleep, I can't help but remember how sad she looked at the discussion of love.

10

LUNA

The layout of the hotel in Athens is different from Berlin. Here, I have my own room that is flanked by adjoining rooms for my bodyguards. I don't feel as safe with this setup, even though they're close by, so I ask Connor if whoever is taking the nightshift can stand outside my door in the hallway.

As it turns out, it's Asher's turn to watch into the night.

Asher, the man who drew me like something beautiful and mystical, too perfect to be real and too human to be anything else.

I lie in bed with just the nightlight casting a yellow glow over the paper, staring at his artwork. It's not as crumpled as before. I covered it with one of my shirts and used an iron to try to smooth out the wrinkles as best as I could.

For all the things I have in the world, this is now one of the most precious to me.

My heart beats in a strange and skittering way when I remember the look on Asher's face as I saw the image, and how he left the table to escape our scrutiny. All afternoon, he was different, as though the weight of the world had settled on his broad shoulders. As though being *seen* had wounded him.

Now, the man who sees me in a way I don't deserve is standing outside my door, and I can't bear the thought of going to sleep without talking to him. I can't leave things as they are.

When I'm sure the rest of Steel 7 are asleep, I slide out of bed, taking a quick look at myself in the mirror. Wide eyes greet me and flushed cheeks. I chose a clingy slip to wear to bed tonight, and I wish I could say it was for no other reason than comfort, but if I did, I'd be lying.

I knew I was going to ask Asher to come into my room.

I know exactly what effect the pale pink silk trimmed with lace will have on him.

At the door, I hesitate, listening.

The silence tells me that the hallway is deserted except for one man whose only duty is my welfare.

When I turn the handle, I hear the shuffle of footsteps. Light streams through the doorway as I pull it slowly open, moving to lean against the polished wooden door frame.

Asher blinks, gazing down first at my face and then at my body. When he realizes his mistake, he looks away, staring at a point far down the hallway, his hand combing through his messy blond hair. "Do you need something?" he asks.

"Can you come inside? I want to talk to you."

"Connor asked me to wait here. He won't like it."

"Connor's sleeping, and anyway, I'm your client. Aren't you supposed to do whatever I need you to do?"

Asher's shoulders drop, his resistance gone with almost no effort at all. I should feel bad for putting him in this situation, but I don't. I feel powerful.

"What do you need?"

"Just to talk. And for you to sit with me while I sleep." I watch the flicker of awareness in his eyes as he understands what I'm asking of him.

"You want me to stay in your room?"

"I can't rest knowing you're standing out here. If I don't sleep, I won't be able to perform tomorrow. You see my dilemma."

The war Asher is having with himself is written all over his face, but I'm not sure if it's because he's worried about what Connor will think or if he's worried about us being in such close proximity. Instead of continuing, I decide to turn and hold the door open for him. The seconds that tick past as I wait feel long and slow. Warm anticipation settles in my belly, although I'm not certain what I'm anticipating exactly.

All I know is that I want to talk to his man. I want to tell him how I feel about the drawing and see if he'll be transparent enough to tell me what motivated him to sketch me and then act as though he's ashamed about it.

Will he take a step over the threshold?

I want him more than I've wanted anything since Blueday Records signed me.

When his foot makes contact with the plush cream carpet of my room, a little puff of air leaves my lips, and when I close the door behind him, the atmosphere seems to change.

Asher heads straight for the couch by the window. Behind the drawn curtains is an exquisite view of Athens, illuminated like the sparkling, glitter-filled world of a children's fairy tale. But none of that is visible. Instead, the room feels enclosed and warm. A private sanctuary, separate from the rest of the world.

He slumps down with a huff of exhaustion, his

shoulders curling as he allows his long legs to flop open. But once he's settled, I don't know what to do. Should I perch at the other end of the couch or sit on my bed? I want to be close to him, but maybe that'll be too much too soon. Maybe he won't be as open with me without a little distance between us.

I go with the bed, sitting demurely with my knees pressed tightly together, close to the nightstand. I finger the paper with Asher's drawing.

"Why did you draw me?" I ask.

Asher's eyelids drop closed, his fair eyelashes casting dusty shadows over his high cheekbones. There's a refined quality to his face that would be amazing to capture in a sketchbook, but I've never been an artist. Nothing I could produce could ever do him justice. Maybe I could write a song about him. That could work.

"Can we just forget about it?" he says softly.

"No." I cross my legs like I mean business. Asher's eyes drift over the bare skin of my feet, then my calves, and then higher. I keep my eyes on him, waiting. Waiting. Waiting.

"I drew you because I like drawing." The tone of his voice is flat and unconvincing, an excuse to cover the truth.

"Bullshit," I say. "There were a bunch of other people you could have drawn, but you chose me. Why?"

When Asher's jaw ticks, I know I'm getting under his skin. "Why do you want to know?"

I hold his gaze, turning the paper and bringing it closer. "Because you captured something about me that I always hoped someone would see one day but never believed they would. I thought I was too broken. I thought I'd seen too much, and that sparkle...that essence was gone. But you drew it."

Our eyes meet, and I hold his gaze, feeling my stomach

squeeze with nerves. Lower, my pussy contracts with arousal and anticipation. The war inside him is written all over his expression again, but I won't let him cop out. I'll keep pushing and pushing and pushing the way I know best.

"It's not gone," he says softly. "I see it."

Now it's my turn to close my eyes, his words slowly slipping inside me and filling parts that have felt hollow and brittle for so long.

"Luna."

My name sounds like a question, and when I open my eyes, I see it in his expression. It's what drives me to slide off the bed and cross the room. It's what propels me to stand between his parted legs and gaze down at him. In the low light, we are both cast in shadows, the light and the dark, the two sides of every person on this planet. I reach out and touch his cheek, finding his skin so much warmer than mine. When his eyelids lower, this time, I know it's with pleasure and longing. This time I feel his desire rather than his conflict. This time I know he's losing the battle to keep his distance, and so am I.

We're supposed to maintain a level of professional detachment. He's supposed to keep his mind on the job, and I'm supposed to stay aloof, but none of that is happening. His left hand drifts until it rests on my thigh, and everything in me heats. The sound that leaves his lips is pained, and I like knowing that this is pushing him past a comfortable place. I like that he's not in control and that I am.

Is it crazy to feel this way?

"When you were drawing me, were you thinking about touching me?"

Asher's fingers tighten, pressing little divots into my flesh. "Yes."

"Where were you thinking about touching me?"

When his eyelids fly open, I realize I've gone too far. He's come to his senses, and this will all be over. "We can't…"

I silence him with a finger pressed to his soft lips. "Can't isn't my favorite word, Asher."

His right hand cuffs my wrist and gently moves my hand away. "It doesn't need to be your favorite word for you to hear it, though." His hand drops from my leg, the spell broken, and my heart tumbles in my chest.

But I was telling the truth about the word "can't." I won't be dissuaded just because Asher wants to hide behind his scruples. Or rather, hide behind Connor's orders.

Connor doesn't rule the world.

Another idea flickers through my mind, taking shape into something sharp and hot and urgent. "I want you to draw me again," I say. "Now."

"I'm working," he protests.

"What better way to closely monitor my safety?" There's a folder on the mahogany desk that contains headed notepaper and a hotel-monogrammed pen and pencil. Before Asher can object again, I take it and hand it all to him, then return to the bed.

The scene from the film *Titanic* floods my mind. The main character lies naked, wearing only a jeweled necklace. I don't think I'm brave enough to do that, although a rebellious part of me that loves to shock would enjoy it. It's more that if I stripped off this scrap of pink silk, Asher would be out the door, but if I lie back, sliding one strap down and find a spot on the floor to stare at, maybe he'll be tempted enough to pick up a pencil.

My hands are shaking as I arrange myself in what I'm hoping is a seductive pose. My hair is loose, so I leave it trailing over the pillow behind me. I don't look at Asher, scared that if I do he'll put a stop to this, so I don't see him rise from the chair until his feet enter my field of vision. He's so tall that he looms over me, obliterating the ceiling. I have no idea what he's going to do, so when his fingers gently guide my hair over my shoulder, I shiver with the sensation, and when he pushes the hem of my slip higher on my thigh, I think he's given up on the idea of drawing, and he's really going to touch me.

But as fast as he rose to adjust my pose, he's back on the couch poised to draw.

The only sounds in the room are our breathing and the teasing scratch of the pencil against paper. I try to keep as still as possible, wanting Asher to have the best chance of creating another beautiful picture and hoping that he'll capture me in that way that touches my heart.

When I chance a glance, his face is a mask of concentration, brow furrowed, eyes lowered, and a serious mouth. When he pulls the side of his bottom lip between his teeth, it does things to me that I could never admit in public.

What would Asher say if I told him I'm wet for him?

What would he feel? Is he hard between his legs as he sketches the swell of my breasts? Is he yearning to touch the skin he's capturing in grayscale?

The urge to breathe faster and deeper is hard to resist. If he could look into my eyes, he'd see that my pupils are blown wide with arousal.

Sometimes, it's not sex that brings the most excitement. It's these kinds of intimate moments that send a shiver of anticipation through me. It's the drag of the minutes that we aren't having sex that I'll remember when I'm old and thinking back across the most erotic moments of my life.

Maybe I'll recount this story at a time when I no longer care about being appropriate. Maybe I'll be like *Blanche* from the *Golden Girls*, still living my best life into old age. I almost snort, thinking about all the things

I'm not doing right now that would constitute my best life.

It's hard to be grateful and ungrateful at the same time.

My mind wanders home to Tyler, and Sandy, and his friends. His profile picture captures them all in their den, six men surrounding one very happy-looking woman. Among them is the niece I haven't met yet but hope to soon. My mind wanders to worrying about my mom, although I know Tyler is going to do his best to take care of her. It wanders to a time when I was lying in a dry field with my brothers, staring up at the sky, talking about all the things we'd do when we were grown up. No one knew that Jake wouldn't get to do anything, and no one would have predicted that I would come so far.

But the truth of it is that I would do anything to snap my fingers and be back in that moment. I'd do anything to change history so that Jake never got on that motorbike, even if it meant I was never in the right place at the right time to become Luna Evans, popstar. It's how I know that deep down, the fame doesn't mean anything to me.

"Are you okay?" I whisper softly. "Can I see yet?"

Asher shakes his head and continues, and I try to stay in the room with him, not drift into my memories again. I think over what I can remember from his written profile. He's an only child from a small town in Utah. Even knowing that about him, I can't picture the light-haired little boy Asher must have once been. He was decorated for bravery despite seeming too gentle to have ever fought an enemy. He's a man who's lived with violence, but who seems more at home wrapped in the quiet concentration of his art.

Eventually, Asher rubs the image with his finger one last time and lowers the pad. His eyes blink and then widen as though he's noticing me for the first time.

"Can I see?"

He nods, then stands slowly to bring me the drawing. I don't move to sit, not wanting to disturb my pose just yet. There's a moment of hesitation where he holds the paper just a little too far away for me to see. When he finally hands it to me, I'm moved by the slight tremble to his fingers and even more moved by the picture.

It's everything I hoped it would be and more. I am me, but I'm better. His pencil strokes have immortalized the wantonness of my pose, and the buzz of anticipation that is fizzing through my body. The girl in the picture isn't just reclining. She's yearning and hungry for something more than the moment. The lump that forms in my throat isn't rational, but it's there anyway. Swallowing it down, I inhale deeply, trying to push down the swell of emotion that's threatening to bring tears. The movement of my chest causes the strap of the slip to slide further down my arm, and the silken fabric drops lower over my breasts, revealing the top of my left nipple.

Asher makes a pained sound in his throat, his eyes falling closed. "Why are you doing this?" he asks. "You know that nothing can happen between us."

"Nobody has to know," I say. "They're all sleeping. How would they find out?"

He mutters an expletive under his breath, this time running both hands through his hair and staring to the ceiling for inspiration.

He'll find nothing there but a smooth, plastered surface. No heavenly inspiration, that's for sure.

I let the drawing drop to the nightstand, and I swing my legs off the side of the bed, moving to stand in front of him and allowing the slip to fully reveal one breast. Reaching for his right hand, I bring it to cup my breast, watching the moment the soft warmth makes contact with his broad palm, seeing the desire building in his eyes. For a long moment, we're both still except for our ragged breathing, then his hand tightens, squeezing my breast, his thumb brushing my nipple.

And then it's like zero to sixty in a second. His hand grips the back of my neck, crushing my mouth to his as my arms slide around his chest, pulling him close.

I'm on my back in seconds, the hard ridge of his cock pressing urgently against my clit as his hand tugs up the hem of my slip. "Fuck," he says again, but this time it's breathy and excited rather than frustrated. I'm so slick between my legs that I'm pretty sure he could just shove his cock right in, and it wouldn't hurt at all. Even through four layers of fabric, I can feel that he's big enough to make me feel it.

The slide of his tongue into my mouth is all about possession. His fingers graze my skin as though he's trying to draw something onto to me. I fumble with his buttons, trying to gain access to his warm skin. His chest and abs are tight and muscular, my hands sliding over them as though I'm trying to read the braille of his body and discover all his secrets.

And inside me, everything is buzzing. It's that same feeling of achievement that I get after a show. The same feeling I got when a pen was placed into my hand, and I scratched my childish signature onto a recording contract. It's about me having the freedom to do what I want. It's about me finding my power and confidence and taking strides away from the frightened little girl I used to be, hiding behind my brothers for security.

Maybe you're still hiding, but this time behind your bodyguards, a small voice whispers in my mind, but I push it aside because Asher has shoved up the fabric of my slip and taken my nipple into his warm mouth.

And oh God that feels good. When he dips lower, nuzzling my navel, kissing my belly, drifting lower, I hold my breath.

Oral sex is an intimate thing. More intimate than penetrative sex in a way, but I don't feel shy when his tongue finds my clit through the sheer fabric of my panties or when he pushes them aside and licks a hot stripe between my legs. I close my eyes and revel in the way he licks and sucks, bringing up my legs to let him go deeper with his tongue.

I hold his head gently, not because he needs guidance but because I enjoy the little flicker of control it hints at, and when he moans, I think maybe that he likes it too.

Asher brings me close, over, and over, and each time pulls back. He's hungry, but he's restrained, and it drives me crazy. He's painting me with his desire but never truly committing to the picture. By the third time, my legs are shaking, and my pussy is leaking between the cheeks of my ass, and the word "please" escapes from my lips. He smiles against the inside of my thigh, pausing for just a moment, then he's freeing his cock and resting in the cradle of my thighs, bending to kiss me deeply as he thrusts deep in one motion.

Everything in me gives way to his power, and the surrender feels so sweet that tears prickle behind my eyes. Instead of letting them fall, I pull him closer, burying my face into the alpine-scented safety of his neck, moving with him until I forget about the past or the problems of the present. There's no time to think about what might happen in the future when this is over. No time to worry that he isn't wearing protection. In a blink, I'm cresting into the sweetest orgasm of my life.

11

BEN

I wake suddenly, feeling as though it's still the middle of the night. My eyes are grainy and stuck together, and my mouth feels dry too. Squinting into the darkness of the room, I touch my phone screen to check the time. It's two-thirty.

All around me, the soft sounds of sleep can be heard. Connor and Mo are out for the count, exhausted from the traveling and the previous late night.

I don't want to disturb them but getting up to check what the noise was that broke my sleep is a more difficult prospect than it used to be.

My prosthetic is propped against the bed for easy access, and I'm so used to strapping it on that I can do it in the dark, feeling for everything with my fingertips. I rush through the process, feeling certain that the noise came from Luna's room. I crane my ear for noise, wondering if Asher heard and has checked on Luna. He has a key card for her room to use in emergencies. The adjoining doors to our rooms are left open on the explicit understanding that no one will pass through them unless there's a risk of harm.

I'm steady on my feet as I pad to the door to the hallway. Turning the handle slowly, I pull it open quickly, confident that Connor and Mo sleep heavily enough not to be disturbed. When I find Luna's door unprotected, I turn my head to check the other hallway, finding Asher is nowhere to be seen.

Fuck.

What the hell is he playing at?

Maybe he needed to take a piss. He had a key card for our room, but when I check, the bathroom is empty. I tilt my ear up again, straining to catch any kind of sound. Disturbing Luna for no reason wouldn't go down well, particularly if Asher has taken a walk to get some snacks or a drink from the vending machine by the elevators. The thought doesn't sit right with me at all. Asher is as diligent as the rest of us about his duties.

I catch a pained sound coming from Luna's room. A whimper.

Stepping closer to the door to her room, I press my ear against the cool wood.

A man's voice growls, and Luna whimpers again and fuck, my instincts go into overdrive.

Asher's left Luna unprotected, and the psycho stalker from Germany is carrying out his threat. I don't wait for another second, tugging the door open and stepping inside the room.

What I see is not what I expect to find.

The lamp on the nightstand illuminates some of the most frantic sex I've ever witnessed. Luna's legs are pinned high over the shoulders of the man who's pumping into her as though he's trying to bury himself between her thighs. Her fingers are pressed into his ass, tugging him harder and harder while she whimpers and begs for more.

But rather than clubbing the stalker over the head, I take a shocked step back because the man on top of Luna isn't a stranger. It's Asher, my buddy, who should be standing guard in the hallway.

It takes a second for them to register the sound of the door scraping against the plush cream carpet, then Asher's head spins to stare directly at me.

Everything goes still: my heart in my chest, Asher's hips, Luna's fingers.

But it's not just from embarrassment. It's with the realization that they've been caught doing something forbidden.

Fraternizing with clients isn't permitted for a good reason. Sexual connection increases the risk for both parties, and it's unprofessional. Something like this, if it got out, could ruin our reputations in the industry. It could even lose us the contract with Blueday Records.

I knew it was coming, though. There's something bubbling under the surface with all of us that I don't quite understand. Maybe we've all been single for too long. Maybe it's being around someone who shines as brightly as Luna. Maybe it's the knowledge that doing anything with her is forbidden.

Don't we all love the thrill that comes with breaking the rules just a little?

"Get the fuck out of here," Asher hisses, coming to his senses. He sounds different, like a man on the edge, poised to do something terrible.

I step out of the room, closing the door as quietly as I can. Connor and Mo are still sleeping soundly, an ability that they probably honed living under fire for so long. An ability that I'm grateful they have.

It takes me a minute to remove my leg, sliding back under the covers and turning onto my side.

But I can't sleep.

My mind is filled with the sounds that Luna was making. Her desperate pleas for Asher to push her over the edge.

I've thought about what it would be like to be with her more times than I can remember, but I'm not a rule-breaker by nature.

And anyway, she wouldn't want me – a broken man – when she could have anyone in the world.

But she chose Asher, my internal voice argues. He's no billionaire. He's not a famous musician or someone who can increase her profile. He's just an ordinary guy.

She's probably just using him for sex. Women have needs too, and if there's no one else around, why not grab hold of the nearest bodyguard? Aren't women's romance novels filled with stories like that?

But what if it's more than that? I've seen the way her eyes drift over us, as though she imagines us with fewer clothes. I've seen her small smiles when we're making jokes or doing things to take care of her. I've seen the softness beneath the hard shell she's constructed to protect her from the world.

I've seen the way the rest of my crew look at her as well, and even the mutterings about Jax's crush and his ramblings about Luna being the perfect woman for us to share.

I observe everything around me, and now I know too much.

Either I keep Asher's secret and risk the fallout, or I tell Connor what I saw and stand by to watch an explosion that could obliterate our bond.

I'm not a rat. I don't snitch on my buddies, but I've never had to cover up something that could have such damaging implications for the group as a whole.

I squeeze my cock, trying to relieve the ache that seeing

Luna on her back has left me with.

Tomorrow, I'll talk to Asher. Maybe he'll commit to stepping back and maintaining professional distance. Maybe he'll want to tell Connor what happened and deal with the consequences himself.

Whatever happens, I'll have to face it in the morning.

But as I slide into sleep, I wonder again what it would be like to have Luna all to myself.

12

MO

Luna is running through the soundcheck while we stand around looking pretty. So much of this job is just passing the time, glancing around, and suspecting every human being you meet of being a psycho capable of anything. Part of that comes naturally to me. The suspicious part. Where I grew up, having that skill was the difference between life and death. Anyone could be your enemy. Anyone could want you dead. Even those who didn't want you dead could kill you by accident. War leaves scars that never heal. The ones in the mind can be worse than the ones inflicted on the body.

Asher is resting after taking the night shift. Connor, Jax, and Hudson are on one side of the stage, and Ben, Elijah and I are on the other. I glance at Ben and catch him biting the skin off the side of his thumb. I know his stress-tells well. Finger-biting tells me he has something on his mind.

"What's going on?" I ask him. "You're going to end up with only four digits on that hand if you keep that up."

"Nothing," he says abruptly without looking at me, but he drops his hand into a semi-flexed fist by his side.

I snort, not believing him for a second. "You can pretend all you like, but I know you, Ben. You have something marinating under all that black hair."

"The only thing marinating under that hair is Ben's crush on Luna." Elijah punches Ben on the shoulder good-naturedly. "I've been watching you all day, staring at her like you've got x-ray vision. And I've seen her blushing too. What the hell is going on between you guys?"

"Nothing," Ben hisses. "As if I'd do something so reckless. I thought you'd know me better than that."

"Jax is reckless," I say. "Asher is led by his heart. Elijah can't decide between left and right."

"And me?" Ben asks.

"You procrastinate behind every decision. Definitely not reckless."

"So why has he bitten his thumb to the point that it's raw?" Elijah probes.

In front of us, Luna's singing reaches its highest, the speakers distorting until they're adjusted to cope with the power of her voice.

"He knows something," I say. "Something he wishes that he didn't. He was like this in Iraq when Jax raided Connor's chocolate stash. He can't take sitting on other people's secrets. He's like a hen sitting on a molten egg."

Ben snorts as though I'm talking garbage, but it's not convincing. I know my friends sometimes wonder if I'm aware of what's going on around me. They think the fact that English is my second language means that I miss the subtleness that bubbles under the surface. They worry that my memories cloud my concentration, but they keep me around anyway because we have ties that bind us. What they don't realize is that I see everything. I notice, and I process. It's why I don't talk as much as the rest. While they are laughing and joking, I'm building a picture of everything they're aware that they're saying and everything that they're not aware of too.

I used to be a translator for the U.S. military. I've seen the way people say one thing but mean another. I've seen how the choice of one word can change a discussion but also how body language that doesn't match can upset everything.

I know people, and right now, Ben is hiding something.

Ben shifts, shoving his hands into his pockets. The strain of sitting on that hot rock of a secret is getting too much for him.

"You know you can tell us, and we won't tell another soul. We keep our promises and our secrets," I say.

He nods, still staring at where Luna is shaking out her hands and stretching, getting ready to run through one song with the accompanying dance moves.

"Tell anyone, and I'll club you to death with my leg while you're sleeping." He sighs long and low, glancing at each of us to witness our nods of agreement. "Asher fucked Luna last night."

"What the fuck?" Elijah has turned to stare at Ben with his mouth flopped open like a landed fish.

"Eyes on the primary," I say. "Or Connor will get his panties in a twist."

"He'll get his panties in a twist even more if he finds out about that."

"Well, he's not going to, is he? Because we keep our promises and our secrets." Ben stares at us both with determination.

"How do you know?" I ask

"I walked in on them. There's no doubt."

"Fuck." Elijah stares into the cavernous space around us, shaking his head. "Lucky bastard."

"Yeah," Ben says.

I chuckle darkly, noticing that Connor is staring at us from across the stage. That guy has instincts like a panther. "Is there a man in this crew who isn't fawning over the pop star?"

"I don't know, Mo. Is there?" Ben's jaw ticks, a little tell of jealousy that he can't keep hidden.

"You know I love a woman with long dark hair," I say. "It reminds me of home."

Elijah raises his eyebrows. "Jax has it bad. And Hudson and Connor."

"So, the answer is no, then."

"But there's a big difference between imagining your cock somewhere and actually putting it in that place," I say. "If we had to face the consequences for our thoughts, we'd all be in hell."

"Asher looked like he was in heaven," Ben says, clearing his throat.

"Lucky fucker," Elijah says. "But Asher's going to get serious shit from Connor. He might even send him home."

"He can't do that. We need seven of us to fulfill the contract."

"Connor has other contacts he could bring in if needed." Elijah holds his hands out and shakes his head.

"It wouldn't be the same," I say. "Separation isn't an option."

"So, keep your mouths shut," Ben says. "I'll talk to him when we get back. Make sure that nothing happens again. If it's in the past, it won't affect the future."

"If only that were the case with everything in life." I know for a fact that the past shapes the future like a child molding a ball of dough.

Luna flicks her dark hair over her shoulder, and my eyes follow her every move. She's a beautiful woman. As mysterious as the moon she's named for and as bright as the stars that surround it. Beautiful enough for me to think past the urges of my cock to something more serious. Could she learn to cook like my mother or be as kind as my sisters? Is she as bright as my cousin, who learned to teach instead of getting married? All my traditional thoughts make me feel ridiculous because I know the men around me aren't thinking of Luna as wife material. They're thinking like animals searching for physical satisfaction.

At least, I think they are.

"Talk to him. Find out what his plan is. That's if he has one outside of getting his dick wet." Elijah pulls a bottle of water from his pocket and takes a long swig.

"Here she comes," I say, as Luna bounds over, avoiding Ben by traveling the extra steps to go around us to the table. She drinks the whole bottle of water in a few noisy, thirsty glugs.

"We're done for now," she says. "Time to get ready."

Connor and Jax have already gone ahead to check Luna's dressing room. I'll be standing to protect the room tonight when there are more people in the stadium.

Connor radios to give the all-clear, and then we escort Luna so she can shower and change out of her casual clothes and into the explicit costume she's going to be wearing for her first three songs tonight.

Angelica is waiting, hustling the hairstylist into the room, so he's ready and waiting for Luna. While she's showering, we take some time to sit and rest, eating delicious Greek-style pastries filled with feta cheese and spinach, and mini crescent-shaped breads stuffed with olives. Although they're not quite the same, they still make me think of home. Connor paces, clutching the phone so tightly his knuckles are white. He's trying to get a handle on the stadium security and who is doing what. I cock my head and raise my eyebrows, code for "Do you need some help," but he shakes his head. Always so independent, he doesn't realize that he could make his life a lot easier by spreading the load a little.

Just as I'm picking up another delicious savory pastry, Ben's phone rings. I catch Asher's name emblazoned across his screen, and Ben hesitates to answer it for a second. "Go talk to him," I whisper, careful to make sure that Connor is facing in the other direction.

"Okay." Ben struggles to his feet and heads for the door, and I decide to follow. Someone else needs to monitor this exchange because it could get heated, and there is no way that a woman, even one as special as Luna, should come between us all.

Outside the dressing-room door, Ben frowns at me. He's annoyed that I'm not leaving him to handle this, and maybe he's slightly justified. Mainly he just has a chip on his shoulder, imagining he's less of a man since he lost his leg.

If he'd only realize that a man's worth comes from inside him, he'd be a lot happier.

"What the fuck were you thinking?" he hisses into the phone. Not the friendliest greeting that Asher will ever have received.

I lean closer, trying to hear Asher's response. "She asked me to draw her. She pushed me and I...I couldn't resist," he says. "Now I don't know what to do."

"Yes, you do," Ben says gruffly. "You know exactly what to do, but you don't want to do it. You have to tell Connor, and you have to insist that it was a one-off with Luna. She has to know, or this is going to get messy."

"It already got messy," Asher says.

"Are you seriously deciding your future with your cock?"

"I don't know...you don't have to tell me." Asher sounds worn down and tired, even though he's probably the most rested of all of us right now.

"Just…just…" Ben seems lost for words, and I don't blame him.

"Yeah. *Just* is about the only word I can think of right now." Asher exhales noisily, making the phone crackle with white noise.

"Maybe one of us should talk to Luna," I whisper. "Find out what she's planning."

Ben nods. "How about I talk to Luna," he relays. "Find out what she's thinking."

"I guess," Asher says. "I won't be able to speak to her until later. I mean, we talked after, but she didn't want to go into anything serious. I just wanted to be able to stay with her…you know, treat her like she deserves to be treated, but after you disturbed us, I knew it was too risky."

"I'll talk to her," Ben says.

"Okay. And don't say anything to Connor. If anyone is going to tell him, it's going to be me."

When Ben lowers his phone, swiping to end the call, he shakes his head. "What the fuck was he thinking?"

"Heat of the moment," I say. "He was rushing to not get caught."

"That worked out well on all counts," Ben snorts.

"So, what do you think Luna's going to say?"

"I have no idea. I don't even know if I'll be able to catch a moment with her alone without drawing attention to myself."

"Maybe Elijah can cause a distraction?"

"Good idea."

Ben re-enters the dressing room with renewed purpose. Luna has already emerged from the bathroom dressed in a plush black robe, with her wet hair wrapped in a towel turban. The hairdresser is new – a very stylish Greek dressed in designer jeans and a white button-up shirt that's left undone at the collar. He's unpacking all the tools of his trade, humming a tune I don't recognize.

"Take a seat, my darling," he says, with a roll to his r's, his dark eyebrows rising expectantly. "I'm gonna make you look beautiful."

Luna sits, distracted by her phone. I try to stand close enough to look at her screen over her shoulder, but it isn't easy. I want to find out if she's messaging Asher but she's swiping through fast and typing in a really small font. Tutting under her breath, she begins dialing a number.

"Greg. What is it?" Her tone is clipped and frustrated.

A man's voice rumbles through the phone, but not loud enough for me to hear. The hairdresser begins combing through Luna's wet hair and she's blocked from my view.

"What?" Luna snaps. "But Tyler promised me he'd look after her."

There's more rumbling chatter before Luna responds, swiping away the hairdresser's hand so she can focus. "Which hospital?" When she hears the answer, her hand flies to her face and rubs over her forehead. "I'm going to have to come home," she says.

Connor's ears prick, and the hairdresser catches my eyes in the mirror, raising his eyebrows and shrugging his shoulders, more excited by the gossip than he is concerned about Luna. We all know that she's contracted for this tour.

"I'm going to come home," she says again, as though Greg is arguing with her on the other end of the line.

"But she needs me," Luna says, tears welling in her eyes. The sight of her distress feels like a shard of glass to my heart. I never was good at witnessing women cry. Instinct takes over, and I drop to my knee, taking her free hand. It's what I would do when my mom or sister was upset. Just the silent reassurance was enough to get them through difficult times. Luna blinks with surprise, then stares down at my hand wrapped around her slender fingers. She doesn't draw away through. "Tyler should have done better," she says. "Can you send me regular updates? I want to know if anything gets worse…okay thanks."

Dropping the phone into her lap, she inhales a shaky breath. "Are you okay?" I murmur. When she shakes her head, I squeeze her hand just for a second. "We're here," I say. "If you need anything."

"My mom's sick," she says, then shakes her head. "She's sick because she started taking drugs again." Her throat moves as she tries to swallow down her emotion. "She promised me she wouldn't go back."

I nod, holding her pretty green eyes with my own. "We can all make promises. Sometimes we keep to them, and sometimes we don't. But always, we disappoint ourselves the most."

"She doesn't care," Luna says. "She never has."

I shrug gently. "We aren't all strong. Some of us have weakness and emptiness inside that we try to hide or fill with other things. Pray for her…if not to God, then to the universe. Ask for her to be filled with light and positivity. It's all you can do, sweetheart because we can't fix what is broken without help."

Luna nods, reaching out to touch my thumb with her free hand. "Thanks," she says. "I'll be okay."

Smiling, I squeeze her hand again, moving to stand so that the hairdresser can get on with his job. But even as I flop onto the sofa in the corner, I can't forget the feel of her skin against mine or the pain in her eyes.

Asher has taken a step over the line, but he's not the only one who wants to hold this girl close and fill her life with happiness. There's a long line of men behind him.

13

LUNA

All the way through my performance, my mind is whirring. My mom is in hospital. Again. I trusted my brother to look out for her, and he's allowed the very thing I didn't want to happen. He's allowed her to go back to her old ways. He's let her hurt herself, and, in the process, he's hurt me. I paste on a smile as I belt out a trivial song about a cheating ex who isn't even real, dancing so fast that my heart feels like it's going to beat out of my chest. I'm aching between my legs too—a memory of another mistake that has bruised my emotions.

Mistake.

That's not the right word for what happened with Asher.

Passionate fits better.

Overwhelming. Deep. Greedy. Desperate. All those words fit better than mistake.

Between Asher and me, there was no error. We both did what we wanted, taking from each other what we needed. It's outside of Asher and me that we've done something forbidden – broken some part of the bodyguard code of conduct. Maybe I could be accused of abusing my position of power too. Even though I should regret it, I can't.

When Asher was inside me, I felt complete. His hands told me everything that his drawing represented was true. His words whispered in my ear settled a restless part of me. Everything about it was perfect, except being discovered.

At the end of the song, the crowd roars, hands clapping and waving above their heads.

There is a sea of phones fixed on me, recording the person they think I am. Luna Evans, pop star diva. They don't capture the churning in my belly or the brittleness I feel. Behind the booty shorts and torn pantyhose, I'm just someone's daughter. I'm a woman barely out of girlhood who half the time feels like I can crush the world in my palm, and the other half is afraid to make a decision about what to eat without assistance.

"This next song isn't on my album," I say, as my mind catches up to my mouth. What the hell am I doing, deviating from the plan? Behind me, I can practically hear the band's thoughts. *What the fuck?* We haven't rehearsed anything that isn't on the album. But suddenly, all I can think about is singing the little song I wrote in when my brother Jake died. The one that poured out of me, tasting of blood and familial love that was lost.

I don't need the band for this. I don't need the dancers. All I need is my voice. At the side of the stage, Ben and Elijah are standing guard. Ben has a stool to take the weight off his leg when he needs to, and I want that stool. I jog to toward him, and he stands ready to do whatever I need of him. That's what they're like, my bodyguards. Ready to lay their lives on the line for me. Ready to service my every whim. I shouldn't enjoy that fact as much as I do, or resent the limitations to their relationship with me.

"Are you okay?"

"I need the stool," I mouth, and smile as he hands it to me. "I need to talk to you later," he says, forgetting that my mic is on and the whole stadium can hear.

"Sure." I beam as widely as I can as I stride back to the middle of the stage, pretending that Ben didn't just request a private conversation in front of half of Greece and the rest of my bodyguards. That's how bothered he is about what he saw.

He might as well just have announced everything about last night in front of the whole of Steel 7.

I drop the stool near the front of the stage and perch on the edge, blinking as the spotlight zones in on me.

"I wrote this song when I felt like my life had been shattered. Sometimes, the only way to get through the tough times is to plow our pain into something beautiful."

The crowd cheers again, because who hasn't lived through pain in some way or another?

I begin to sing the words.

The chair will never know the shape of you again.
The bed will never feel your weight.
My heart will never heal because you're gone.
And I'm left to live on.
All I can do is hope that one day,
we'll meet,
in another place,
another time.
And I can tell you all the things I stored inside,
imagining that I will tell you in life,
what you mean to me.

Looking up for the first time since I began singing, I realize that the whole stadium is silent, craning to listen, holding phones high to record the words that up until now have been private to me. My throat tightens, but I continue, my voice rising, rending open my chest with the memories of my brother's face. I close my eyes again, dwelling in the song, then trying to pull myself out of the pain, finding solace in the memories from last night. Asher's touch, the weight of his body on mine; everything made me feel better, bigger, stronger.

And at the end, when I drop my head, allowing my long intricate braid to flop over the top, I know.

The only way that I'm going to get through this tour without being dragged back into the negative place that my life was in before I was discovered by Blueday is with men in my bed. Sex helps me forget my worries. I can work out my frustrations and find inner peace. I need a distraction. I need a Band-Aid for my emptiness.

I can fuck my pain away with seven men whose job it is to take care of me. Taking care of my body in public and private will be their mission.

Sandy's not the only girl who can have a harem of men at her disposal. And mine will keep it a secret because they have as much to lose as I do.

Ben can talk to me all he wants about what Asher and I did – the wrongness of it – but when he does, I'll show him just how right it felt.

I'll drag these men into my web, like a black widow spider. I'll eat them up, satisfying my hunger with their bodies, pushing down all the fears I have with their cocks.

I'll drown in their passion and be smothered by their weight.

And when this tour is done, and I can finally go home, I'll have to find a way to deal with everything that I've been burying for too long.

When the performance is over, I'm hurried backstage and to my dressing room, finding Mo, with his kind black eyes, standing guard. At least now, I can be confident that I'm not going to find anything funky in my room. The thought of that bloody underwear sends a shiver through my sweaty body.

"I need another shower," I announce, strutting into the bathroom and slamming the door, content to leave the six men out there to wallow in whatever conversation is going to happen in my absence. I don't switch on the shower immediately, though, choosing to press my ear against the door, straining to hear whatever I can. Almost immediately, Connor growls, "What the fuck was that out there?"

"Fuck."

I'm assuming it's Ben who swears. He must not have intended Connor to know about Asher and me. He must have been hoping to keep it a secret. I guess I should respect him for that. No one likes a snitch, especially among friends.

"Fuck, what?" I picture Connor's face screwed up and angry, covering the deep worry he has about what's going on with his crew.

"It's not my information to share," Ben says. "Can you just leave it?"

"If it's something that can negatively affect Steel 7 or Luna, then no, I can't leave it."

"I'm in a situation where I know something that I shouldn't know and sharing it just wouldn't be fair."

There's a pause, and my heart thuds against my ribs, waiting for Connor's reaction.

"For us to work as a group – as friends and work colleagues – we have to be honest about things. Keeping secrets risks our safety and security. You know this."

"I know, Connor. I do. I just…"

Deciding that putting Ben in this position for any longer isn't fair, I throw open the door and stride out. "What Ben is trying desperately not to share is that me and Asher fucked last night," I blurt without regret. "He tried his best to resist, but I guess I'm just irresistible. Ben walked in on it. Asher is riddled with guilt for doing something that is against your bodyguard bro code. As far as I'm concerned, we're all adults, and we can do what the hell we want. I don't regret it. It was awesome. And, as your client, I would appreciate it if you didn't make a big deal about this. Asher is a grown man. I'm a grown woman. And that's it." Putting my hand on my waist, I cock my hip, wanting to demonstrate that my body language matches my tone. Staring at Connor, I wait for him to react to my challenge.

"Fuck," Connor says, lowering his lids and shaking his head. The way his shoulders slump speaks of great disappointment, but I'm not having that.

"Fuck, nothing," I say. "Orgasms should never be something that we regret. Put yourself in Asher's shoes. If I dragged you into my room and made you sketch me wearing next to nothing, wouldn't you be tempted to cross the line? If I took your hand and pressed it against my breast, would you have the restraint to resist? If no one was looking, wouldn't it cross your mind to just go for it? Be honest."

As I gaze around at the six men in front of me, I swear I can see arousal painted across all their expressions. There's a power in this feeling. Power in owning my sexuality and my needs. Power in being unapologetic about indulging them.

"We all would have been tempted," Jax says. "Hell, I couldn't say if I could have resisted you if you did all that to me."

"You've been thinking about it, haven't you?" I take a

few steps closer until I'm just a couple of inches from his body, gazing up into his soft brown eyes. "You've been thinking about what it would be like to make a move on me. What it would be like to taste me." I let my hand trail his lapel, watching as his lids lower with arousal.

"And you..." Turning to Elijah, I raise my hand to his face. "I've seen you watching me. I've seen the sex in your eyes." His cheek is rough with stubble as I stroke it with my fingers.

"And you..." Hudson doesn't move when I slide my fingers into his palm. "When you were reading to me about Berlin, and I rested my feet against your thigh, you imagined what it would be like to run your hand up my leg."

Gazing into Ben's gunmetal gray eyes, I see the worry there that he's messed everything up for his friend. "And you touched yourself when you got back into bed last night, didn't you?" Ben shifts uncomfortably, and the truth of my words is obvious to everyone who's watching.

"And Mo. You might hide behind your serious facade, but it's there in your eyes and the way they linger on my curves. It's there in the way you touched my hand earlier." The small smile he gives me in response just confirms what I knew.

"And you, Connor?" Reaching up, I take hold of the long part of his tie, adjusting it to make it straight and proud. "I've seen the look in your pretty green eyes. I've seen it all. You can rail on Asher, but any one of you could have been him last night."

As the words leave my lips, I realize that I've given away a lot in that statement. It's as much about them putting themselves into Asher's shoes as it is about my feeling toward all of them. If I was anyone else, I'd be worried that there are seven men in my life that I like enough to invite into my bed. But knowing that my brother lives in the very same setup means this doesn't feel taboo or wrong to me. It's just another way of living. Something that consenting adults can do and should be able to do without judgment.

"I would have resisted, Luna," Connor says softly. "I would have because I understand the risks."

"You really think that in the heat of the moment, when it's dark, and there's no one around, and you're horny, and I'm there, willing and waiting, that you would have put business first?"

"It's not just about business," he says, his voice tight as though he's holding pain behind a veneer of normality. "It's about your safety."

"My safety? You think that you can't keep me safe and fuck me at the same time?"

"My mind would be compromised," he admits.

"Don't you think it would make you more protective? Heighten your instincts? If you loved me, wouldn't you go further to preserve my safety?"

"It doesn't work that way." His tone is flat and final, but I won't accept it. I might be a belligerent bitch, but that comes from growing up with two determined brothers and living in situations where I had to fight my corner or suffer the consequences.

"So if I did this…" Pulling down the strap of my top, I expose the top of my breast and just a centimeter of my nipple. Connor's eyes drift down and then close as he sees what I've done. Around the room, there's an audible inhale of shocked breath from the other men. "And this…" I take Connor's hand firmly, resisting when he tries to pull it away, pressing it against my soft flesh. "And this…" I rise on my toes and take his bottom lip between mine, sucking gently.

A groan leaves his throat as he pulls back. "Don't," he says, but it doesn't sound firm. There's no backbone to his statement. He's just saying what he thinks he needs to say.

"I rest my case."

Turning, I stride back to the bathroom, my heart pounding in my chest like the feet of a stampeding rhino. Connor can say whatever he wants about Asher, but now he'll have no conviction because he knows he would never have said no, in the dark, with temptation urging him forward. None of them would.

And the truth is that I wouldn't have said no to any of my bodyguards, even if they came to my bed all at once.

14

CONNOR

What can I say after Luna's rant and display? What can I say to my crew with conviction when I have none? Luna's right. If it had been me in Asher's place, I would have buried myself inside her and pushed all of my hesitations aside. I'd have done exactly what he did and would have had to deal with the guilt and the consequences the next day.

My eyes meet Ben's, and he shrugs. "I'm not a snitch, Con," he says. "It wasn't up to me to tell tales on Asher."

"All of this is unacceptable," I say. "What the fuck did we learn in Iraq? A team is only as strong as its weakest link. If we're doing things behind each other's backs and keeping secrets, this whole thing is going to go to absolute shit."

"I agree," Mo says. "But Luna was right. If it had been me who she'd set her sights on, I'd have caved too."

"And me," Jax and Hudson say in unison.

I guess it looks like this whole team has a crush on our

client.

Not good.

But there is no point in dwelling on the past. There is no way of changing what is already done. All we can do is change what we do going forward. "Tonight, we need to have a serious conversation, Asher included."

"Okay, boss." Jax throws me a crisp salute, and the rest of the crew nod, which is reassuring. As long as we get back on the straight and narrow and keep our minds on the job, everything will be fine.

Luna doesn't take long in the shower, emerging smelling sweet with a freshly scrubbed face and wet hair twisted into a tight bun at her nape. She cocks an eyebrow at us as though she's daring another confrontation, but I'm not going there. She's on a mission to prove that we're all weak enough to give in to temptation. Pushing harder in that direction isn't going to prove anything good.

"Ready to go?" I ask.

"Sure," she says. "Let's get out of here."

Back at the hotel, Luna disappears into her room, and we all troop off to find Asher. He's resting on his bed reading a crime novel, but looks up when we all appear.

"We need to talk," I say firmly.

Asher's eyes immediately flick to Ben, and I catch him nodding. The twitch in Asher's jaw is noticeable, so I need to quash his assumption that Ben snitched on him.

"Luna told us what happened last night," I say. He straightens immediately and lowers the book to the comforter.

"I know it was wrong." His hands fly up, palms forward. "It was stupid. I should have been stronger, but…"

"You were tempted," I say. "We all get that."

"You do?" Sliding off the bed, he stands, meeting me eye to eye.

Glancing around at the rest of the crew, they all nod. "She's sexy as fuck," Jax says before I can cut him a disapproving look.

"We would all have done the same in your position," Mo says softly.

"You would?"

"But we should all know better." I shake my head, disappointed in my own weakness. "This job is important because there is a real threat to Luna's safety and because it's our most high-profile client since we set up Steel 7. We can't risk any negative stories getting out. It could ruin Luna's career and put an end to our business."

"I'm sorry, Connor." Asher's lids lower, and he shakes his head.

"It's okay. As long as we learn from it."

"Was it good?" Jax asks, his eyes bright with curiosity.

"Don't answer that," I bark. "There's already too much rogue testosterone in this place. We don't need mental images to drive us even crazier."

At that moment, the door that opens into Luna's room clicks, the handle turning. It's pulled open slowly from the other side, and we all stare in through the doorway as Luna takes a seat on a chair. The black lace lingerie that she's wearing hugs her perfect curves and makes her smooth skin glow in the low light. But what's glowing even more are her catlike green eyes. There's mischief there; mischief and challenge.

In my pants, my cock stirs before I can tell myself that this is wrong. I have to stop her.

Luna squeezes a bottle of something into her hand and begins to rub what I'm assuming to be lotion into the skin of her arm. It's a slow and seductive stroke across her own skin, which sets more blood rushing into my cock, and when she slides the strap of her bra down over her toned shoulder, exposing just the top of her nipple as she did back in the dressing room, my mouth waters.

Eyes fixed on her; I do nothing to protest.

I need to be strong and push my craving for Luna aside, but how can I when she's making it so hard? Jax makes a low whistling sound, and the rest of them watch with lowered lids and bottom lips drawn between teeth. Not a man among us, for all our good intentions, has the strength to turn away from temptation. Luna pushes the cup of her bra down, revealing one perfect, round breast, tipped with a tightly drawn rose nipple that's just begging to be sucked.

If I was closer, my fingers would twist it with just enough pressure to send a jolt of pleasure and pain through her body. I'd watch her flinch and then soothe her skin with the warmth of my mouth. I'd dip lower, pushing aside the sheer fabric of her panties and pushing my tongue into her most private place. She'd have to wait for her pleasure, though. Hearing her beg would be the sweetest part because I'd know then that I was under the thick skin she's crafted to hide behind. There would be no keeping me at arm's length. There would be no shielding her vulnerability from my eyes or my body.

She'd put up a good fight, but I could break her.

"Fuck," Asher mutters, as though the memories of last night are surging through his mind.

And still no one tells her to stop, even when she reaches behind to unclip her bra, even when her hands massage slick cream into both her breasts, and lower over her belly, and even when her finger dips underneath the fabric of her lace panties and her eyelids lower.

Letting her legs drop open, she touches herself without a care for who's watching. Her pretty pink lips part, her tongue darting out to moisten them, and her hand moves, but we can't see what she's doing. We can only guess that her index finger is circling her swollen clit. From the enraptured expression on her face, we can only guess how good it feels. And maybe it feels even better because she knows she has seven sets of hungry eyes watching her.

I need to pull myself together and walk across this room to pull the door closed, but she was right. Luna is a temptation that I can't resist.

Turning to my team, I search for someone who will put an end to this madness, but they're all frozen, watching and enjoying too much to even think of doing anything else.

A moan leaves Luna's lips, and then her eyes spring open, scanning over all of us. I'm surprised when she stands, freeing her hand from between her legs and walking slowly forward. I expect her to head to Asher first because he's the one who she's already known intimately, but she doesn't. Instead, with her shoulders back and her hips switching, her eyes catch mine.

My instinct is torn between taking a step back and a step forward. My whole system is confused, so instead I remain where I am, even when she's close enough for me to smell the sweet scent of her lotion and feel the heat radiating from her skin. She raises her hand, and for a second, I expect her to press it to my cheek but that's not what this is about. Luna slides the finger she used to touch herself across my bottom lip and then into my mouth, her eyes never leaving mine.

Oh God, the taste of her fills my senses, my eyelids dropping as though I'm savoring a delicious dessert, and I hear her sigh of satisfaction. "You don't have to resist me," she whispers, stepping even closer. "You can have me, any time you want. Nobody has to know."

As I open my eyes, she turns to the rest of the group. As she moves, her hair shifts, revealing her breasts in a way that's so tantalizing, someone groans. "There's enough of me to go around," she says, running her hands over her waist, hips, and then thighs. Turning, she gazes over her shoulder so she can watch us all salivating at the sight of her ass in high-cut lacy panties. I want to growl at the tingle in my palm to slap that flesh until Luna's whimpering. She thinks that she can tempt us this way and suffer none of the consequences. Well, she's got another thing coming.

"Am I going to have to make myself come, or will you help me?" she asks.

My gaze flicks to Asher's, then Ben's, Hudson's, Mo's, Elijah's, and lastly to Jax. They all have the same desperate plea in their eyes for permission to do what they're craving. They're looking to me to decide something that could bring all of us to our knees.

I know what I need to say.

No.

In no uncertain terms, we cannot do this. It would be better to contact Blueday and tell them to hire different bodyguards. At least then, Luna won't be compromised. We can move on and work for a rich asshole CEO type who won't ever pose any kind of temptation or risk.

But I can't do it.

I don't want to walk away and spend every moment of every day wondering who's taking care of this beautiful, frustrating, brilliant girl. I don't want to lie awake at night wondering if another bodyguard is keeping her warm.

If not us, then who?

Isn't it better the devils I know?

My mind is so jumbled with urges and rationalizations that nothing makes sense except for the gorgeous, crazy woman standing in front of us, beckoning seven men into her bed.

Seven.

I know her brother shares a woman with his five

friends. I've seen them together and imagined what it must be like to stand on the outside looking in as your buddy, or your brother fucks your girl. I thought it was crazy, but now I find myself being drawn into a similar situation there's no madness. Only perfect and unadulterated lust.

I'm a strong man. I can bench two hundred and seventy pounds, and destroy a man with a single punch, but this tiny woman is bringing me to my knees.

"Decide," Luna whispers, and then she tosses her long hair over her shoulder, walking back to her room with a switch of her hips.

Decide.

This rests on my shoulders. I'm the boss, even though it's a position I didn't really want. Now the pressure to lead in the right direction weighs like the world on my shoulders.

No one else says a thing. Seconds tick past, and I close my eyes, drawing in a deep, deep breath and holding it.

I know what's right. I know that walking away is the only way to stop this madness. My team will follow me because that's how things are. But I'm tired of always doing what's right. I'm tired of being responsible and putting my own feelings and desires to the side.

When I open my eyes, I take a deep breath and follow Luna into the darkness of her room, and behind me, the six men I love most in the world, trail me into what might be the best and worst decision of our lives.

15

JAX

When Connor follows Luna, I almost drop to my knees in shock and relief. One minute he's telling us all that we have to be strong and stick to the rules. The next, he's trailing our half-naked client like a puppy on a leash.

And what do the rest of us do?

We follow, of course. We go where Connor goes. He's in charge, and he's just made an executive decision that will earn him the Best Boss in the World certificate for the next decade at least.

Oh my God. Luna looks so hot. My cock is harder than granite, and my balls are drawn so tight it's uncomfortable to walk.

But I do it anyway because there's no way I'm getting into Luna's bedroom last. I'm the one who's been imagining what it would be like to date her when this job is done. Asher managed to get between her legs first, but I'll forgive him for that. His so-called mistake is what's gotten us to this amazing place where one of the most adored pop stars in the world is climbing onto the center of her bed in panties so small that they don't count as clothing. I've seen spiders' webs thicker. It's Asher's weakness that has convinced Luna that this is a good idea. It's his failure to keep to our code that's driven Connor so deep into his arousal that he's ignoring his own advice.

We've all been hypnotized by the prospect of Luna's pussy and I am in no way sorry for being led by what's between my legs.

Seven of us crowd the bed, all of us still fully clothed in our suits. We all still have our communications equipment on too.

Seven men have been drawn like bees to nectar, and now comes the realization that there is only one pot of nectar to share between us all.

How will that even work?

I mean, I'm not ignorant of what it takes for multiple men to fuck one woman. I've seen enough porn on the subject to earn myself a doctorate in gangbanging. But that's very different from this. Those men are fucking for their own satisfaction and the pleasure of the men watching. They don't give a fuck about the woman they're using. She's just a vessel with orifices to slide their cocks into.

Luna isn't like that.

That isn't how I want this to be for her.

But we've never fucked together before. We haven't worked out the rules, and so there is no finesse to this situation. And Luna deserves finesse. She deserves our absolute best. She needs all the skills we can bring to give her pleasure. It's the only way I can guarantee that this won't be a one-off.

We're on the road for weeks, always together in whatever hotel we're staying in. As bodyguards, we have unfettered access to more and more of this. A dull tour filled with duty could become something so much more interesting. It could give us the chance to show Luna that we're men she wants to keep around. This is our moment.

So why do I feel so worried that we're all going to fuck it up?

We can't get to know Luna the way she deserves like this.

We won't be the men she needs if we run in, all guns blazing. If our military experience has taught us anything, it's that a meticulously planned operation will turn out better ninety-nine percent of the time. A rushed operation will nearly always fail or at least result in some casualties along the way.

Sex and casualties are not a good combination.

I need my crew to understand that simple fact. They're all thinking with their dicks right now, not their heads. Touching Connor's shoulder, I whisper, "There's too many of us," close to his ear. "You go first. Then, if she wants more, come get us one by one." When his eyes meet mine, an understanding passes between us. He knows how much I want this, but I'm offering to give up my place at the table for the greater good.

I start to back off, clearing my throat so that the others can see that there's been a change of approach. Connor nods his head at the door, and the rest of the crew gets the message quickly. Luna's eyes follow us all as we leave, her mouth opens in protest, but when Connor begins to loosen his tie and unbutton his shirt, her gaze drifts to his muscular chest. Ben is the last to leave, but I hesitate with my hand on the door handle. Luna wasn't looking for privacy, so maybe I don't need to close it. Maybe we can watch, listen, and learn from a distance.

As Connor loosens his belt and unbuttons his black pants, I watch Luna push up on her elbows and spread her legs. There's an almost palpable crackle of electricity buzzing between them as he climbs over her, dipping to kiss her lips, tentatively then deeper. He presses his knee against her barely covered pussy, eliciting a moan that forces me to take hold of my cock and squeeze. But when he kisses slowly downward, sucking her pretty nipples and nuzzling her navel, I have to rest against the wall to stop myself from falling.

It's not normal to like a girl and get turned on by watching her fuck someone else. Or is it? Who knows what's normal when it comes to sex? We all have our own kinks and fetishes, the little things that turn okay sex to amazing and mind-altering sex. Maybe I just found mine.

"I don't know how you can watch," Hudson says. "That shit would just about stop my heart. I don't have the restraint. I'd be back in there, shoving Connor out of the way, the lucky fuck."

"You should try watching," I say. "Because today, we're taking turns, but it might not always be that way. You know that in situations like this, taking turns isn't the norm."

"Luna can't take us all at the same time. She's too fucking tiny." Hudson folds his arms and shakes his head. With biceps straining the sleeves of his jacket, his six-four frame is certainly intimidating. He might dismiss the idea now, but if he was watching Luna and Connor grasping at each other as though they want to rip each other's skin off, maybe he'd have a different opinion.

"She'll take us all," I tell him. "She can take it."

"So why the fuck did you usher us all out of the room?" Elijah says.

"Because we need to learn how to be with her first," Mo says, resting his hand on my shoulder. "This man can be serious when it counts. What he did was right."

"It had better be," Asher says. "Because if you just fucked things up for all of us…"

Mo shoots Asher an exasperated look. "You've already

had your fun. You're the last of us who should be feeling annoyed right now."

"Jax shouldn't get to speak for all of us," he replies, shrugging his shoulders. "He's not the boss of any of us. Most of the time, he's not even in charge of his own mouth."

As Connor sheathes his cock, lining it up with Luna's entrance and thrusting, Asher's frustrated insinuations dull into the background. What would it feel like to be surrounded by that tight wet heat? How would her hands grasping first at my biceps and then at my ass make me respond?

Maybe Connor will satisfy Luna enough, and she won't want the rest of us. Maybe he'll make her come so hard that any prospect of future orgasms will feel like too much.

"Harder," Luna hisses, which grabs Hudson's attention. Moving closer, he watches as Connor hitches Luna's leg over his shoulder and thrusts deeper. Fuck, he's working so hard that his back muscles are rippling, and a sheen of sweat is forming over his skin. He's pounding so fast that it matches the beat of my heart, and all of us, even Hudson, are straining to watch through the narrow doorway, leaning in to hear the whimpering sounds Luna makes as she gets closer.

"Fuck," Hudson growls, and Luna's body goes limp. It doesn't take Connor long to reach his own pinnacle of pleasure, his back arching and a rumble coming from his throat that's loud enough to wake Hades.

"It's looking like that will be it for the night," Ben mumbles.

But as Connor leans to kiss Luna lazily, her eyes meet mine across the room, and I'm not so sure.

16

LUNA

Oh my God. I think Connor just broke my brain.

How many times have I looked into his mysterious green eyes and wondered what it would be like to be under him, feeling the power of his body over mine? And now I have been, he's confirmed all my fantasies and more.

All my fantasies involving just one man. But there are six others in the next room, standing in the doorway with their eyes feasted on their very own little porn show.

And I've imagined too many times what it would be like to be surrounded by these men. The sun at the center of a universe of masculine planets. They can orbit and orbit until my energy is depleted.

But they seem to be more cautious than me. One minute they were all in the room. The next, they were all leaving except Connor. Are they worried about being too much for me? Are they worried about rushing things? Or is it something else?

Do they not want to get up-close-and-personal naked?

Surely it can't be that. They've all bunked with each other. I can't imagine that privacy is a big thing between men when they are living in close confines in a warzone.

It's not like they'd need to touch each other either, but perhaps I'm further along in imagining this. It could be that I need to provide some encouragement.

As Connor kisses me, I slip into the sensual movements of his lips, loving the slickness of his hard body after all the work he put into pleasing me.

And when we eventually draw apart, I glance over to the door, finding Jax and the rest of my bodyguards watching everything. But it's Jax who's closest. It's Jax who seems the most eager to be next, and I like eager.

"Jax," I whisper, watching as he starts to loosen his tie before he makes his way nearer to the bed. Connor's face hardens, the complex situation that surrounds us suddenly coming into focus. I place my hand against his cheek as he starts to pull away. "Stay," I say, leaning up to kiss his lips. Turning in his arms, I face Jax, who's definitely understood what I need. He's left his clothes in a messy trail across the room, but I don't give a shit about tidiness. All I care about is how sexy he looks climbing onto my bed naked while I'm wet from fucking another man.

"Are you still needy, baby?" Jax asks, his eyes as soft as melted chocolate. Smiling, there's a cheekiness about him that contradicts the roughness of his broken nose and torn left ear. It's as though light pours from inside him, covering my face in a glow that's uniquely his.

Behind me, Connor snorts. "You think I didn't get her off?" he grumbles. "I have never left a woman needy in my life."

"I'm needy," I tell Jax as I slide Connor's hand over my breast. "For both of you."

"Fuck," Connor huffs, his fingers already playing with my nipple, his pride forgotten. My eyelids drop closed as

Jax presses a kiss to my lips, his rough palm already caressing the curve of my hip, moving lower until he's gripping my ass.

"I'm needy for all of you," I say.

"All of us?" Jax dips his head to kiss me, drawing my bottom lip between his and sucking gently.

I smile against his mouth, and when he pulls back to gaze into my eyes, I nod. "All of you. At the same time."

"Are you sure?" he asks. "Are you sure we won't be too much for you? None of us wants to hurt you."

"I'm sure," I say. To be honest, I'm not as certain as I'm making out. I have no idea what it will physically take to please seven huge muscular men at the same time, but I'm eager to find out. I trust that these men will always put my safety and happiness above their own, even in the heat of the moment. Time and time again, they've proven to me that they are good and decent.

Jax nods again with a solemn air. I'm used to him being the joker of the group, but where it counts, he can be serious and considerate. I like that combination a lot.

He pushes himself up on one arm, his bicep bulging deliciously, and waves to his friends from the doorway. "Get in here."

Connor rolls slowly away to give the others space to slot in next to me. As each of my bodyguards remove their shirts and pants and kneels on the bed, my heart thuds a drumbeat of expectation.

Oh God, they are all gorgeous. Toned and muscular from years of making their bodies into worthy fighting machines. Some have tattoos like Connor, whose script isn't something I can read, and Hudson, who has the name Hartley inked across his heart. Some have scars, like Mo, whose back reveals the crisscross lashes of a whip, and Ben, who's lost a whole limb during his service. Connor's back is scarred too, a lattice of wounds that could be shrapnel or maybe something more sinister left over from childhood. I saw kids like that in foster care and group homes. Battle-weary from shitty childhoods.

They're all different but all perfect.

"Luna, baby. We'll be careful with you," Elijah says, bending to kiss my calf.

"All you've got to do is tell us if it's too much, and we'll stop," Mo says softly. His hand hesitates over my skin, and he takes a deep breath, allowing his eyelids to drop before he finally allows himself to touch me.

Ben hangs back as though he thinks I'm going to be bothered about his disability. He doesn't know how much his sacrifice means to me or how the extra effort it takes him to do his job has inspired me. I know that he must carry emotional scars, but he pushes forward, and for that, he's earned my admiration. Plus, with his coal black hair and cloud gray eyes, he's sexy as hell.

Jax impatiently leans in to kiss my lips, and I close my eyes, wanting the security of the darkness behind my eyes while I get used to the feeling of so many men around me.

Hands explore my body as though they're mapping out an undiscovered land. Lips find parts of my skin that have never been kissed before, my ankles, the backs of my knees, the small of my back. I'm shivery with anticipation as Jax's fingers slide between my legs, searching for my slick and swollen clit.

When I moan, it's followed by the growl of at least two men. Mo slides in behind me, using his big hands to cup my breasts, driving me crazy with the tempting press of his cock against my ass. "You ready for me?" he murmurs against my ear, nipping it before I have a chance to nod.

He's notched against my entrance so fast, and with Jax's finger still working my clit, my pussy accepts him in with no resistance.

"Fuck, you're wet."

Wet and about to come, I'd say if my tongue wasn't stuck to the roof of my mouth and my brain cells hadn't upped and left the building.

Two thrusts are all it takes, and I'm bucking against Mo, making noises that don't even sound human.

"Shit," I hear Jax say. "She comes like a fucking rocket."

Mo, who's thrusting faster through it all, grunts, "You have no idea."

Even though I'm done, Mo doesn't race to his own finish line. There's a finesse to the way he fucks into me with rolls of his hips, gripping onto my hips so I fit perfectly into the curve of his body. When he comes, I don't even get to enjoy the feeling of him softening because he pulls out quickly so that Jax can take his place.

I'm rolled onto my back, and Jax holds himself over me on thick, muscular arms. "Ready for number three?" he says.

In my mind, I register that there are still four men waiting at the sidelines for their own satisfaction, but rather than feeling overwhelming, a buzz of sensation skitters up my spine. With so many men, there is never going to be that moment when I'm still needy for more, but my man is already sleeping. There's never going to be a time when I'm left unsatisfied.

Fucking Jax is hot as hell and sweet too. He kisses the corner of my mouth with a smile curving his lips. He nuzzles my neck with his nose and tells me I smell like summer blossoms. When I get close to coming again from just the graze of his hips against my clit, he teases me for being so easy to please, but when I come, things get serious. Just like the two sides of a coin, the flip side of Jax is completely different. When it's just about him, he's overcome with intensity and pounds so deep and hard it's as though he wants to bury himself inside me. When he comes, the softer Jax is back, flopping on top of me and panting into my hair, laughing with a little bubble of delight, like a kid who just got given ten dollars to buy candy.

He's not selfish either, pulling back quickly like the others did to let his friends come forward and take his place.

There are still so many of them waiting.

And I'm as hungry for fourth, fifth, sixth, and seventh helpings as I've ever been for anything in my life.

17

ELIJAH

Waiting on the sidelines while Luna fucks my friends fucking blows my mind. I've seen this shit in porn and understood the appeal, but being here in person is different.

I'm close enough to touch her. Close enough to see her eyes screwed up before she comes and the whip of an orgasm that turns her body rigid. I'm close enough to hear how turned on Jax is and to witness the sensations that he's experiencing.

My cock is like a nightstick in my palm, hot and heavy and ready to slide into Luna's tight, wet heat. I'm so ready that when Ben takes a step forward, I almost grab him by the shoulder to pull him back. But knowing what I know about my friend since the explosion he lived through, there's no way I'd push him aside. If he's feeling confident enough to rock Luna's world, I want him to take his chance.

Kneeling on the bed, his prosthetic juts out awkwardly.

Luna, sensing that there might be physical limitations, sits up and shuffles closer to the edge. Her hands graze his chest, trailing the ladder of his abs, eyes glowing with appreciation. "You're so fucking sexy," she says, and Ben's bunched shoulders relax immediately.

"Not as sexy as you," he says, gazing down at her body. She's got that toned look about her, honed by hours of practicing dance routines and eating right. Her skin is even all over, and her pussy has a little strip of soft chestnut curls that makes my heart clench. She's a woman of contradictions; soft and hard, bright, and shadowed, gentle, and fierce. But it's her gentleness she shows Ben, tugging him until he's resting over her, hooking her leg around his hip on the side of his prosthetic. "Thank you for not telling on Asher and me," she says softly, running her hands over his back.

He kisses her, smoothing the hair from her face, using that tender moment to ease inside her with one slow thrust that causes her back to arch. Scooping beneath, he pulls her closer, their bodies moving in a synchronized rhythm that I match to my hand. Closing my eyes, I can almost feel what it will be like to be with Luna. The perfection of her surrender, the sweetness of her pussy. I wish I could spend a whole evening worshiping her body, but there are too many of us. Getting that kind of one-on-one time wouldn't be easy with so many other men waiting to share.

"Don't stop," Luna gasps, her fingers reaching to tug at Ben's ass, giving him some resistance to move against, and he doesn't stop. He keeps the perfect rhythm until Luna is losing her mind and so is he.

Our girl flops back onto the bed, her arms splayed. She looks as though she's done, the four men who've gone before having wrung her body out like a soaked rag. But what about the three of us who are left?

As Ben rolls to the side, trailing his hand over Luna's stomach while he catches his breath, her eyes open and scan the room. "Elijah, Hudson, Asher…"

"Yes," we all say in unison, stepping forward like we choreographed the move.

"I want you."

I glance at my friends, not knowing what to do next. Am I right in thinking that she's going to want us all at once rather than one at a time? I'm cool with that, but one of us will need to choreograph. There are only so many ways to accomplish something like that.

As though Asher read my mind, he lies on the bed next to Luna, encouraging her to roll on top of him. He's pushing her hips down until she's impaled by his cock, and I get to watch it all from behind. "Can you suck Hudson while me and Elijah fuck you?" he asks. "Could you take us that way?"

I don't see her expression, but I hear the breathy "yes" slip from her lips. Oh fuck. This is about to get real.

Hudson climbs onto the bed next to Asher and I move closer, watching the rhythmic movements of Luna's hips, desperate to feel the sweetness of her pussy. My hand rests on her hip, soothing like I'm trying to sooth a skittish animal. She stills, anticipation bubbling in the room. "I'm gonna push," I say. "Just relax…it'll all be fine."

I say that but I have no idea if it will be. My cock is big and so is Asher's. It's a lot for one woman to take, but Luna shivers when I press my cock at her entrance, and exhales as I ease myself inside. Asher grips Luna's arms as though he's fighting for control, and I know exactly how he feels. It's so tight in her pussy, so hot and perfect that my whole body is primed to fuck, but I need to be careful. I need her body to adjust and more than anything, I want this to feel good for her.

When Luna's lips wrap around Hudson's cock, I know she's ready. The first few movements in and out send white hot sensation up my spine. Asher's head whips back, his face scrunched up and Luna groans around Hudson's cock.

Around the room, the rest of Steel 7 gather closer, watching everything with a fascinated interest and a hunger about what the future might hold for all of us.

There's a crazy intimacy in this moment that I didn't anticipate. There are four of us experiencing this pleasure, four of us working to get to the pinnacle of release. My balls draw tight, watching Hudson's cock disappear deep into Luna's throat, as his abs ripple with the sensation. Luna's pussy squeezes tight as I pump deeper and faster, forcing her clit to graze Asher's body with every thrust.

I'm close, but there is no way I'm going to come before the rest. In this position behind Luna, I'm the ringmaster, controlling everything. A little slap to Luna's ass has her rhythm faltering, but Hudson doesn't seem to care. He growls as he releases into her mouth, holding her face as she swallows it all. Asher chooses that moment to begin to thrust upward in little jerking movements, until Luna is begging us not to stop, her legs trembling until she comes like a firework, exploding with pulsations that feel like heaven. Asher is next to give in, his cock pulsing against mine and I can't take it anymore.

I can't hold back.

I have to let go.

And fuck it feels good. I pump Luna full, releasing deep inside her, the deliciousness of it all almost taking the top of my head off.

Someone in the room swears, and someone else whistles but all I can do is laugh.

Bubbling up from a place deep inside comes so much happiness that I don't know what to do with it.

And Luna's laughing too. It's contagious and perfect, and I gather her against me, kissing her neck and her back, showing her just how much she means to me.

This crazy girl who's managed to illuminate my life and the lives of my friends.

This girl whose heart is as big and bright as the moon.

When we've cleaned up and Luna is sleeping peacefully, we all draw back, looking down on the most beautiful girl that any of us have ever been with. A shiver of something passes between us; a shared rush of affection for a person who pushed hard to make all of us see how awesome this crazy thing between us could be.

We leave her to sleep, slipping back to our own rooms without saying a word.

How we each feel individually remains unspoken. All I know is that we shared the most unbelievable sex I've ever experienced, and, in the process, I realized that I want so much more from Luna than just physical satisfaction. I want to be someone she cares about. Someone she cherishes. And I want to hold my moon-girl in the palm of my hand like the treasured pearl she is.

STEEL 7

18

HUDSON

The next stop on the tour is Barcelona. It's my first time in Spain, but Mo has been there before. It doesn't look that different from Athens until you hear the people talking and observe their slightly different mannerisms. The woman at the front desk of the hotel has the softest accent, and eyes that sparkle with youth despite her being at least thirty years older than me.

"Luna, over here," a fan shouts from where they are being held at the doorway by the hotel's security. We were warned in advance that the hotel was already overrun with Spanish teens just desperate for a photo or a video of their idol.

Luna's in a good mood. I guess multiple orgasms have a long-lasting positive effect on her. Unfortunately, they've had a less positive effect on our crew. Connor is stressed. I can see it in the way his jaw ticks as he grits his teeth and the intermittent flex of his hands into fists. His eyes are dark, flitting around for threats, landing on Luna with a fierceness that's different from yesterday.

STEEL 7

Everything is different from yesterday.

We're still focused on our job but keeping Luna safe has gotten personal. Maybe that's why this is forbidden by the bodyguard code. Fucking your client changes your mindset. It changes a role that should be wholly objective into one that's emotional, no matter how much you might want to separate the job from your personal life.

The elevator is slow to arrive, and when it does, it's filled with Luna's dancers who arrived on an earlier flight. "Luna!" they all shout, seemingly unaware that they're drawing attention to her. This kind of exposure only makes protecting her more difficult. Mo is there, ushering them out of the mirrored interior as quickly as he can. It's not that quick. Half of them are on their phones, and the other half look as though they're still recovering from a hangover. I heard last night was busy outside of Luna's bedroom too. The nightlife in Athens is crazy, especially when there is live music and ouzo involved.

On the journey up to the top floor, Luna tips her head so she can stare around at us all. She's so little in comparison, and somehow, it's even more apparent when we're standing and clothed than it is when we're naked.

"Just looking at you guys all dressed up in your suits gets me wet," she says.

"Luna," Connor warns in a low voice. "Keep that kind of talk to the room."

Taking hold of his lapel, she tugs him closer. "There's no one here. Only us. If this hotel had more floors to travel to, things could get messy."

It's at that moment that the elevator comes to a stop, and a bell dings to announce our arrival.

"You're going to kill me," he whispers softly, his shoulders dropping.

Luna's grin is wicked. "That's my aim."

"We don't have time for any death tonight, even a little

one," Mo says, striding into the corridor and glancing left and right. "Luna is performing in a few hours."

"Just enough time for someone to get me off," she says, trailing her hand over Mo's chest as she makes her way to the huge mahogany door to the penthouse suite.

"We're going to need to invest in a seven-sided dice to decide that shit," Jax says. He taps the keycard to the lock and strides inside with Elijah, clearing the room for Luna to enter.

"Maybe I should just choose." Luna lets her eyes trail up and down our bodies as though she's assessing who would be the best candidate for the job. We've all proven our abilities, so it's just a tease. Even so, Connor and Ben both shift so that their shoulders are back, and their chests puffed out.

Damn, it's so hilarious to watch all the posturing, even though there shouldn't be any need for competition between us all. Luna hasn't shown any favoritism so far, that's for sure.

"Maybe you need to keep your mind on tonight's performance, and my men need to keep their minds on the job at hand."

"*My* men," Luna emphasizes to Connor, but as soon as Elijah gives the all-clear, she's striding into the room and disappearing behind a closed door.

Jax releases a long hissing breath. "That girl is going to put an end to all of us. I think we've created a monster."

"A perfect, sex-hungry monster," Ben sighs.

"Is there anything sexier than a woman with a high sex drive?" Elijah asks.

"I can't think of one," Mo agrees.

"Less sex-talk and more preparation," Connor says. "Get yourselves organized. We need to leave in an hour."

Luna flings open her door, staring into the room. "If

we have an hour, I definitely need some sex. Hudson." She beckons me, and even though I know going to her is in direct conflict with Connor's orders, I go with it.

She's right. We might all work for Steel 7, but we're Luna's men now.

When I close the door behind me, her sassy and demanding mask drops away immediately. A blush rises on her cheeks and her eyelids lower. It's as though she finds it easier to demand what she wants in front of an audience but much harder when it's one on one.

"What do you need, princess?" I ask, tucking her loose chestnut hair behind her ear. "Anything you need, I'll give it to you."

"Can I…" she falters, glancing at the sofa in the corner of the room. Is she remembering the night I read to her in Berlin? We were close that night. Closer than friends. More familiar. Last night she made me come in her mouth, and it was awesome but not intimate.

I want intimate, and maybe Luna does too.

Maybe we can recreate that Berlin night, but this time take it further. I reach for her hand, sensing that she needs a steer. Slumping onto the sofa, I pull her into my lap, tugging her hips possessively until we're close enough for my cock to feel the heat between her thighs. I slide one hand into the warmth of the hair at her nape, bringing her sweet lips close enough to kiss. I'm slow and lazy about tasting her mouth, savoring every second. When she's melted all over me like butter, I draw back, searching her eyes. "I can lick you, baby, or you can ride me. Anything you want."

"I can ride you, but I've never come like that before," she says, surprising me. I always thought it helped a woman to be in control of the pace and depth. But I guess everyone's different.

"Let's try."

She scoots up, pushing down her sweatpants and panties as I free my cock. I'm cool with it being functional. It's good that she can admit to needing sex. So many women bury their urges, waiting for men to take the lead. I scramble to find the condom in my wallet, sheathing my cock as Luna straddles my lap again. I'm hard as a rock, gazing at her spread pussy as the latex unfurls.

"That's it, baby. Sit on this cock."

Luna moans softly, shifting closer and rising until her entrance notches at the head of my cock. Our eyes meet, her hands grasping onto my shoulders, but when she pushes herself down, her lids lower with pleasure.

"Fuck, you're tight," I say.

"You're big," she gasps.

"We're a perfect fit."

The smile that pulls at her lips is sweet and happy, sliding warmth into my chest.

"That's it," I say as she bottoms out. "Just move in the way that feels good to you. It'll all feel amazing to me."

The first roll of her hips is pure pleasure. I close my eyes, resting my hands on her waist, feeling her movements. As she grinds harder, I open my eyes to see her mouth dropping open and lids fluttering shut. "That feels so…"

"…good?"

"Good." Smiling again, she slides her fingers over my still-clothed chest. "Perfect."

"Just relax and take your time," I murmur, squeezing her breast and rolling her nipple between my thumb and forefinger with just enough pressure to elicit a moan. God, I love bringing Luna pleasure. I love seeing her coming undone and the look of pure surrender that softens her expression. In her day-to-day life, she has to be so tough, but here, in this room, with our bodies fused, we can both be something else. She can forget all the pressure that she has to face with her job, and I can lift myself into a place where I don't feel the ache of Hartley's loss quite so keenly.

As if she can hear my thoughts, she begins to undo my tie and the buttons to my shirt, all the while maintaining the rolling rhythm of her hips. When her hands make contact with my bare chest, the coolness of her skin makes me shiver.

From beneath, I begin to thrust upward in tiny little jerks that I know will hit her just right inside. A tiny squeak leaves Luna's lips, and she starts to lose focus, hands grasping onto my shoulders as I take hold of her hips and move her body in the way I know will get us both off in record time.

When her head lolls back, I know I've got her close. My thighs are screaming from the effort, but I don't give a fuck. All I want to do is fill this girl and feel her pussy clamp around my cock. I want her to let go of all the tension inside her. I want my friends outside this door to know exactly how good I've made her feel.

"Oh fuck, Hudson…don't stop…"

Oh, I'm good at taking orders. I've had years of experience of being told what to do and how to do it. I'm a good soldier.

The rippling feeling of Luna's orgasm just about blows my fucking mind, and I'm letting go inside her in a flash, our sweaty bodies flopping together like rag dolls.

It's only after, when we've both caught our breaths, that I wrap my arms around her tightly, holding my bossy girl, so she feels safe and cared for. Her fingers trail over my jawline, down my neck, over my collar bone, and lower, leaving a trail of gooseflesh in their wake. When they rest over my heart, I know what's coming.

"Who's Hartley?" she asks softly.

"My twin," I say, swallowing the lump that always

forms in my throat whenever I'm forced to remember that my brother, the other half of me, is dead.

"I had a brother, Jake, who died," Luna says. "He was killed in a motorbike accident."

"I'm so sorry to hear that, sweetie," I say, holding her a little closer.

"What happened to Hartley?"

"He was killed in service," I say flatly. "We were close to discharge. It shouldn't have happened."

"I think death always feels that way," she says, resting her head on my shoulder so her forehead is tucked into my neck. "I always think of things that I want to tell Jake. He loved dessert, especially ice cream sundaes. He loved country music and baseball. All the things he loved bring him back to me."

"It's hard that way," I say.

"I think it gets easier with time." Luna exhales softly as though admitting that fact makes her feel bad. "And I'm happy about that because I want to be able to remember my brother without feeling as though a javelin has pierced my heart. I want to be able to laugh about the things we got up to because he was always full of humor. I want to be able to accept it and live with it, not feel like hurting my other brother out of blame or resentment."

I know exactly how she feels. "Life is for the living," I tell her. "There's no point in blaming anyone for something that was just fate's responsibility. Family is important. You have to focus on the family and friends you have left."

"Is that what you're doing?" she asks.

Nodding, I run my hand over her smooth thigh, pulling her closer. "Every day that I get since his death feels like borrowed time. Like a clock started ticking the minute he was gone, measuring every single second that I get more than him. I want to live my life to the full because I have the chance to be here, and he doesn't. It's why I won't ever walk away from my friends. They pulled me through, and in the process, they became my brothers."

"They're all good men," Luna says softly. "You all are."

Smiling, I press a soft kiss to her forehead. "And you, Luna, are a very special girl."

She doesn't say anything after that. We cuddle for a few more minutes, then Connor knocks on the door to warn us that time is running out. She slips off to shower, and I clean myself up, getting ready to switch roles again.

For a while, I was Luna's lover.

Now, I'm back to being her bodyguard again.

The Luna who performs in Barcelona seems different. She has a lightness to her that wasn't there before. Her eyes are bright and alive, and maybe the audience can tell because this show feels so much more engaging than her others. The song she sang in Athens isn't repeated, and instead, she ends by repeating her biggest hit and encouraging the audience to join in with the chorus.

The only time my eyes drift from her, they settle on my crew. We've always been close. Maybe finding yourself in a life-or-death situation with people helps to fuse relationships in a way that's special. I'm not really sure. What I do know is that there is an added element to our relationship now. A shared connection with another person. A connection that links us all physically and emotionally.

I don't know what's going to happen in the future. I can't tell what Luna is looking for outside of human connection and maybe some control. She knows that being with us all means she has tied us to her in a stronger way than she was as just our client, but that doesn't mean that she will want this to continue when the tour is over.

"Keep your eyes on the client," Connor growls into my

earpiece. "Keep your mind on the job." He's not necessarily just talking to me, but I feel it probably more than the others. She chose me today. That means something. Maybe Asher feels it, too, because he was her first. Maybe we'll never stop thinking about our connection in parts and pieces and as a whole. I think we need to think about it as a whole for it to work the way her brother's relationship is set up. There can't be any singular thinking.

"Thank you, Barcelona. I love you," Luna shouts, bringing both her palms to her lips to blow kisses into the seething masses cloaked by darkness. She waves for longer than she did in Berlin and Athens and even embraces her dancers before jogging off the stage.

Luna's buzzing in the dressing room and all the way back to the hotel. Our plan is to collect Mo and head out to a casino for some fun, but when we get up to the top floor, we're greeted by police at the door to our room.

"What the hell?" Connor shouts. "Mo, where the fuck are you?"

Mo's voice sounds from inside Luna's room, and Connor, Elijah, and Jax stream inside, leaving the rest of us to huddle around our worried-looking client. A heated discussion begins as Connor tries to get to the bottom of what is going on. From what I can hear, someone left a box outside Luna's room, and when Mo took it inside to check its contents, he found something bad.

"Again?" Luna says, gazing up at me. Resting my hand against her arm, I stroke in a way that I hope is reassuring.

"Remember when we told you that we'll keep you safe and that you need to trust us? Well, this is one of those times that it's better that you don't ask any questions about the specifics. Whatever happens, no one is going to get close to you. They might try, but between you and them are seven huge men who would fight to the death to protect you, okay?"

"To the death?" Her smile is fleeting. Does she think that I'm being overdramatic? She'd be mistaken if she did. I've seen my friends step directly into danger to assist each other. When Hartley was injured, there was no question that my friends would step in to help him. That's the way we are together, and that's how it is with Luna.

"To the death," I say.

Connor appears in the doorway. "Take Luna to your room," he says, "and keep the door closed." And to Luna, he says, "I'm sorry, honey, but there's no way we can go out tonight."

Rather than kicking up a stink about it as she did in Berlin, Luna nods once. "It's okay. I have a pack of cards in my suitcase. We can play strip poker instead."

We all chuckle, and Luna beams, happy that she's lightened a tense moment.

That night, we play cards, agreeing to save strip poker to another night. And later, when Luna is sleeping, Mo tells us what he found in the box. A picture of Luna's pretty face, stuck onto the body of a naked woman in a compromising position, but it's the handcuffs and the knife that cause us all the greatest concern.

Whoever this psycho fuck is, he better fade into the background because if one of us catches him, he's never going to recover from his injuries.

19

ASHER

The tour continues through Europe, stopping in Rome, Prague, Helsinki, Brussels, Warsaw, Stockholm, Dubrovnik, and Paris. Although I'm certain that Luna would have liked to roam the streets and see the sights, she never raises it. I guess she understands the risks now. Or maybe it's because we spend all our nights working to keep her happy.

Happy might be the wrong word. We spend all our free time sending her to heaven and back. I smile at the memories of last night when we fucked her so good that she called out for heavenly intervention.

Now we're on a flight to Australia, buzzing with excitement. None of us have ever been "down under," and because the flight is so long, I find myself imagining that things might be a little different once we get there. Whoever has been following Luna around Europe trying to scare the bejesus out of her could travel easily and cheaply. A flight to Australia is a whole other ballgame.

This time, we're flying with other members of the entourage, and the plane is filled with noisy chatter. I could do without it, to be honest. All I want to do is get to the hotel and decompress.

"Can you believe that they're serving us another meal?" Luna says, shaking her head. "I feel as though I just finished that chicken, and it's not like we're expending any energy."

"I know a really fun way to remedy that," Jax says, keeping his voice low so Angelica and the others can't hear.

"Oooo…the mile-high club," Luna exclaims. "Are you a member?"

Jax shakes his head, pasting a disappointed hang-dog expression onto is face. "You could change that, baby," he murmurs.

"Connor would have my head on a platter for corrupting you on the job," she says.

Connor, who's had his face buried in a free copy of a newspaper he picked up in the airport, lowers the black and white pages and looks at us all in the same way my father used to look at me when he caught me dancing in the kitchen. He's playing at being disappointed, but it brings back difficult feelings.

"You've corrupted all our mortal souls," he says, but it's accompanied by a fleeting smile. I know Connor is the most worried about this situation. He's the one who's internalizing all the risks, but we're in too deep to change things now. Luna's so happy, and none of us want to change that.

I'm happy too. For the first time in a long time, I feel lighter. Luna presented me with a sketch pad and a box of art pencils in Prague. I have no idea how she got hold of them. Maybe the concierge was drawn into procuring the sweetest gift I've ever been given. As she handed them over, she told me to draw whatever inspired me and that she would love to see whatever I sketch.

It's not like I get much time to sit around drawing when I'm employed to ensure Luna's safety though. We're working around the clock and are all as confined to hotel rooms as she is. Even so, I've been inspired to sketch a few times. My favorite is a drawing of Luna sitting on Jax's knee, her arm thrown around his shoulder, laughing at the conversation she's having with the rest of Steel 7.

She loved it too.

It seems like every sketch I make of Luna fills her with light. Her joy at my creations fills me with a sense of satisfaction that I've struggled to find for a long time.

"What are we going to do when we arrive?" Luna asks Connor. I can tell she's trying to keep the hopefulness out of her voice, but it's there in the way her sweet voice turns up at the end.

"Crash out, I expect," Connor says.

"You should sleep," Angelica pipes up. "The jet lag can be really bad."

"Sleep is for old people," Luna says, reminding me of the age gap between us. Ten years ago, I would have been as buzzing as her to get out and explore.

"What do you want to do?" Hudson asks.

"Swim," she says.

"There's a pool at the hotel," Mo says. "It looks awesome."

"In the ocean," Luna adds. And then, more quietly, she says, "I've never seen the ocean before."

"You've never seen the ocean." Ben sounds as shocked as I am, but I guess lots of people Luna's age, who've been born into landlocked states, won't have seen the sea. My parents used to take me to Florida each year, so I can't even remember the first time I heard the lap of waves against the shore or tasted the cool salty water on my tongue.

To rescue Luna, I jump in with a distraction. "I've heard Bondi is the coolest beach."

"If you like surfer dudes with blond locks and board shorts," Elijah says.

Luna shoots him a look. "Surfing isn't just for men."

"Bondi could be good," Connor says. He catches my eye, a slightly worried look passing across his face. This is what he was talking about when he worried that our relationship with Luna could put her at risk. If he didn't feel tenderly for her, would he care if she was disappointed about not going to the beach? No, he wouldn't. He'd be a professional and put his foot down. He'd do the job he's getting paid to do.

But we all feel tenderly for Luna. It's there in every touch and caress. It's there in the way we all want to please her. There in the way that we take it in turns to cradle her while she's sleeping. It's there in the way that Connor will give in and let Luna do something that will make our job so much harder.

Luna blinks her pretty green eyes as though she can't quite believe the four words that just left Connor's lips. "Are you serious?"

He shrugs, and Luna erupts into squeals, her hands clapping frantically.

"Does anyone have any sunscreen? Because we're going to need it." I catch Ben glancing down at his leg when he says that. Even though he seems okay with Luna seeing it, he's still not wholly comfortable about baring it in public. With our smart work attire, it's not as though he's regularly in shorts, but Australia's going to be hot, and you can't exactly wear a suit to the beach.

"You guys are worried about a little sun," Mo scoffs.

"We can't all have your Middle- Eastern complexion."

Everyone laughs because I'm the fairest in the group. In the sun, my eyelashes change color until they are almost transparent, and without a high factor sunscreen, my skin turns a shade that looks better on lobsters.

Connor's lucky. We may share Irish ancestry, but he managed to inherit the dark, swarthy looks that are more practical in the sun.

Even in heat that could cook an egg, Mo somehow manages to stay cool, calm, and collected. The man has a super skill.

"Luna definitely needs sunscreen," Angelica says. "She can't get too much of a tan. It will ruin her aesthetic."

Mo frowns, his face expressing the emotion we are likely all feeling. "A tan will ruin her aesthetic?"

"Yes. Luna has a look, and she needs to maintain it across the whole tour."

"She has to look the same across forty performances?" Hudson glances at our girl, and I know he's as frustrated as I am at the rules and regulations she has to live with every day. Being famous sure has its limitations. I always thought that fame would bring freedom, but it's actually like having a shackle on your ankle. A shackle that's secured to a giant fucking annoying boulder.

"Yes." Angelica is firm, and she picks up her phone and starts tapping away to make it clear that the conversation is over.

Luna's staring at the floor, the corners of her mouth turned down. Just as she thought she was going to have a little piece of freedom, Angelica had to weigh in with something to curtail it. Now, Luna will be worried about being in the sun for too long. Even with sunscreen, she'll tan. It's inevitable.

I want to scream at Angelica that all these rules and regulations are out of order. Luna needs to be free to live her life. She can still perform with a tan. Are Blueday seriously worried that her fans won't like her if she looks even slightly different?

"We'll find some sunscreen," I say softly. "And a wide-brimmed hat. I'm sure they'll sell them at a tourist shop near the beach."

"Maybe you can get one with the corks hanging from strings," Jax says. "Will that fit with the aesthetic?"

Angelica scowls at Jax's facetiousness, but she doesn't reply.

But Jax's humor achieved one important thing. He got Luna smiling again, and for that, I want to hug him.

Angelica was right. We are all shattered when we arrive at the hotel in Sydney. The hotel is surrounded by crazy fans, and hotel security who look as though they grew up on a diet of nothing but grass-fed Australian lamb. We're hustled in through the staff entrance at the hotel and end up making our way through the hallways adjacent to the restaurant kitchens. And even though we've eaten like kings on the plane, my stomach rumbles.

It doesn't take us long to change into our beachwear. Luna braids her hair and wraps it with a patterned silk scarf. Dressed in a white bikini and a lace beach cover-up, she looks like a pin-up girl from another era. In contrast, the rest of us look like extras from that awesome 1980s show about lifeguards.

Ben shifts uncomfortably, taking the weight off his prosthetic. It isn't obvious that Luna has noticed his discomfort, but she chooses that moment to pay him some special attention, wrapping her arms around his neck and pressing a soft kiss to his lips.

That's all it takes to draw him out of his self-conscious funk.

It feels like we're in a Hollywood movie when we all make our way back through the staff areas to the rear door and jump into the two waiting vehicles. Even though we're dressed for the beach, all of us are on high alert, keeping Luna safely between our huge bodies.

When the sea comes into view Luna squeals again. "Look at it…look at the waves."

We all crane to see the gorgeous bay that is one of Australia's most famous beaches. With light sand and vivid blue waters tipped with foaming white waves, it sure is a sight to behold.

Luna's hand squeezes my knee, and I smile at her efforts to share her bubbling joy. "Look at that," I say. "Isn't it something?"

"It's more than something," Luna whispers. "It's everything."

At Bondi, Connor asks the driver to stop. Jumping out, he heads into a nearby shop and returns with a wide-brimmed straw hat for Luna and four large bottles of sunscreen for us all.

"If anyone recognizes Luna, we'll need to get off the beach as quickly as possible," Connor says. "We're good until then, but just keep a low profile."

"That's going to be easy with seven huge guys who look like a cross between The Rock, Chris Hemsworth, and Mark Wahlberg," Luna snorts.

The driver advises us to head to the end of the beach, where there are fewer people. We try to make it look like we're a group of buddies out for an afternoon rather than seven bodyguards surrounding a celebrity, but I'm aware of the intrigued looks of the surrounding beachgoers. Luna's disguise is good enough that she's not easily recognizable, but how long before people put two and two together? There must be a few people at the beach who have tickets to her concerts. Her tour is a sellout, and she's playing all the major stadiums around the world. It won't take much for them to notice us.

I really hope that they don't. I want Luna to have fun for at least an hour. I want her to wade into the ocean and feel its power. I want to watch the light pour out of her as she experiences this momentous thing for the first time.

Because who knows how many first times we'll have together?

This thing we're doing has to have an expiration date. Celebrities don't just leave their careers to shack up with their seven bodyguards. Even movies haven't stepped that far.

When Luna strips off her cover-up, we all gawp at her like starving puppies. It's not like we haven't seen her naked before, but in this tiny white bikini, with straps that could come untied so easily, it's so much more of a tease. Before we can insist that she applies the sun cream, she's dashing across the sand, clutching the hat onto her head. Stopping abruptly at the shore, she seems to take a few seconds to look out toward the horizon. There are so many other people in the sea, laughing and splashing, but it's as though she doesn't notice them at all. There's only Luna and the roaring power of the ocean. Luna who was named for the moon, the celestial body whose movements control the ocean's tides.

The first time the water laps over her foot, she takes a step back. Then she turns, not realizing that Mo, Connor, Elijah, and I all followed her closely. "We're going to come in with you," I say softly.

"I can't swim," she admits. "I don't think I understood how big and crazily powerful it would be."

"Not all sea is the same," Mo tells her. "Some seas are warm and calm; some are freezing and angry. This is a mixture of the two."

"Warm and angry. Sounds a bit like Connor," Luna says, and when he growls at her joke, she dashes into the water. Soon we're all up to our waists, the seven of us surrounding Luna, eyes scanning for threats and making sure she's safe in the water too.

We manage to enjoy thirty minutes before a girl with red hair and freckles dusting her nose approaches to ask Luna if she can have a selfie. Ben steps in to say no, but Luna puts a hand on his arm and lets the girl come closer.

"I didn't recognize you at first," the girl says, her face flushing. "But then…"

"Are you coming to the show tonight?"

The girl nods enthusiastically. "My mom bought the tickets for my birthday."

"Well, that's awesome." Luna puts her arm around the girl and smiles for the selfie. With her hat shading her face and her huge sunglasses, it'd be hard for anyone to really see that it's Luna in the flesh, but at least the fan is happy.

"Thank you so much," the girl says, waving to her mom, who's waiting on the shoreline.

"Anytime," Luna says.

When the girl dashes back to show her mom the photo, Luna gazes out the horizon again. "I guess it's time for us to leave."

"It's probably for the best," Connor says.

"I'm ready for my bed anyway," she says softly.

Who knows if it's the truth? But what I do know is that Luna is learning what it takes to be a real celebrity. I just hope that, in accepting the restrictions of her new lifestyle, she doesn't lose a part of herself in the process.

20

MO

Luna is playing three shows in Australia. Two in Sydney and one in Melbourne.

It turns out that the girl at the beach was the daughter of a journalist for one of the major Australian newspapers, and she writes an article about celebrities who show real kindness and appreciation to their fans. The sweet selfie of a disguised Luna and a very happy fan is splashed all over the front page of the Entertainment section, and Blueday Records are ecstatic at the exposure. They are less happy that Luna is, in their words, "out in public in a way that's dangerous." Connor patiently explains that she can't be expected to be a hermit and, in the politest way, that we're not getting paid to be her jailers.

Luna then receives a phone call warning her of the dangers of over-exposure and, for the rest of the day, is walking around with her eyes lowered.

Anger bubbles away in my chest.

No one should act in a way that takes away someone's

sparkle. I saw it often with my cousins. They'd get married to a man who, on the surface, seemed okay, but then over time, they'd change the way they dressed and how they'd express themselves in public. It was like the marriage sucked out their true selves.

I read somewhere once that affairs happen because a person is looking for another "self." We mold to walk beside the people we love, and sometimes we don't like the person we're shaped to become. Will that be the same for Luna? Walking arm in arm with the phenomenon of celebrity is going to shape her for sure.

There is not a man among my friends who wants to mold Luna to be anything other than she is.

The trouble is that everyone she works with seems intent on shaping her to be something totally different.

We're on our way to Melbourne. It's a short flight, and once again, we're traveling with the dancers and the band, and even some of the technical team too. Luna has a great relationship with most of her supporting crew, but there is one guy, a lighting technician called Marcus, who makes the hair at the back of my neck prickle.

There's no reason for the strange sense that I have about him. He hasn't, to my knowledge, done anything wrong. There's just a feeling of wrongness about him. The same kind of wrongness that I sensed in my cousin who ended up in jail. An emptiness in his eyes. A smirk that doesn't touch the rest of his face.

I start to tell Connor about it, but I hear the vagueness of my own words and cut short before I spill it all. My crew already thinks that I'm superstitious. They don't believe in the evil eye, but I've seen the consequences of people's jealous thoughts. I know how much damage they can do.

It's why I try to surround myself with positivity.

It's why I value my friends so much.

STEEL 7

Friends are the family we choose for ourselves.

Luna reaches across the aisle and touches my arm. "You're looking very serious today," she says. "You got something on your mind?"

"Just ghosts." I cover her tiny pale hand with my broad darker one. "But all the ghosts disappear when you're around."

Her hand squeezes my arm gently. "Mine too," she whispers.

We smile at each other in that warm, melted butter kind of way that comes with being completely comfortable in another person's presence.

When she draws her hand away, looking around, conscious that we are surrounded, I do the same.

We need to be watchful, Connor said. We need to make sure that our feelings for Luna don't blind us to any potential threat.

As I scan over the other people on the plane, my eyes meet Marcus's. He nods and curls his mouth into that smirk, and unease snakes through me.

Maybe he's just being friendly and polite. Maybe he's just one of those people who never quite fits in wherever he is but keeps trying anyway.

Or maybe he's trying to tell me without words that he saw the intimacy between Luna and me.

Paranoia isn't a good feeling to live with.

I've gone years suspecting everyone around me, never certain who was a friend and who was foe. I don't want to experience that again.

Our ghosts continue to shape us unless we work on dealing with them.

I haven't done that yet, but maybe it's time.

Maybe I can only be the man Luna deserves if I try.

We land in Melbourne and spring into action, hustling Luna into a new waiting car and then into a new luxurious suite on the top floor of Melbourne's most prestigious hotel.

It's evening, so I'm expecting Luna to tell us to lock the doors and come into her room. I'm expecting her to beckon us until we're all sliding between her thighs, finding pleasure and peace in her body, reveling in those feelings for as long as it lasts.

But she doesn't.

"I want to swim in the ocean now," she says.

"But it's dark." Ben glances at the inky black sky visible through the floor-to-ceiling windows that make up one side of the VIP suite.

"That's why," Luna says. "No one will be there. I can enjoy the water and not have to worry about paparazzi or fans or crazed stalkers."

"You don't have to worry about those things," Connor says. "Those things are for us to worry about, and we worry about them as much at night as we do in the day."

"I know." Luna pads toward him, throwing her arms around his neck. "You take care of me as if I'm priceless."

"You are." He dips down and gently kisses her lips.

"I'm just a girl," she says softly. "Just a girl, asking a boy if he'll take her swimming in the dark, away from prying eyes."

"You know that you don't play fair, Ms. Evans," Connor says.

"It should be okay," I say, never wanting to see Luna as down as she was in Berlin. "Some of us can stay on the shoreline."

Luna shakes her head. "I want us all to do this. I want to make this memory so I can hold it in my heart. The other day it was nice, but I couldn't relax. There were too many people, and you guys couldn't just hang out and be yourselves. I want this time for us."

Connor scans the room, meeting the eyes of each of us. He's seeking out our approval to do something that we all know could be dangerous. He's tired of shouldering all of the responsibility alone, and I understand that.

We're all in this forbidden relationship with a girl who is still trying to find out how to be happy and live her dreams. We're struggling to work through our own feelings and pasts in the process. He's not the only one who should be making these decisions. We are eight people. We all need to take responsibility for ourselves and for each other.

"Okay," Asher says, reaching out to take Luna's hand. He broke first once, and it seems he'll always be the one to give in where Luna's concerned.

She beams and hugs Asher, taking time to send each of us a smile so grateful that it should warm us to the bottom of our damaged souls. "I won't be long." Trotting off to get changed, we trudge off to each root around in our cases for swimwear that we packed, never believing we'd actually need it.

We never believed that we'd allow ourselves to step so far over the line with our client.

It's funny how little we really know ourselves until we're tested.

The sea at night is a totally different animal.

Water, which during the day is clear enough to see your feet, suddenly becomes opaque and inky black. It turns from something welcoming to something with unfathomable dangers.

After scanning the shore and finding that we're alone, we strip silently, as though each of us understands that Luna wants this to be a tranquil memory. She's chosen to wear a black two-piece that perfectly fits with the oil-slick sea, and she's the first to dip a toe into the water.

"It's still warm," she says in a voice that is high with surprise.

"The sun warms it during the day," Asher says. "This time of year, it probably never gets much cooler."

As we wade in, I watch my Steel 7 brothers, taking in their constant watchfulness but also the other element of their protective feelings toward Luna. I see the beginnings of feelings of tenderness and care in the way they gather, careful not to cramp her style. I see their gentle touches to her arm and brief caresses to her face that have nothing to do with sex and everything to do with love. I see all the things that we shouldn't be feeling, and I see them in Luna too.

"This is perfect," she says. Then she holds her nose, dipping under the water and rising with her hair slicked around her face and trailing down her back. Her shoulders rise and fall with a deep breath as though she's trying to draw in everything around her for safekeeping.

"The smell of the sea is intoxicating," I tell her. Beneath the water, her hand finds mine, and my heart skips a beat.

When she moves closer, her wet skin already cooler than mine, I don't tell her that it's a mistake. We're in public, and we made a promise not to do this, but with the darkness resting like a cloak around us, all caution seems to slide away.

Her wet lips find mine, and as I kiss her back, I taste the salt of the sea and the unending sweetness that is Luna. All around us, the other six other people who make up our strange relationship gather closer. Luna, conscious always that there are many of us, slides out of my arms and into the waiting arms of another. Elijah cradles her to his chest, nuzzling into the warmth of her neck. Then she's moved to embrace Ben, touching his face softly, and his hands graze her body beneath the water. Asher is next, his artist's fingers tracing circles through the beaded water resting on her shoulders. She shivers, breaking out into goose flesh as Connor embraces her from behind. She's so tiny between the protective bodies of my friends, but she doesn't rest there long. Jax, with his ever-present smile, swoops in for his own embrace, and lastly, Hudson waits patiently for his turn.

It's seamless, the movement between us. As liquid as the ocean that surrounds us. As natural as anything I've ever experienced in my life. And although I know that this kind of relationship would never have been what I dreamed for myself, I find that I'm drifting weightlessly in the perfection of it.

And I will drift for as long as it can last.

I've learned that you can fight the paths that life creates for you, or simply walk them, soaking up all the experiences that you never believed would be yours. My paths have been challenging, but there is little I would change. Our days are like the glittering links in a long golden chain. Break one, and everything unravels. I preserve my chain, even when experiences feel more like dreams that reality.

We all need to wake from our dreams sometimes, but we can fight to stay slumbering in them for as long as we can.

21

LUNA

I feel weightless during my performance in Melbourne. Maybe it's because I'm now a quarter of the way through my tour and well-practiced at all the routines. I know what's expected of me and can replicate the dance moves without even thinking.

Maybe it's that I'm becoming the professional singer that I didn't even have the courage to dream I could be, back when I was in the small town where I grew up, with only my two brothers to hold me together.

I tell myself it's those things because the alternative reason scares me too deeply to contemplate.

When my Steel 7 bodyguards cover me with their kisses, envelop me with their arms, and push inside my body, my mind drifts to a place where I feel like I'm flying. And after, the bubbling feeling that rests near my heart doesn't settle. If anything, dancing in front of a sold-out crowd, knowing that their eyes are settled on me protectively, the feeling of weightlessness only gets stronger.

Connor is resting back at the hotel tonight, and even though I know the rest of my bodyguards are more than capable of taking care of me, I feel his absence.

Is it weird that I want us always to be together? We're like a toddler's puzzle; eight pieces that need to fit together to make a single bright and colorful picture.

As I finish the penultimate song, I tell myself that I should be worried less about the weirdness and more that this thing between us has become so much more than just sex.

My plan was to indulge in a fling that would keep me from worrying about everything at home. Having company in my bed pushed away the anxious feelings that come with every new photo or incident related to my stalkers. It's helped me to focus on what this tour is about, delivering great music to my fans.

It's working, but I know it's not just a fling. How could I ever keep my heart separate when these men are all so perfect for me? How could I hold them at arms-length when they fit so perfectly against me?

My throat is a little dry, so rather than push through and risk being hoarse tomorrow, I dash to the side of the stage to grab a bottle from the table set up for me. Unscrewing the lid, I take a long gulp of the room-temperature water that is best for my vocal cords, except it isn't water. It's something terrible and bitter that burns and stings the inside of my mouth. Retching, I start to spit on the floor, the screaming of panic in my ears dulling the rising noise of the crowd and the music the band is playing as an interlude until I return. Resting my hand on my thigh, I retch and retch, my stomach racking my whole body as my stomach empties over my feet. Tears are streaming from my eyes before Elijah's arm goes around my body.

"Luna...are you okay?"

I hold out the bottle, coughing, and spluttering. "It's…it's not water."

He lifts the bottle to his nose and winces at the smell. "You drank this?"

"It went in my mouth…I don't think I swallowed, but it's burning."

"Fuck."

Pulling a bottle from his pocket, he quickly hands it to me. "It's okay. I brought this from the hotel. I've tasted it. Wash out your mouth with it and spit on the floor."

He touches his lapel. "Luna's water's been contaminated. She needs medical attention. She can't go back on."

"Fuck," I hear in response, sensing the movement of people gathering around me. Hands touch my shoulder. Someone pulls out a stool, and I'm urged to sit. I retch again, bringing up yellow water, coughing, and spluttering until my face is wet from tears and my nose running.

I don't care what I look like because it doesn't matter how much I wash my mouth out with the fresh water Elijah gave me, it's still tingling.

"What the fuck is it?" Mo asks. "It's not…?" When he trails off, I know what he couldn't bring himself to say.

Acid. Poison. It could be anything.

"It smells chemical-y," Elijah says. "How the fuck did it get in with Luna's drinks?"

"Deliberately," Jax says, holding his hand out for the bottle so he can smell it too.

I open my mouth to speak, my throat feeling raw. "It's not acid, is it?" I whisper.

It's at that moment, two paramedics arrive. One drops to his knee in front of me. "Open your mouth."

He presses my tongue down with a flat wooden stick, shining a light into my throat. "It looks pretty red. We need to get her checked out."

"Shit," Hudson says.

I blink, tears leaking out of the corners of my eyes leaving cool trails over my cheeks. The crowd is cheering restlessly as they wait for me to go back on and sing my number-one hit. They're going to be disappointed.

The paramedic stands, and before I have a chance to think, Elijah has scooped me into his arms.

I burrow into the warmth of his neck as my whole body trembles. "Where shall I take her?" he asks.

"Backstage," Angelica yells, coming into view. "Keep her away from the crowds. I'll sort out the end of the show. Go."

Elijah doesn't hesitate and follows the paramedics, flanked by the rest of Steel 7. "Bring the bottle," the paramedic calls over his shoulder. "They'll want to identify the liquid."

"I've got it," Jax yells.

Behind us, Angelica announces that the support act will be coming back on due to unforeseen circumstances. The crowd whistles and the ominous rumbling of booing follows us down the hallway, but when the band starts playing their biggest hit, the disgruntled response is drowned out.

I shouldn't care, but I do.

This is my show, and I can't finish it.

I pour more water into my mouth and swill it around. "I need to spit," I tell Elijah, and he pauses for long enough to allow me to relieve a little of the strange feeling.

"Don't worry," he says as we emerge into the warm evening. "Everything's going to be fine."

He's just trying to make me feel better. He's a good man with a good heart, but he doesn't know that.

Nobody knows that.

STEEL 7

And for the first time ever, I find myself doubting him and the men paid to protect me.

22

CONNOR

Ben calls me on route to the hospital to tell me what happened, and I'm up and out of the room so fast, I forget to pull the keycard from the doorway. The concierge hails me a cab, and I urge the driver to speed as much as he can.

All the way, my heart pounds in my chest, imagining Luna feeling hurt and scared. I curse myself for not being there when she needed me. I don't blame my team or imagine that it wouldn't have happened if I'd had been working tonight. I just hate that I wasn't there to give her comfort.

Food and water are Angelica's area. She organizes Luna's rider. She's responsible for letting this happen.

At the hospital, the receptionist doesn't want to tell me where she is. The information is for family only. "I'm her fiancé," I tell her. Anything for her to let me up to the floor where Luna is being treated. I find everyone apart from Elijah in the waiting room. "What the fuck?" I say, not caring that there are other people waiting too.

"Someone tampered with her water," Mo says. "The hospital has it and is trying to identify the substance. It's lucky she didn't swallow, or it could have burned her throat. As it is, her mouth is a little red, and she's hoarse from vomiting and coughing.

"Hoarse? Her voice?"

"Yeah," Jax says.

"Do you think that's what this is about?"

Everyone shrugs. "Who knows, Con? Why put something that smells corrosive in a bottle unless you want to damage someone's mouth?"

The rage I feel bubbling up wedges in my throat. Someone hurt my girl, not just inadvertently, but with purpose and malice. They tried to damage her body and her livelihood.

Who would do something like this?

"Did you see anyone? Anyone hanging around? Someone standing near the table?" Everyone shakes their heads. "Well, it couldn't have just happened. Someone did this."

"The only people allowed back there are…" I raise my hand before Ben can finish.

"Remember the torn-up panties…someone got through that time."

My phone starts to ring, and as I pull it out of my pocket, I see it's my contact at Blueday Records. Shit. They must have heard already.

"Hello."

Adam begins asking a ton of questions that I don't have answers to, so I cut him off by saying that I need to talk to the doctor, and I'll call him back.

He's still talking when I swipe to disconnect the call, but I can't worry about that right now. I need to get in there and see Luna for myself and talk to Elijah, who's the only one who's been allowed to go into the room.

The door to Luna's room is open, and she's lying back on the bed, looking as small and frail as a child. Someone has covered her with a blanket, probably because her stage costumes are always tiny and revealing. Elijah stands from his seat in the corner and moves closer to Luna's side. "She's okay," he tells me. "It could have been a lot worse, but thankfully she realized what was in the bottle before she swallowed it. Her tongue is a little pink, and her throat is a little tender, but she's going to be okay. Luna blinks up at me, the corner of her mouth twitching. "The doctor told her not to talk. She needs to minimize potential damage."

I exhale a long breath, relieved to know that there aren't going to be any long-term problems caused by this incident. Luna's had a scare, and one concert has been affected, but she's not due to sing again for three days. Maybe that'll be enough time if she has total rest.

I nod my head, indicating to Elijah that I want to talk to him in private. In the corner of the room, I whisper, "This can't happen again. Nothing that isn't vetted by us will pass Luna's lips."

"Seriously. I don't understand how this shit is getting this bad." Elijah says. "We've worked with big stars before, and none of them have had people infiltrating their rider items."

"This might be the last time we work for Blueday," I say. "Adam was raging on the phone."

"I'm raging in here," Elijah says. "Someone out there is trying to make a mockery out of us, and I'm not going to stand for it."

"When will they release Luna?"

"They want to keep her in for a couple of hours."

I glance at my watch, mentally calculating forward. "We'll make the flight tomorrow then."

"Yes," Elijah says. "Do you think London is going to

be less crazy than the rest of the countries we've been to on this tour?"

"Somehow, I doubt it. Trouble has a tendency to follow."

There's a knock at the door, and I turn to find Mo, grave-faced, holding his phone.

"What is it?" I ask impatiently.

"You've got to see this, Con. We're fucked."

"Stay with Luna," I tell Elijah before I follow Mo out into the sterile white corridor. My feet squeak on the linoleum as my chest tightens with dread. When Mo passes me the phone, the first thing I see is a murky night image. Bringing the phone closer, it takes me a few seconds before I realize what I'm looking at: images of our swim with Luna last night were taken with a high-tech nighttime camera. There isn't just one either. Seven snaps show Luna in the arms of each of us, and the headline reads "Luna Evans in a seven-times-lucky shocker."

Shoving the phone back into Mo's hand, I slump back against the wall, dropping my head into my hands and tugging on my hair with frustration.

This was always the worst-case scenario that I had in my mind when we started this crazy relationship. Luna didn't want to hear it. She had her own ideas about the risks, and they were a lot more cavalier than mine. And I was weak. We all were.

And look where we are now.

Luna's in more danger than she's ever been before, and in a matter of minutes, Adam is going to be on the phone railing at me for another reason.

We're going to lose the Blueday Records contract, but that isn't the worst of it.

When we lose the contract, Luna's safety will rest in the hands of another security firm, and we'll have no way of protecting her.

23

JAX

We decide between us that we won't answer any calls or tell Luna what's happened until morning. Connor messages Adam to inform him that Luna's wellbeing is our priority, and we need to focus on getting her ready to fly tomorrow. He tells Adam he'll speak to him when we arrive in London, but he doesn't get a reply.

Keeping Luna away from her phone isn't easy, but Asher finds ways to distract her, and Hudson places her purse into the trunk.

It's so strange to spend time with Luna when she's not able to speak. She's such a vocal person, always chatting, humming, and singing. Luna's voice is one of the traits that makes her larger than life, and without it, she seems diminished.

I didn't realize how much I love her being strong and loud and capable until she isn't. I didn't know how much I would struggle to see her weakened.

When we get back to the hotel room, Elijah runs Luna

a bath filled with the subtle fragrance of luxury bath salts. Before she has a chance to object, he undresses her and helps her into the water. The bath is big, and to continue the distraction, he drops his clothes to the floor and climbs in beside her. There's space for another, and I don't wait to be asked.

Climbing into the water feels so good. Even though the night at the beach is going to be our undoing, I can't feel anything but happiness for the time we've spent together and the experiences we've had. I hope that Luna will feel the same when she finds out that the whole world knows our secrets.

I find Luna's hand beneath the water and squeeze it gently, hoping that she's finding mine and Elijah's presence reassuring. She squeezes back, gazing at me with green eyes that always hook me in the heart. "Thank you," she mouths to me and then Elijah.

He presses a finger to her lips. "Rest," he says. "You have to rest. Let us do the talking."

So that's what we do.

We play a silly game where I come up with two possible questions to ask Elijah, and Luna gets to pick which one he answers just by pointing.

"What's your most embarrassing sexual experience?" is the first one Luna chooses.

Elijah shakes his head. "The first time a girl put her hand into my pants, I came in exactly three seconds." I snort with laughter, and Luna places a hand over her mouth, shoulders shaking with amusement. "Thankfully, I've learned to last a lot longer than that since."

"Only just," I laugh, and he punches me on the shoulder.

"Choose a question, Luna," Elijah says, his eyes focusing on the ceiling as he tries to come up with questions that will embarrass me as much. "Worst sexual experience or most extreme place you've ever fucked?"

There's no way I'm going to go into my worst sexual experience, so I opt for the second. "Most extreme place I ever fucked was the backseat of my girlfriend's truck when her mom popped into the store to buy milk. We were in the parking lot and not tucked in the corner either. Her head was thumping against the side of the car, and she came so loud, I swear the store manager must have heard."

"Wow," Elijah says. "That was ballsy."

"Horny teenagers will do anything to nut."

Luna snorts a puff of air from her nose but somehow manages not to use her voice at all.

"Okay," Elijah says, splashing water at me. "The most disgusting thing that ever happened to you or the weirdest thing that ever happened to you."

"Where the fuck are you getting these questions?" I ask.

Elijah shrugs. "When I was a kid, there wasn't a lot for us to do, so we used to ask each other twenty questions. They'd be different every time, but we always ended up in stitches."

I watch as Elijah's face goes from happy amusement at the memories to sadness. He hasn't spoken to his family in years. Not since he decided he didn't want to be part of the religious life they'd imposed on him since birth. I've never asked too many questions about his past. There's always a melancholy that comes over him whenever he's forced to think back. It's not only his parents. It's his brothers that he left behind too.

"Okay, most disgusting thing," I say.

"I'm not sure I want to know," Elijah says, holding his hands up. Luna nods enthusiastically, moving her hand in a quick circular motion, trying to tell me to get on with revealing the answer.

"A dog once shat on my pillow," I say.

"Gross." Elijah screws up his face, but Luna makes the hand gesture again, not believing my answer.

"You think I've got a grosser answer?" I ask her.

When she nods, Elijah splashes me again. "Are you holding back, dude? Not cool!"

"Okay…how about this one. I was with this girl in a club. We both drank way too many tequila shots. She decided it would be a great idea to go down on me in one of the club booths. So she's there, bobbing away enthusiastically and I don't know if it was the amount of alcohol she consumed or the difficult angle, or the fact she was rushing in case we got caught by one of the burly bouncers, or you know, the sheer massiveness of my cock…"

Luna rolls her eyes, Elijah snorts, and I pause for dramatic effect.

"…but she vomited all over my dick, and my trousers and my shirt."

"For fuck's sake." Elijah's face scrunches, and Luna is laughing silently.

"I had to tuck my huge boner into my soiled pants and head home stinking of tequila vomit."

"That is really fucking gross."

Using my arms to make a bowing gesture, I enjoy their laughter, but it's tainted because I know this isn't going to happen again. These stolen moments with Luna are going to get taken away by people outside of this room. They're going to judge us without knowing anything about how awesome it feels to sit in a hot tub with a woman who makes your heart feel full to the brim and your friend who can make you laugh without even trying. They're not going to know how real and pure this feels. All they're going to care about is slandering Luna and destroying us.

The press is going to do what they do best and stoke the fire of public opinion. No one will believe how being in this relationship has changed all of our lives for the better. No one will ever know because Luna will be forbidden from discussing it and we will be pushed out of the public eye, restricted by our non-disclosure agreements and the need for us to try to rebuild our reputation that is going to be shattered, maybe irreparably.

All of that is coming tomorrow.

Luna slides closer, her arms wrapping around my body until her head is resting on my shoulder. Beneath the water, she hooks her legs over Elijah's and pulls him closer. Her forced silence makes everything feel more serious, and I'm not good with serious at all.

Serious takes me to dark places.

"I know you can't talk," I say, "but if you promise not to make a sound, we can fuck you nice and slow."

Luna nods, and without needing to move much, Elijah pushes inside her. Gripping tightly onto me, she keeps her promise, gritting her teeth against calling out as Elijah rolls his hips, shifting the water enough that it overflows the tub. My hand grazes her nipples and grips the softness of her breast, watching all the tiny flickers of arousal in her expression, keeping track of her responses in a way I've never needed to before.

The forced silence makes everything seem furtive. Even Elijah is biting his lip as he thrusts faster. Luna's eyes scrunch closed, the concentration wrinkling the top of her sweet nose. I press a kiss there, wanting to commit everything that's happening to memory for cold nights in the future. My finger finds her slick, swollen clit beneath the water, rubbing in tight circles that mirror the tempo of Elijah's movements, and I watch the moment Luna starts to come apart with absolute awe.

She keeps her promise, swallowing the moans that she usually makes, shuddering through her pleasure. Elijah pulls out, using his hand to finish.

Wasting no time, I pull her onto my lap, wrapping her limp legs around my waist. It takes nothing to push inside her. Elijah's made her slippery and stretched her open nicely. The first thrust feels like heaven wrapped around my cock. Luna's arms hook around my neck to stabilize her, and even though he's still reeling from his orgasm, Elijah is there to kiss the back of her neck and finger her nipples. God, it's something to watch Luna's head drop back with ecstasy as the two of us work to satisfy her. Two of us master her body and scramble her mind enough that the incident that happened tonight seems forgotten.

We lift Luna from the trials and tribulations of her life into a place that's safe and filled with satisfaction, and for the minutes that I'm buried inside her, I go to that safe place too. When she comes around my cock, I'm not expecting the vice-like pulsation of her pussy to trigger my own orgasm. My cock, buried deep inside her, releases a rush of heat from my body to hers and I groan so loudly it'd wake the neighbors.

We're all panting and hot, the water and exertion bringing a pink flush to our cheeks.

And as I come down from the most intense orgasm of my life, it's only then that the outside world creeps in again.

I hold Luna tight against me, knowing that this will be the last time we're this close.

Sometimes love is fleeting.

It sweeps into our lives, taking us by surprise.

Sometimes love can't be the permanent state we want it to be, no matter how much we want or how much we fight.

Sometimes we have to let go because it's the only way to save the person we love. Luna can't be the superstar she is with seven lovers.

Tomorrow will be a terrible day, but for now, my girl is

STEEL 7

in my arms, and everything is okay.

24

LUNA

I can tell that there is something going on.

All the indications are there in the constantly worried looks passing between my bodyguards. It's there in the fact that I heard Angelica banging on the door to the hotel suite, but nobody let her in. It's there when I go to look for my phone, and it's not in my purse.

I don't ask what's happening, though. I've learned to trust that my men are doing everything they can to shield me from stresses in the outside world, and I'm tired. So tired of trying to keep me together.

I miss home. I miss my brother and my best friend, Jordy. I miss having my feet firmly on home ground.

So instead of asking why, behind all the bright smiles, there's an atmosphere similar to a funeral, I settle into bed with Connor and Mo and let them shoulder the burden. I keep my worries stuffed down deep the way I'm used to doing. I swallow my fears and rest my voice like I've been ordered to do. In the morning, we're flying to London.

STEEL 7

At daybreak, when everything is packed, Connor gives me a black baseball cap, sunglasses, and a scarf to try to shield me as much as possible from the prying eyes of the pap photographers and rabid fans. "Keep your head down," he says.

Then Mo hands me some earbuds and a phone that isn't mine. It's already playing some calming music, and I don't question why they want my attention focused elsewhere.

I'm hustled into the waiting car so fast I feel as though my feet never touched the sidewalk. At the airport, we enter into a VIP security area, and all the checks are handled by Steel 7. Today, they seem even fiercer than usual, their eyes darting in a way that seems fearful, muttering observations into their audio equipment.

I have to take off my hat, scarf, sunglasses, and earbuds to pass through the scanning equipment, and it's then that I hear "Is that really them?" and notice some of the security team whispering behind hands cupped furtively over their mouths.

Someone whistles the way people do when they get a bill that's too high, or they see something surprising. I'm used to unwanted attention, but this doesn't feel right.

When I'm approved to fly, I reapply my disguise like a shield that I'm grateful to cower behind.

As soon as we board the flight, the atmosphere changes. Connor sits on one side of me and Hudson on the other. The weight of unspoken words curls Connor's shoulders and prevents Hudson from directly meeting my gaze.

As I fasten my seatbelt, I pull a sheet of paper and pen from my pocket that I stashed for emergency communication.

Please tell me what's going on, I write.

Connor exhales, his shoulders slumping even further.

"Someone took pictures of us in the sea in Melbourne," he says. "They've been published worldwide."

A shivery feeling passes over my face, and my grip loosens on the pencil. Even though Connor warned me about this possibility, I never imagined it would come to pass. We were careful. The only time we did anything in the open, it was so dark I could barely see who was in front of me. How did they get pictures? *Stupid question*, I think. When people want to uncover dirt badly enough, they'll find a way to dig.

What's going to happen? I write.

Connor shrugs a single shoulder; the hopelessness he's feeling is evident in every movement and gesture he makes. "Blueday is going to fire us. Most likely, we'll be relieved of duty when we land in London. I've avoided talking directly to my contact so we can get you safely to your next destination. You will need to speak to your agent and to the record company and decide whether you will comment on the photos or not. How you deal with it from your side will be up to you. From our side, we won't make any comments about the images. Everything that happened will remain a confidence between us."

As I take in what Connor is saying, tears prickle my eyes and constrict my throat. These men who are such an important part of my life will be removed from it, and I don't have the power to disagree. They're losing their jobs because of what we've done, and their first thought isn't about themselves. It's about protecting me and my reputation.

I don't want them to leave me. I don't want to face the rest of this tour without them. I won't feel safe, even in the care of another bodyguard team. I don't want to be protected by men who don't care for me. I want the love and affection that we've built up together.

But I can't tell them any of that. My voice has been taken in more ways than one.

Reaching for Connor's hand and then Hudson's, I hold onto them like I never want to let them go. Tears slide down my cheek, but I don't bother to wipe them. I'm so sad inside; my heart is broken into shards that radiate ache right through me.

I don't even care about my reputation. I don't give a fuck that Blueday is going to be raging about the damage I've potentially done. I mean, what parent is going to want to bring their child to see a singer who is sexually promiscuous? Not exactly ideal role-model material.

This tour is already sold out. The tickets have been purchased. Blueday is going to make their money whatever happens, and I will too. The only people losing out here are my bodyguards.

"It'll be okay," Hudson says. "Blueday will hire you a great team, I'm certain of that. Your performances are perfection. All you've got to do is keep going the way you have been. Keep your mind on the job this time, and everything will be fine."

I pull my hand from his to write. *No one they hire will be as good as you guys.*

"I'm sure they'll protect you just fine. And they'd better keep their hands to themselves," Connor growls.

We all laugh at the ridiculousness of the idea that anyone could replace what they are to me. We laugh because Connor's jealousy doesn't fit with a relationship that started the way ours did. I made it clear what I wanted was men in my bed. They don't know that I've fallen in love with each of them. They have no idea that when they walk away from me in London that they'll leave me bereft.

Even though I know it's impossible, a childish and ridiculous part of me wants them to fight for me. It wants them to argue with Blueday and demand that they stay on to look after me. It wants them to be willing to tell the world that they love me and show that the love we share is the most important thing.

I don't really know what love is supposed to be like. My parents didn't love me in any kind of way that I could feel nurtured by. If they did, it was a selfish love that was more about using me and controlling me than it was about supporting and cherishing. My brothers loved me but in an imperfect sibling way. Looking back, I don't know how much of it was real love and how much was about duty and desperation to have something to cling to when everything around us was falling apart.

In the movies, love takes two forms: the sickly-sweet love of Christmas movies where even the most difficult of challenges are easily overcome, or the crazy psycho love that drives people to do all kinds of insane things.

As much as I'd like to believe that these men have feelings for me, I'm obviously kidding myself. They have a duty to protect me that I've built into some greater level of care. They're good, responsible men, and that's blinded me to the fact that this situation is all my creation.

Men love sex. They're biologically driven to fuck as much as possible. So, if a woman offers it on a silver platter, they're likely to take it. Sex for women has a greater emotional element. Sex for men is a functional need.

All I've done for them is fill a desire for physical release and provide them with some fun on the lonely nights on tour. The same as they've done for me, except I've been an idiot and let my heart get involved.

If I tell them how I feel, would it make a difference? If they fought to stay with me, what would the end result be? I'd lose my contract with Blueday. That's a certainty. We'd all end up resenting each other. Their life is on the road, and mine is too. I convince myself that this thing only worked because of the forced proximity of the tour.

Swallowing everything down tastes as bitter as the

drink I almost swallowed yesterday. To my dying day, the loss of these men and that terrible experience will have the same flavor.

For all of our sakes, the best thing I can do is let my bodyguards walk away.

25

BEN

It's raining in London; weather fitting with the mood we are all doing our best to conceal. As we disembark, the stewards shoot us pearly-white smiles that don't quite meet their eyes. When we're through the immigration checks, we're stopped by a troop of men in black.

"Steel 7 Security?" the biggest one with the shaven head asks.

"Yes." Connor's shoulders rise as he takes a steadying breath, and my knee feels weak.

These are our replacements.

"We'll take it from here," he says. "Miss Evans, your car is waiting outside. I'm Mr. Wright, and this is the rest of your team. Can you follow me, please?"

"Hang on a minute," Asher says. "We're going to need to see some documents before we release the primary. Show us your contract."

Mr. Wright reaches into his inside pocket, pulling out a roughly folded bundle of papers. "Here's the contract from

Adam at Blueday. I take it that it's the same one as they sent to you."

Connor looks over the details, nodding as he reads the relevant sections. Mr. Wright takes a step forward impatiently, but Connor puts up his hand, and the rest of us gather closer to Luna. Eventually, he turns to her. "Luna, these men are going to be looking after you from here."

I can't decipher her facial expression because her eyes are obscured by her oversize sunglass. She can't speak either.

Connor reaches for her hand, but Mr. Wright clears his throat. "Can I suggest that goodbyes are kept to a minimum? Who knows who's watching and recording right now? Luna needs to maintain distance."

As Connor's hand drops to his side, my heart feels like a missile dropped from the belly of a plane. We're not even going to be able to say goodbye properly. I'm never going to feel the soft press of her lips on mine or the gentle touch that told me I was enough.

"Luna, we wish you all the best with the rest of the tour. If you need anything, please call any one of us anytime." Connor's voice is flat and defeated, and I get the urge to shout the words from his tattoo: *Tada gan iarracht*. There's never been a moment in our lives when it has meant more.

Nothing without effort. It would take effort for us to fight to be together. Luna would lose the most. She'd have to give up her career and the wealth that it's set to bring her. It's a lot, but we've never asked her how she feels about us. We've never given her the chance to make a choice.

I want to step forward and give her that choice right now, but if she says no, if she chooses to walk away, I don't think I could take it.

It's not kind to force her into a corner, not kind to her

or kind to us.

Sometimes the end of a situation is the best thing for everyone. Fighting doesn't always lead to victory.

Luna nods at Connor's best wishes, wrapping her arm across her body in a way that seems as though she's trying to hold herself together but could just be impatience.

I thought I felt the emotion behind her kisses and in her fingertips, but we never made each other promises. Now I wish I had the courage to tell her how much better my life has been with her in it. Maybe it would sound selfish, or maybe just pathetic.

"Anytime," Asher says.

We all mumble our agreement because it's the only thing left to do.

She brings her hand to her lips, kisses it lightly, and blows it; then she breaks out of the protective circle that we've gotten too used to forming around her and into the circle of new bodyguards.

They're an older group than we are. Maybe Adam at Blueday selected them because they'd be less of a temptation. Still, if Luna was really driven only by her physical urges, maybe she'll indulge in the same kind of arrangement with her new security team.

I feel sick at the thought and sick with myself for imagining she'd think so little of us.

Luna's a great person. Kind and thoughtful. Bright and bubbly. Confident yet vulnerable.

I'd trust her with my life, just as I trust my Steel 7 brothers.

I'll keep the memories of our time together wrapped up tightly next to my heart.

As Luna disappears through the doors, we stand frozen for a few seconds. We have no purpose now – no reason to be in London at all.

"We should have told her," Asher says softly as we gather our luggage and make our way to the exit.

"Told her what?" Hudson shrugs, his huge frame carrying the air of the defeated. "That we love her? I told her that in a hundred kisses and touches. She knows, Asher. It just wasn't enough."

As I step into the London rain, I have no idea what to believe.

But either way, none of it really matters anymore.

26

LUNA

As soon as I switch on my phone, I am bombarded with messages. The screen lights up with icons that tell me my voicemail box is swamped, and WhatsApp has gone mental.

In the back of the limousine, surrounded by strangers, I feel so alone. I can't face listening to the ranting of anyone who cares more about money than they do about me, so I ignore everything apart from the messages from my friends and family.

Jordy is first. **What the fuck, girl? You look like you're living some different dreams from the ones I expected from you. Seven bodyguards, eh? I would call you Snow White, but those hulking dudes look nothing like dwarves. Can you call me or something? I mean, I'm sure this radio silence breaks the bestie code in some way. Shouldn't I be the first one to know your gossip? Or should I say, shouldn't I be the first one to hear the juice. Sex gossip is definitely bestie territory. Did I say call me? Call me!**

Damn, I want to hear my friend's voice. I want to joke with her about guy stuff like we used to. I want everything to feel less like it's shattering my insides, but there is no way I'm making juicy confessions surrounded by my new bodyguards, and anyway, I'm pretty sure I couldn't mention the names of the men she's seen me with in the pictures without breaking down.

Tyler's messages are more worried-sounding. **Sis, are you okay? I've seen the pictures and no judgment from me. At least, what I mean to say is that I'm good if you're loving life. Just want to check that you are loving life, and the pictures aren't anything a big brother should be worried about. Not even sure if what I've just said makes sense. Love you baby girl.**

I smile at his rambling because I can tell he's treading on eggshells, not really sure how to be toward me. There was a time when he would have just said exactly what he thought, but we're not there right now. Maybe one day we will be.

There's a message from Sandy, Tyler's girlfriend too. **Just to let you know that your momma's doing well in the facility. She's talking about a release date, but I think she needs to stay longer. Oh, and by the way, I'm pregnant. Ready to be an auntie?**

Auntie Luna. It has a cool ring to it.

For a second, I wonder if she knows that it's definitely Tyler's baby, but then I realize that it doesn't really matter who the biological father is. All the men in their relationship will step up to be a parent to their child. That baby is going to have six amazing daddies. How cool is that?

I type out congratulations and tell her how happy I am. Then I sign off **Love Auntie Luna** with a smiley emoji, but inside, slithering jealousy takes place in my gut. Sandy has everything I really want. Men who love her. A home that's safe and secure. A family on the way. Her life is illuminated with a soft yellow warmth that I want to climb into. By contrast, my life feels as though its tinged with icy blue. Glancing around the vehicle, I'm struck by the emptiness, the coldness, and the absence of all the things I crave.

Where is the fun, the warmth, the laughter, the love, and the affection? Where is the safety and security? Where are the people to rely on when times get tough or to giggle with when life is great? I'm back to being alone.

Drawing in a shaky breath, I keep scrolling. Beneath is a message from Greg, Tyler's friend. He's a hulking great man who's covered in tattoos and has eyes as dark as hell itself, but underneath the fierce exterior, he's a stand-up guy with a heart of gold. **Luna, girl, I hope you're looking after yourself. Let me know if I need to break any bones. Remember that you're a queen and that any man who comes near you should be treating you like royalty.**

As I said, he's the kind of guy that every girl should have in their lives.

No bone-breaking required, I reply, **but thanks for the offer. Do relationships ever get any easier?**

Even though it's the middle of the night back home, I see Greg begin to reply. **Baby girl, relationships are a journey, not a destination. All we can hope is that we'll find the right person or people to walk next to. You okay? Those men in suits treating you well?**

Blueday fired them, I type. **Relationships in the public eye are a whole different ball game.**

I'm sorry about that, he replies. **Your focus has to be on your job right now, but you have time. Look at me. I just found my girl.**

You're gonna make a great dad, I tell him. **I'm so excited to hear your news.** I sign off, blaming my schedule, but really, it's because I can't deal with the feelings of longing for home and for people who are familiar to me.

At the hotel, it gets even worse. My new security detail doesn't consult me on our food order. They just use the nutritionist's plan. I end up with an avocado and chicken salad, which I want to throw out the window more than I want to eat. Just the smell makes my stomach turn. What I'm craving is a green tea and a plate of steak and fries. They talk among themselves as if I'm not even there, so I leave the plate on the table and return to my room, closing the door behind me.

There's no Jax to make me laugh or Asher to draw something pretty. There's no Mo to make me see the philosophical side of life or Connor to step in like a big brother to sort out any situation. There's no Ben with his kind hands or Hudson with his voice like silk. There's no Elijah to encourage me to stick up for myself. The Steel 7 men made me feel at home wherever I went in the world. Knowing they were around made this tour bearable, but now I'm out on my own.

I glance at my phone, tabbing through my contacts and looking at the profile pictures for each of the Steel 7 men, longing to be in their arms again and wishing that they'd contact me. Just one little message to find out how I'm doing. That's all it would take for me to know they care.

But there's nothing.

Then the phone lights up. It's a Blueday Records number. My heart skitters, knowing that when I pick up this call, I'm going to have to face up to what's being said about me. I'm going to hear how disappointed the record company is about my behavior. I'm going to be told how much I've damaged my reputation.

But I can't put it off any longer.

The next ten minutes are the worst of my life. I have to bite my lip until it bleeds to stop myself from telling the five balding assholes on the conference call to fuck off. My manager doesn't support me. It's clear all he's interested in is securing his percentage. I want to tell them that they loved making me into some kind of ingénue sex object, but when I actually have sex, they don't like it. I want to scream that my body is mine to decide what to do with. They might contractually own my singing voice and my performances, but they don't own me. I want to tell them to shove their contract up their asses. I want to rage and sob and throw expensive objects in my hotel room and take no responsibility for my anger.

I don't do any of those things.

I swallow it when they insinuate that I'm a slut who's allowed men to use my body. I swallow it when they tell me I cannot talk about it. I even agree when they tell me that I'm not allowed to be seen with another man for the rest of the tour.

I let them talk about me as though I'm an object and not a person and I appreciate the irony. My Steel 7 bodyguards never made me feel like an object. They saw me, the real me behind my ridiculous public image, the real me behind the toughened exterior I've fashioned to protect myself. They saw the good and the bad and didn't ever make me feel lesser.

My manager and the Blueday Record Executives say they have my best interests at heart but what they really mean is that they want me to sit down and shut up so that *their* best interests aren't damaged any further.

The next evening, I perform in a huge stadium in London. It should be one of the highlights of the tour, but inside, I feel dead. The crowd whistles when I dance. There's a raucousness about their cheering that I sense is leery and disapproving rather than appreciative. In my skimpy costume, I feel like a sex object rather than sexually empowered. Around the edge of the stage, my new bodyguards watch with crossed arms. When I go to get a drink, I'm handed one from Mr. Wright's pocket. He watches me with a cool expression as I take a tentative sip. It's water, but that doesn't mean that I don't flinch when it passes my lips.

After the show, my dancers all disappear quickly, and Angelica keeps a frosty distance.

Nothing feels good now the men I love have gone.

27

ELIJAH

London is a city of contrasts. One moment, you can be walking down a street flanked by buildings as old as Dickens, and the next, you're faced with a huge skyscraper in the shape of a cucumber.

The people walk around as though they don't see anyone else. Everything is a rush.

And the rain. It's something else.

To be honest, the weather fits our collective mood. Everything feels gray now we're not with Luna. We've lost our purpose and left pieces of our hearts behind.

Even a shopping trip for tacky souvenirs doesn't cheer us up. It's on the biggest shopping street in London that I think I hear my voice being shouted. When I stop walking, Connor turns, and the rest of the crew slows down. "What is it?" he asks.

"Did you just hear someone shout Elijah?"

"It's not an unusual name, dude."

"Elijah," I hear again, and everyone turns, searching the crowd. People stream past us, some tutting at the way we're blocking the sidewalk.

"Come on," Connor huffs. "They're shouting for a British Elijah, not some American dude on vacation."

"Is that what you call this?" I start walking but then two voices shout my name, and when I turn, I see familiar faces. For a moment, I'm frozen in place, slowly closing my eyes to wipe the weirdness from my vision. Then my brothers get close enough for me to accept that I'm not seeing things.

"What the fuck?" I mumble. The last time I saw them, they were sixteen, and I was walking away from our family. The last time we were together, they had chosen to remain part of a cult where travel outside of the compound wasn't permitted. And here they are in London.

When they throw their arms around me, tears burn in my throat. They're grown. The skinny teenage years have been left behind. Now they're two huge men with beards, and eyes just like mine.

"Elijah. What the fuck are you doing here?"

"What the fuck are *you* doing here?" I counter, hugging them again and slapping them both on the back hard enough to raise interested expressions from passers-by.

"We're traveling the world," Isiah says.

"Enjoying the freedom we never had," Josiah grins. "What about you?"

Glancing around my friends, I swallow down the truth. "We were working, and now we're on vacation. What are the odds that we'd be in the same place at the same time?"

"Who the fuck knows." Josiah runs his hand over his beard. "You're looking good, man. Old but good."

There was always a rivalry about the age between us. They hated the fact that I was two years older and was always the one our mom trusted the most.

"Less of the old," I laugh. "These guys are my brothers from other mothers." I point at each of my friends in turn, introducing them to my flesh-and-blood brothers who have been strangers for too many years.

"Shall we go and grab a drink somewhere," Connor says. "I want to try some Irish beer if we can find it. And I reckon if we don't move, we're going to get knocked out by a raging Brit for blocking the 'pavement.'" He uses his fingers to make air-quotes around the word Londoners use for sidewalk. We've been trying to pick up the differences in language as something to improve our mood. It hasn't worked.

Hudson pulls out his phone, already on the case. "With Google, anything is possible," he says, but it's not true. Google can't give us back Luna, and that's the only thing I really want.

It takes us ten minutes to find an Irish bar, or as the Brits call it, a pub. It takes another ten minutes to get served and receive our drinks. Thankfully, there is a table free at the back and, as we all take a seat, I feel strangely awkward.

My friends are like oil, and my brothers like water. They've never mixed before, and now we're in the same place at the same time, I feel trapped between them, not really sure which version of myself to be. They're not that different beneath the surface though. I'm hoping that some time spent together will iron out any creases.

"So, where are you guys staying?" I ask to break the silence that's settled over our group.

"A hostel in Kings Cross. It's basic and expensive but the cheapest we could find. What about you?"

"We've got rooms in a chain hotel. Nothing fancy," I say. I don't tell them about the penthouse and VIP suites we've been staying in or our travels around the world.

They don't need to know about Luna at all and to be honest, talking about her would be like picking open a wound. "You gonna share what happened...how come you've left the family?"

Josiah nods, taking a sip of beer, which leaves white foam in his blond beard. "Same as you, brother. We got to an age when we realized that there wasn't anything for us there."

"I'm surprised they didn't marry you off by now," I say.

"They tried, but we grew up with those girls. They all felt more like sisters than potential brides, and we didn't love them. What kind of marriage isn't built on love?"

"My parents only met once before they married," Mo says, sipping his Coke through a straw. "They're happy together."

"I guess it can work some of the time," I say. "But I get where you're coming from. I wish I'd known, but I couldn't get in touch with you. I tried, and Dad would always put the phone down. I just believed that I was never going to see you again."

"We didn't take it personally, El," Isiah says. "We knew you weren't leaving us; you were leaving the life. We knew you were doing the right thing for you."

"It was hard to leave everyone behind," I say. "I used to dream I was home, and then I'd wake up in some dusty tent in Iraq and wonder how the fuck I got there."

"We prayed that we'd find you somehow," Josiah says, revealing that it's not their faith that they left behind, just the restrictive lifestyle our family enforced.

"It looks like those prayers were answered," Connor says. He holds up his glass, "To Elijah and a surprise family reunion." We all clink glasses, but the toast is followed by another awkward silence.

"Love always finds a way to bring people together." Isiah nods knowingly, suddenly seeming older than his years. I wish I had the same faith as him. My whole life seems to have been about leaving people I love – first my family and my friends back home, now Luna. I don't get why holding onto love can be so hard.

"Love always finds a way to fuck you in the ass," Jax says, tipping the rest of his beer down his throat as though he's trying to drown his melancholy.

"Not love," Josiah says. "It's everything we put before love that does that."

"Your brothers are very wise," Mo says, nodding.

"But that's life," Hudson says. "There's always something that comes to test us."

"And what do you do when that happens?" Isiah asks.

"Whatever is best for everyone," Hudson says.

Isiah nods knowingly, slumping back into his chair. "Our parents would say that they did that for us. They would tell whoever asked that all their decisions had the best interests of their family at heart, but they never asked us what we wanted. They never asked us how we felt. Our real wants and needs were pushed aside for what they believed we should need and want. In the process, they squashed us until we didn't know whether we were coming or going. Elijah was the strong one. He was the first to break out of that and find his own place in the world. We waited for longer, hoping that our mom and dad would learn that they were doing wrong by losing one son. It turns out they lost all three of us and still haven't learned."

"That's sad," Jax says. "Why do parents fuck us up so bad?"

"They say the worst preparation for life is a happy childhood." Connor says it bitterly, but I understand why that might be true. When things are too easy, we don't build the fortitude to resist difficult times.

I think over what we just went through with Luna. As soon as the going got tough, we did what we thought was best and left her to live the life we assume she wants. We made the decision without even consulting her. We acted like my parents, overriding another person because we thought it was the right thing to do, but is it?

What if Luna really wanted us to fight for her? What if she's sick of a life that's taking so much from her and would have been happy to settle down into a relationship with us?

Maybe we've just left behind the best thing that's ever happened to us and made the girl we love think we never cared about her. Maybe we've broken her heart.

Mo leans over and rests his hand against the top of my arm. "I know what you're thinking," he says, "But it's too late."

"Too late," I murmur as the rest of my friends all shake their heads.

I guess we'll never know what she really wanted, and maybe that's a good thing.

As Isiah and Josiah talk more about their travel plans, I try to stay engaged, but all the while, my heart is telling me that I'm a fool. A fool who let the girl of my dreams slip through my fingers without ever asking her what she wanted.

A fool who repeats the mistakes of his parents.

28

MO

Everyone starts the next morning with a full English breakfast, which turns out to be a huge plate of eggs, sausage, bacon, black pudding – which is actually blood sausage – fried tomatoes, fried mushrooms, fried bread and some beans in tomato sauce. I opt for oatmeal which is definitely a healthier option.

The group is trying their best to keep spirits high. Jax is reeling off joke after joke, and Isiah and Josiah are getting involved, oblivious to the involvement of their brother in the Luna Evans scandal that is still blowing up across the newspapers of the world. I guess it's good that they're not interest in celebrity gossip otherwise I think Elijah might blow their minds. They might have stepped away from their traditional upbringing, but not that far.

I'm so far out of the realms of my past that sometimes I don't even recognize myself.

Is it a good thing? I'm not sure.

I miss my family, but there's no way I can go back

safely. That's what happens when you work for a foreign force. You end up blacklisted by your own people. I don't regret becoming a translator for the Americans. I do regret that it's caused me to separate from my old life.

I'm also thankful that I gained a new family who are as loyal and goodhearted as my real family.

There's no point in looking back when the journey is in the opposite direction.

It's funny that I don't feel that way about Luna, though. With her, I want to gaze into my memories and hold them close.

When a call comes through to my phone from an Australian number, I know it's going to be the police. I'm still listed as a contact, and I guess the record company hasn't thought to replace our details with the new teams. I'm eager to answer to see what they've found out about the stalker, and when they relay that they've connected all the incidents to one person, I can't wait to tell the rest of my boys. We finally have a lead.

"We have to tell Angelica," I say.

Connor flairs his nostrils, expelling a noisy huff. "Are they sure Angelica isn't the one responsible? She had access to the dressing room and the rider table."

"Angelica may be snarky and hardnosed, but I don't see her as a stalker," Hudson says.

"The messages sounded like they were from a man, not a woman," Asher recalls.

"For Luna's sake, we need to get back in touch to discuss this with Angelica. She's the one running things. She's the one with the power to make a difference."

"She's not going to be interested," Jax snorts. "That woman doesn't give a shit about Luna. She's just there to push her out on stage so that Blueday can extract their money's-worth."

"Then those elderly meatheads they've hired to replace

us need to step up," I say.

"Well, maybe you should call Angelica and get Mr. Wrong's number." Jax screws up his napkin and tosses onto the table in frustration.

"I could mash that guy's face into the ground with the heel of my boot," Asher says, in a surprisingly vicious way that doesn't suit him.

"They all look like they should have retired a few years ago," Hudson grumbles, downing the last of his coffee and slamming the cup on the table. The sharp noise draws the attention of other customers but he's oblivious. We're all taking the separation from Luna badly.

"Let's just hope they're doing a decent job. I don't think I could sleep at night if I was seriously doubting their capabilities."

Connor nods at my comment, his eyes closing slowly. He's going to that solitary place where he searches for solutions to problems. He's always been bad at asking for help but good at working out what to do. The trouble is, when you face problems alone, you miss the chance to get other perspectives. "If we call Angelica, what will her incentive be for handing over that number? As far as she's concerned, we're off the security detail. She doesn't need to have anything more to do with us."

"All we can do is try," I say. "Appeal to her better nature."

Connor rubs his face and drops his hand into his lap with a thud. "I would recommend someone other than me handles this. Angelica doesn't hold much affection for me, especially when I didn't let her into Luna's room the night that we left Australia. She will probably hold a grudge about that to her deathbed."

"Mo's always had a cordial relationship with her," Asher points out.

Everyone turns to stare at me. "I try to have a cordial

relationship with everyone."

"Well, that's it, then." Hudson balls up his napkin and tosses it at me, narrowly missing my head and landing it on the floor behind me. "Luna's safety now rests solely in Mo's hands."

"Way to put pressure on him." Jax turns to me, and grins, reaching out to pat my hand. "You can do it, Mo. Just turn on that Middle Eastern charm. Angelica has a soft spot for your dark eyes and smooth tanned skin. You know there's a whole romance genre featuring sheikh billionaires that she probably reads every night."

"Can we make this sound less sexual?" I say. "I'm phoning the woman to ask for a telephone number, not calling to propose to her."

"Sheikhs don't propose," Jax laughs. "They kidnap and seduce."

"I think that might be taking things a little too far." Grabbing my phone from the table, I rise and walk to the front of the restaurant to secure a little privacy. "Angelica."

"Mo, I don't have time for this right now," she barks. "Everything's a disaster."

"I'm so sorry to hear that," I say, keeping my voice low and smooth, hoping that it might have a calming effect. "Is there anything I can do to help?"

"Not unless you can find me a missing lighting rig. I swear, the thing is huge, and it has somehow managed to go missing."

I think again of Marcus, the weird lighting guy, wondering if he might have anything to do with Luna's troubles. Then I squash my suspicions because I have no proof that he's anything other than a stand-up employee.

"I can't do anything about the rig," I say. "My mom always told me to go back to the first place you thought to look. Sometimes, we're in such a panic to find something that we skip over it in our haste."

"I'll bear that in mind," she says. "So what can I do for you?"

My heart skips a beat. I've gotten her to listen. "I need a number. The telephone number for Mr. Wright, Luna's bodyguard."

"What's this about?" Angelica's voice has gone from laid back to suspicious in the blink of an eye. Time to get her back to feeling comfortable.

"Nothing important. We just wanted to make sure that the new team has everything they need. I'm sure that Blueday has set them up well. They're meticulous like that, but just in case. For Luna's safety."

There's a pause and I sag against the wall, already thinking the worst. If she doesn't give me the number, our only option will be to try and crash one of Luna's concerts or find a way to get into the hotel. That would leave us looking like stalkers and potentially upset Luna. We walked away to create a clean break. Going back would just muddy the waters.

"For Luna's safety, I'll message you with his number. But listen Mo, if anything happens and I find out it's because I trusted you with this, you and me will have a serious falling out."

"Nothing's going to happen, Angelica. You can trust me."

The words hang between us for a few seconds. I guess maybe Angelica is thinking about the photos in the newspapers and how we abused the trust of everyone by breaking our code of conduct with Luna.

"Okay," she says eventually. "It's on its way."

The relief I feel is immense, not just because I can now do something with the information that I have but also because I haven't let my friends down. They were relying on me, and I delivered.

When I slump down at the table, six pairs of eyes fix on

me expectantly. "So, did you get it?" Jax asks.

"That Angelica is a real hard-ass." I sigh, hoping they're all going to take the bait.

"I can think of other way less polite words to call her," Connor grumbles. "Can't she see that we only have Luna's best interests in mind?"

"She can," I say. "I have the number."

Four napkins fly across the table at my head and Elijah slaps me on the back. "Sheikh Mo did it again." When I grab a balled napkin and aim it at him from close range, he puts his palms out to bat it away. "She fell for your exotic charm."

"Like Luna," I say, wiggling my eyebrows, but my attempt to keep things light only sends everyone back into gloom. "Maybe I need to become like one of the sheikhs in those books you were talking about and just kidnap her. Would that put the smiles back on your faces?"

"It wouldn't be what she wanted, so no," Hudson says.

"Let's stop wallowing in this," Connor huffs. "Pass me the number."

He grips my phone in his left hand and his own in his right, tapping Mr. Wright's number onto the screen with his thumb. Connor chooses not to leave the table for privacy, so we all sit in silence, waiting to hear the conversation.

"Hi, this is Connor, from Steel 7. I have some news from the Australian police."

There's a pause but all we can hear is the rumble of conversation on the other end.

"It's relevant because you should know what you're dealing with."

Connor's jaw ticks as he waits for a response.

"It's one individual. They have matched the prints...I know you've got her covered. What I'm saying is that one crazy person is following her around the world. You need to up your game. Stick to her like glue. Don't let a single thing pass her lips if it hasn't been checked. Don't let her out of your sight, even backstage, even with the crew. Who the fuck knows how this asshole is getting so close?"

There's a louder rumble of speech audible through the speaker and Connor pulls the phone from his face and stares at it.

"Seriously, dude. If you have a problem with me, that's fine. I get it. But don't let that affect your professional judgement because if anything happens to that girl...I swear to God."

The phone goes dead, and Connor tosses it onto the table, cursing. "That idiot has a fucking boulder for a head. Nothing I said went in."

"He's arrogant," Asher says. "But maybe he's just pissed off that you're telling him what to do. Maybe he heard you and he'll take action."

"Or he's going to ignore me and do the opposite." Connor slams both his fists onto the table, making the empty plates and cups bounce and the silverware clatter.

"Fuck," I mutter, the joke I made earlier suddenly seeming less crazy. I could kidnap our girl and ride into the sunset. We could all go to ground somewhere no one knew us until all the bullshit blew over. I've gone to ground before. With preparation, it was okay. And with Luna, we'd have no need of entertainment. She could keep us all satisfied without even trying.

"We can't leave London," Ben says. "Not until Luna moves on. And when she does, maybe we need to go too."

"Shadow her, you mean?"

Ben nods in response to my question. "Until the stalker is caught."

And in my heart, I feel so twisted because staying close to Luna is what I want, and if catching the stalker means that we'll have to leave her and go home, maybe I don't want that to happen too soon.

29

ASHER

I'm sleeping when my phone begins to vibrate on the nightstand. I've never been one for leaving my phone on overnight but since we left Luna in the airport, I haven't been able to switch it off. The thought that she might need me has been lingering at the back of my mind. I'm just one of seven men who was caring for her, but we had as strong a connection as any.

I reach over to grab it, my sleep-addled mind anticipating it's going to be a nuisance sales call from the U.S. They won't know that I'm in London or realize that I'm in a different time zone, but when I crack one eye open to see who it is, I find Luna's name on the screen.

"Hello," I whisper, scrambling out of bed. The air in the room is cool, but even in just my sleep shorts, I feel warm.

"Asher," Luna's voice is so soft I can barely hear it. I make it to the bathroom and close the door so that I don't disturb Ben and Elijah.

"What is it, honey? Are you okay?"

"It happened again," she says, then I hear her sniff in a way that sounds like crying.

"What happened?" I think I know but bringing up the stalker in the middle of the night when Luna's already upset wouldn't be sensitive.

"The stalker. He sent something else. The bra that went missing from my dressing room in Berlin, covered with more blood. My bodyguards have given it to the police but I'm freaking out. How the fuck is he getting so close to me, and no one is catching him in the act? I don't understand. To get backstage you have to have a pass. Whoever it is has followed me from city to city."

"We don't know that everything is connected. What happened in Australia could be someone totally different." I say, trying to find a way to calm her. Is it better to tell her the truth or pretend I'm not sure? We've always tried to keep the darkness away from her, and in the middle of the night, when she's so far away, how does it benefit her to know?

"More than one stalker?"

"I'm just saying that it hasn't been confirmed."

"He's getting closer all the time," she whispers. "It doesn't matter how many burly men I have around me, he's there." Her breath hitches with what sounds like real fear and my arms break out in gooseflesh.

Rubbing my hand over my face, I take a deep steadying breath. My grip tightens on the phone as my frustration passes through every limb into every tendon. "I wish I could be there with you," I say. "I wish we'd done things differently."

"You think what we did was a mistake?"

"No. I could never see it as a mistake. It was a mistake that we weren't more careful."

Luna exhales lightly, and her phone rustles as she shifts

around. It's hell to hear her voice and not be able to hold her. It's hell not to be able to help her directly when she's in distress, but at least she called me. At least she still reached out.

"Mo was on the phone to the police in Australia yesterday. They're making progress, honey. We've just got to be patient. Stick closely to your new team of bodyguards. Don't go anywhere that isn't an absolute necessity. Don't eat or drink anything that they haven't checked first, okay?"

"Okay."

Seconds of silence tick past while all of the things I want to say to her stick like wool in my throat. It's not fair to tell her that I miss her when there's no hope of anything happening between us. It's not fair to draw her into something that isn't going to bring her happiness. The scandal will die down in time and she can go back to the career she's so driven to pursue. Protecting that has to be all of our priorities.

"I miss you," she whispers. "I know that wasn't part of the plan for any of us, but I do."

I slump against the wall, the biting cold of the tile against my skin matching the ache in my heart. "I miss you too," I say, my resolve drifting away. "We all do. But you have so much going on and none of us want to mess it up for you."

It's her chance to tell me what she wants. It's her chance to step forward and say that our relationship is worth fighting for.

The silence between us echoes louder than church bells. Is she angry with me? Did she want me to say something different? Every man in my crew would fight for Luna if we felt that it was the right thing. Letting her go has been the hardest thing I've ever had to do, but it's for her own good. If she chose us over her career, there would always be a part of her that would regret it.

"How are you all?" she asks eventually. "How was the journey home?"

"We're all good," I tell her. "We're still in London, taking some time off. Elijah ran into his brothers yesterday so it looks like we might stay for a few more days."

"You're in London?" Somehow the news that we're close has made Luna's voice brighter.

"Yeah. Probably not that far from you."

"For now," she says.

"When do you move on?" I ask, not remembering the tour schedule in detail.

"Two more days," she says. "I have a TV show tomorrow night. Blueday have briefed them that I won't be answering any questions about the pictures, but that doesn't mean that they are going to listen."

"You think they might try it on?"

"I think they'd be mad not to get the scoop if they could."

"Shit," I say. "What will you do if they ask?"

"Smile and thank them for letting me perform my new single on their show. At least, that's what Blueday have told me to do."

"Sounds like a plan," I say slowly, worrying that things could get very awkward for her in front of a huge TV audience. "Are you sure that you want to go through with it? Could you make an excuse?"

"It's great exposure," she says, but there is definitely doubt in her voice. "I have to brave it at some point. I can't hide at my own shows forever. The tour needs to build publicity. That's the whole point of it."

"It must be tough, always thinking about pushing yourself further into the public eye."

"You wouldn't like to be a famous artist?"

"I'd like for people to love my work, but if that could

happen without anybody ever needing to see my face, I'd take the anonymity over fame any day."

"Really?"

"Really."

"I never believed that anything like this would ever happen to me. It started off like a fairy tale, but it's starting to feel like a nightmare."

"Don't say that," I say. "It's just a temporary blip and when it's passed, you'll feel like you're in the fairy tale again. How could you not? You're a superstar, Luna."

She sighs softly and I hear the rustle of her bed covers as she shifts position. "I'm just a girl, Asher. Whatever happens in my life, however famous I get, I'll still be just a girl."

"You're so much more than just a girl," I say. "You sparkle like the brightest diamond. Don't ever forget how special you are."

The cool tiles of the bathroom floor are starting to make my feet cold and outside, a car horn sounds despite the late hour. If I could click my fingers and find myself in Luna's bed, tucked up warm and tight away from the world, I wouldn't hesitate. Even though seeing her again would make our eventual separation harder, I'd put myself through it if I could be a comfort to her.

"If I forget, all I have to do is look at your drawings of me," she says. "You drew me in black and white, but somehow those drawings seem to convey me in vivid technicolor."

"That's all you, sweetheart. I just captured what I could see."

I think she smiles then, at least, I imagine her pretty face resting against the pillow and a soft curve to her pink lips. I imagine her delicate collar bones and strong toned arms revealed by the sheet, and a swathe of shiny chestnut hair spread out behind her.

"Do you think we'll ever see each other again?" she asks.

"You know we would in a heartbeat if it wasn't going to mess with your career," I say.

"My career." She says it as though her teeth are gritted. Two simple words laced with a bitterness I can almost taste.

"Just know that the time we spent together was everything we could ever have wanted," I say, swallowing around the ache in my throat. "Just know for that short amount of time, you were all we wanted."

"Goodbye, Asher," she whispers, and then the phone line goes dead.

I stare at the phone in my hand, hoping that she was cut off accidently, praying that she'll call back, but she doesn't.

For a long time, I stare at myself in the mirror, replaying our conversation in my mind. Did I say what she needed to hear? Did she understand that we love her and would do anything to be what she needs in her life? Did she appreciate that we're sacrificing the best thing that's ever happened to us so that she can keep the fairy tale?

As I splash some water onto my face, I can't shake the feeling that the fairy tale Luna has isn't the fairy tale she really wants.

Maybe I'm just overlaying my own hopes. Maybe I'm reading something into nothing.

All I know is that she'll have to be the one to tell us that a life with us is her true happy ever after. We could never make that decision for her.

30

LUNA

Calling Asher was a mistake, not because he said anything wrong. He didn't. Not really.

It was a mistake because it just brought back everything that I lost.

I can't sleep without my men around me. I can't sleep knowing that they aren't close by. I pace around my room, feeling hollow-stomached and weary. I have an urge to eat a huge rack of ribs with a side of sweet potato fries, but I also feel as though I might throw up at any second.

Anxiousness is wreaking havoc with my digestion and my state of mind.

Maybe I'm being an idiot for not trusting Mr. Wright and his team. They haven't done anything wrong as such. Well, apart from the slightly leering looks they give me and the fact that they don't really care if I'm happy or not.

The Steel 7 men were a different breed of bodyguard. They were more than just contractors looking out for my safety. They were like friends before they became more.

And now I have no one.

Jordy and Tyler, the only people in the world who really love me, are so far away that they feel lost in a mirage of the past.

Eventually, I slump into bed for a few hours of what feels like half-awake sleep. When there's a knock on the door to wake me, my eyes are dry and stuck together, and my shoulders feel tense.

Breakfast is yogurt and berries when all I want is waffles with butter and maple syrup. Conversation happens around me but never includes me. It's as though I'm invisible, and it makes me feel even hollower inside.

This was the day I'd planned to go sightseeing in London. I imagined taking an open-top red bus tour around the city. I'd picked out places that I wanted to see. Big Ben, the Houses of Parliament and Westminster Abbey. Tate Modern and St. Paul's Cathedral. Buckingham Palace and some shopping in Regent Street. I imagined strolling around with my men, laughing, and having fun. Instead, I'm trapped in my hotel room all day, waiting for the limo to pick me up to take me to the television studios later.

I watch TV, enjoying the numbness of mindless entertainment. I keep my phone on silent because there is no one that I want to talk to right now. My aloneness has become a cocoon of safety. Any kind of conversation would just bring my sadness welling back to the surface.

I don't bother putting on makeup before we head out. I wear my slouchiest jumper, a warm coat, leggings, and a baseball cap to travel to the studio.

When we arrive, I'm hustled into my dressing room for the evening and fussed over by a team of people who are there to make me beautiful. The hairdresser uses a giant curling tong to set my hair into large, loose curls, then pins it up on one side with a diamante clip. The makeup artist focuses on my eyes, making them dark and smoky and using thick false lashes to exaggerate them even further. The dress I have to wear is made from jade-green satin. It has cut-out sides and wraps across my breasts in a way that enhances my curves. When I'm ready, I stand in front of the mirror, and I almost don't recognize myself.

They've made me beautiful, yes. But somehow, it's erased the essence of me at the same time. The outfit and makeup are like a disguise. Is this what happens to all celebrities? Their image smudges out the authentic truth of who they really are?

I warm up my voice, going through the motions but not really focusing on my actions. My stomach roils with nerves as I go to wait in the green room, coming face to face with a Hollywood actor who ignores me and a British comedian who doesn't stop telling jokes. I try to smile in all the right places, but I'm not really listening. My fingers twist in my lap as my nerves build and build.

It's not like me to feel this trembly. Even when I first started singing, I went out into each performance too hyped up to feel the flutter of winged creatures in my belly. When I had the Steel 7 around me, I fed off their appreciation and confidence. Now, my team of bodyguards stands around the perimeter of the room, making everyone feel on edge, as I watch the other celebrities being interviewed by the annoying host.

My performance is last, which means I have a long time to wait. There's a live studio audience who clap and cheer in all the right places for the other talent. I just hope they'll be as kind to me.

Eventually, I'm called to take my place on a stage to the side of the main interview area. The stage is dark, and the audience is focused on the Hollywood actor who is now all smiles and filled with entertaining stories. Such a fake. There's no stool for me to perch on, just a single microphone standing like a lonesome baby tree in the middle. My silver sandals click on the hard floor as I make my way to my mark. The stage manager smiles, checking the microphone by tapping in gently. "You ready?" she asks.

I give her a simple nod, but inside, I feel anything but.

I try to feel the words that Asher spoke to me last night. You sparkle like that brightest diamond, he said. He called me a superstar. That's the Luna they want me to be. It's the Luna that everyone wants me to be, but who do I want to be?

I don't even know anymore.

The crowd begins to clap, and from the other side of the stage, I hear the host begin to introduce me.

"Discovered on the side of the road, singing for change, Luna Evans' rise to the top has been remarkable. She's here to sing her new single tonight. Give a round of applause for Luna Evans."

The spotlight focuses on me, and the huge cameras in front of the stage begin to move. The backing music begins to play, sounding out the first bars. Listening for my cue, I start to sing a song I'd know in my sleep. The words pour out of me, but I don't feel them. The song doesn't match my mood at all.

A stabbing pain rips through my stomach, stunning me momentarily, but I push through. Professionalism has to be my priority. I'm making up for mistakes right now. I'm under the microscope, and the world is poised to notice even a tiny error.

The audience is in darkness, but they're close enough that I can see people whispering to each other. My paranoia flares, imagining that they are saying negative things about me. Slut. Whore. All the things I might have thought about a girl caught with seven men before I'd been in that kind of relationship myself. My head begins to throb, but I carry on, feeling sweat prickling under my arms and running down the small of my back.

STEEL 7

All I have to do is get through the last verse. I'm nearly there. This is the home straight, except it isn't.

I know I'm falling before I hit the ground...then there's nothing.

31

HUDSON

When Luna collapses live on TV, all of us are on our feet, hands flying to our mouths, eyes staring as an A-list Hollywood actor leaps across the stage to put her in the recovery position. The camera pans away, focusing on the host who's adlibbing while on the other stage, while our girl is unconscious.

"What the fuck?" Jax says. "Why won't they show what's happening?"

"For her privacy," Asher says. "Shit."

"I'll call Angelica. Find out what's happening." Connor begins swiping through his contacts, and heads toward the corner of the room so he can have a conversation away from the disruption.

"She'll be okay," Ben says.

"She's probably fainted because she's not eating enough," Mo says. "That fucking nutritionist had her on child portions."

"Whatever it is, we need to get down there," I say.

"They'll take her to the hospital to check her out, won't they."

Connor nods. "Angelica says they're going to take her for a full checkup. With everything that happened in Australia, they're not ruling out foul play."

"Shit," Elijah says. "You think someone got to her food or water again."

"Those assholes were supposed to be checking everything she ordered." Connor's jaw ticks at even the thought of the rival bodyguards not doing their jobs properly.

"Do you know which hospital?"

"Angelica didn't want to tell me. She's pissed about what happened. The whole tour could have been called off, and that would have been money out of her pocket."

"Let's try the dancers," Asher suggests. "One of them will know what's happening. They're the kings and queens of the gossip grapevine."

"Okay," Connor says. "Everyone call somebody. Between us all, we'll find out what the hell's going on."

We each call out the name of a person who's part of Luna's tour and start to phone around. Within five minutes, Asher has a hospital name.

It takes us two minutes to get downstairs to the hotel reception and another ten minutes to get two cabs ordered. The hospital is only five miles away, but with London traffic, it seems to take hours.

My hands are sweating, and my eyelid is twitching with worry. I replay the moment that Luna's eyes rolled back over and over in my mind. I'm not a religious man, especially since my brother was killed, but I say a silent prayer for her safekeeping to anything out there with power.

"We should have been there," I say to Connor. "We should have been the ones there to catch her when she fell."

"We should have. We would have been if I'd just stuck to my guns."

"You think you could have resisted her? Luna was persistent and irresistible," Jax says.

"Infuriatingly persistent and irresistible," Connor mutters. "If those assholes have done anything to her, I swear to God."

"Let's just wait until we get there," I say, trying to keep tempers as calm as possible. No hospital is going to permit seven raging men to enter.

"How much longer?" Jax asks the driver.

"Five minutes," he says. "It's just further up this road."

Eventually, he deposits us on the sidewalk outside a huge modern hospital building. The inside is cavernous, and there are signs pointing in every direction for every type of medical department known to man. In the corner, there is a small reception. "Over there." I point.

The man behind the counter must be around sixty, with a shiny bald head and huge white eyebrows that tickle his eyelids. His eyes are bloodshot, probably a result of working the late shift at his advanced age.

"We're here to see Luna Evans. Can you tell us where she is?"

"Date of birth?" he asks, tapping her name into the computer.

Connor confirms the detail, and the man continues staring at the screen. "She's in the Elizabeth Ward. It's on the eighth floor. You can use the main lifts." He points further into the hospital to what looks like two closed elevator doors. His eyes scan our large group. "Only relatives will be allowed into the ward."

"I'm her fiancé," I say.

"Tell the nurse on the ward. I'm sure that will be fine."

As we make our way to the elevators, I catch Connor looking at me out of the corner of his eye. "Fiancé? Does that mean you want to be the one to go in?"

"Yep," I say with determination. I might be one of seven men that were in a relationship with Luna, but all that means is I have as much right as anyone else. I know I can be a comfort to her. We built up a loving connection in the time we spent together that was closer than any other relationship I've had in my life.

"Hudson's going to be the one to go in," Connor says. It's a clear order, not a statement to be disputed or argued over. I know every one of my brothers would want to be the man to get into the hospital ward with Luna, but they also know that having a fight about it in the hallway isn't going to help anyone.

In the elevator, I take a deep breath. I have no idea what I'm going to find. Luna might be really sick. She could still be unconscious. How will I deal with seeing her like that?

It would kill me to see her in pain.

"Make sure you ask the doctor questions," Ben says. "We want to know exactly what's going on, so you're going to need to find out."

"Make sure she's got enough water," Asher says. "This hospital is so hot. She's going to get dehydrated really quickly."

"Reassure her," Mo says. "Tell her that everything's going to be alright. She'll need to hear it."

"Hold her hand," Elijah says. "Physical contact's important."

"Don't be too serious," Jax says. "She'll need you to cheer her up. She'll be scared, so make sure you at least try to make her laugh."

"Are you saying I'm not funny?"

Jax shakes his head. "We all have our strengths in this

group."

"And our weaknesses," Connor says. "Just be her rock. Be the man she needs."

"I'll do my best."

At that moment, something passes between us. I've felt it before when we've been in the line of fire. There's a bond that runs a deep connection from man to man, and it's been activated again by our joint love of this one woman. They're placing her wellbeing in my hands. Trusting me to do whatever needs to be done. In this moment, I feel our connection strengthening. The unity we need to do right by Luna is there. We're not seven individual men who want one woman, we're a pack who are seeking their mate.

At the huge double doors to the Elizabeth Ward, there's a buzzer to gain entry. I push it and wait, bouncing on my toes. "Elizabeth Ward," a deep voice says.

"I'm here to see Luna Evans," I say. "I'm her fiancé."

"Are you really? I haven't read about an engagement in the newspaper," the nurse replies with a smile in her voice. I'm about to answer when the door clicks open.

"I'll call you guys when I know anything, okay?"

Inside, the hallway is clean and smells fresh. Everything is modern and organized. The nurse who buzzed me in is at a desk. "So you're the fiancé," she says with a wink. "Our resident celebrity already has more of an entourage than we usually allow." Nodding her head to the corner, I can see exactly what he means. Two bodyguards stand like sentries at the foot of a cubicle surrounded by curtains. "Where are the rest of them?" I ask.

The nurse smirks, her brown eyes widening with amusement. "We sent them down to the coffee shop. This is a secure ward, and it's intrusive to the other patients. She also has another visitor. A woman."

I nod, expecting to find Angelica inside the curtains,

and I'm bracing myself for her wrath. If she wanted us to come, she would have told us the hospital.

"You can go on over. I'm taking it that the two bodyguards know who you are."

"They do," I say.

As I near the cubicle, the bodyguards step forward. "You're not supposed to be here," one of them says.

"We've had orders not to let anyone in," the other growls.

"I don't give a shit what you've been told. I'm going in to see Luna."

"Let him in." Luna sounds furious and frustrated, but all I care about is that she's awake and speaking. The bodyguards look at each other, then the biggest one shrugs.

"Her majesty has spoken," he mutters, and for a flash, I get the urge to punch this asshole in the face. Then I remember where I am and how important it is that I don't get thrown out of this hospital for violent behavior, so I cut him a narrow-eyed look as I walk past.

I find Luna tucked into a hospital bed inside the cubicle, still covered in her performance makeup. Angelica closes her eyes and grits her teeth when she notices me, but I guess she feels that making a scene wouldn't be appropriate under the circumstances. "I'm going to go get a coffee," she says to Luna. "Do you want anything from downstairs?"

Luna reaches out to touch Angelica's hand. "It's okay," she says. "You can go home. Get some sleep. I'll call you if anything changes."

Angelica nods curtly. "Just remember what you've been told, Luna. There won't be more second chances. Don't throw away what you've worked for."

Luna's lips twitch as though she's swallowing down something she really wants to say. It's not like my girl to hold back when she doesn't agree with someone. Seeing her like this hurts my heart.

As soon as Angelica has left, I move her chair closer to the bed and take a seat.

"Did you draw straws?" Luna asks.

"No, but that would have been a good idea if someone was in the habit of carrying seven straws." I reach out and take her hand. "What happened, honey? How are you feeling? What did the doctors say?"

"I fainted," she says. "They don't know why. They've done some blood tests, and we're waiting on the results."

"Have you been eating properly and drinking enough?"

Luna shrugs her shoulders, rustling her white and blue patterned hospital gown.

"Have you been sleeping?"

She shrugs again, and I shake my head, knowing that it's all our fault. If we'd just kept to the professional arrangement, we'd have been there to ensure that nothing like this happened.

The curtain is pulled back roughly, and a man in scrubs steps into the cubicle. His gaze drifts from Luna to me, then back to Luna. "I have your blood test results. Would you like to hear them now or in private?"

"It's okay. You can tell me with Hudson here," she says.

"You're healthy. We couldn't find anything that would cause you to faint, so it must have been to do with the pregnancy."

Pregnancy?

Luna's hand slides out of mine, and she rests it over her heart.

"Sorry, doctor. Could you say that again?" I say.

"Ms. Evans is pregnant." He takes a step around to the other side of the bed, focusing on Luna. "Didn't you know?"

She shakes her head, her throat making a gulping sound as she swallows. "I was late on my period, but I thought it was all the stress and exertion from the tour." When her eyes meet mine, they're wide and glassy. Resting my hand over her blanket-covered leg, I try to get my scrambled mind to focus on what the doctor is saying, but all I can think about is telling my boys that Luna's having a baby. How will we find out whose baby it is? None of us even thought about using protection. A full medical is part of our contract and we assumed Luna would be on some kind of birth control. I mean, she's a popstar at the height of her career. Why would she risk all that with risky sex? Will she even want to keep the baby? What would that mean for her touring schedule? What will it mean for us?

But I don't get any answers to my questions, just a quizzical look from the doctor who must have noticed my confusion.

"You'll need to make sure that you're eating, drinking, and getting enough rest. These first few months can be tough. Are you getting morning sickness?" The doctor looks at me as though I should know how she's been feeling. I'm the fake fiancé, after all. Knowing nothing about any of this makes me feel sick.

"I've felt a few waves of nausea, but I haven't thrown up."

"Well, not all women do. Maybe you'll be one of the lucky ones who get through the first trimester without any trouble. Anyway, we want to keep you for a few more hours. We'll get you something to eat and drink, and once you're feeling better, you'll be free to go home." Turning to me, he says, "You'll need to stay with her. Keep a close eye on her for the next forty-eight hours."

"Of course," I say. It doesn't matter how difficult that might be, I'm going to make it happen.

Nodding curtly, he leaves the cubicle, tugging the

curtain briskly.

And then we're alone.

"Pregnant," Luna whispers, her hand drifting until it's resting over her belly. She stares down at her body as though it's suddenly a strange and unfamiliar thing. I guess it must feel like that to find out that you're growing another human being inside you, especially when it wasn't something that you planned to happen.

"Whatever you need, whatever you decide to do, we'll be by your side," I say softly. I know I'm making promises on behalf of six other men who haven't even heard the news, but I feel okay to commit to this. Luna has to come first.

I expect her to breathe a sigh of relief and maybe reach out for a reassuring hug. I don't anticipate that she will begin to sob, clutching her hands over her distraught face. "I'm so sorry," she says. "All of this is my fault. I've ruined everything."

"Luna," I whisper, rising to sit on the bed next to her and pulling her against my chest. "You haven't ruined a thing. Don't you know that we'd do it all over again just to have that time to love you? None of us would change a thing."

"But I'm having a baby and I don't even know which of you is the father."

"It doesn't matter which of us is the father. We'll all treat the child as our own." As soon as I've spoken the words, I know them to be true. This baby might not have been planned but it will be loved. Of that I am certain.

She twists her face from my chest, blinking up at me with eyes surrounded by makeup smudges. Even blotchy and messy, she's still the prettiest girl I've ever seen. "You will?"

"Of course. We love each other like brothers. We love you. We'll love the baby if that's what you decide."

"You will?"

Pressing a soft kiss onto her forehead, I stroke away the tendrils of damp hair from her cheeks. "We will. But what about your tour? What about your career? How do you feel about all this?"

Luna closes her eyes and shakes her head. "I love singing, Hudson. I really do. It's the thing that brings me the most joy, but the touring, the fame, the psycho assholes…those parts just make me sad."

"What are you saying, honey?"

"I want this baby, Hudson. I want this baby more than I've ever wanted anything. If you guys aren't ready to step in and be fathers, I'll understand. This isn't exactly a normal situation, and I'm sure that some of the guys will have a problem not knowing who the biological father is. I just…I don't want anyone to feel trapped. What we had was convenient at the time, but this is a lifelong commitment."

I snort, hugging her closer. "Nothing about being with you was about convenience. It was about desire and longing, and eventually about care and love. We would never have walked away if we didn't think it was what was best for you. The past few days, we've been walking around London like half-dead men."

"You have?"

"We have."

Her arms wrap around me more tightly, and a small sigh leaves her lips. "I missed you all so much."

"We missed you too, honey."

"Those new bodyguards weren't a patch on you guys."

"Now that, I'm glad to hear."

Swatting me on the shoulder, Luna smiles broadly. Our eyes meet, and then our lips, and I kiss my girl long and slow and deep. I kiss her so that she can feel how much I love her. I kiss her so our unborn child will know too.

And when I feel that I've made my boys wait long enough without news, I put a single message on our group chat—**Luna's pregnant. We're going to be daddies.** And I wait for six heads to explode!

32

LUNA

I'm pregnant.

I still can't believe it. The doctor's words didn't register at first. It was only when he left that it hit me.

A wave of panic so strong that it stole my breath until Hudson held me close and told me everything I needed and wanted to hear.

I'm pregnant, and it's going to change everything. If I'm well enough, I might be able to finish this tour, but the timings for recording another album will be difficult, and who knows if Blueday will be interested in continuing to push my career. Do I even want them to?

I know there are women out there who are moms and still killing it in their careers. There are pop stars and celebrities who take their kids with them on tour and somehow manage to do it all. I'm sure they have a lot of help, which is fine. I'm sure they feel torn between the two loves in their life because how could they not?

I felt torn enough when Connor and my boys were

forced to leave me. I felt torn over whether I should pursue my career or pursue the men that I wanted. I guess when it came down to it, I just didn't feel secure enough about their feelings for me. But now Hudson has told me they love me. He's told me they would want to be there for the baby, and he said it all in a way that didn't feel as though it was pressuring me to do anything.

He acknowledges that the decision about the baby has to be mine. What he doesn't know is that I would have wanted to have my baby whether my men wanted me to or not.

I grew up a child of parents who never showed me that they valued that role. They always put themselves and their addictions first. Their lives were not anchored to mine in any way. But even though this baby is tiny, and even though I've only known about it for a few hours, I feel completely tethered to it already.

I just want to be a good mom. I want to give this child everything that I didn't have. Safety and security. Love that fills their heart. Enough money to always be able to put food on the table and a roof over their heads. Daddies who will love them.

"Are you ready to go?" Hudson asks, appearing through the gap in the curtain. I nod, standing slowly just in case I get lightheaded again, and he rushes to my side to take my arm.

"Woahhh...that's some kind of dress you have on."

"I came straight from the show," I say, looking down at my ridiculous attire. If I could, I would have left the hospital in a gown. At least I would have drawn less attention.

"Here." Hudson takes off his jacket and helps me slide my arms into the warm sleeves. Hugging it around myself, I hook my arm into his.

"Didn't you have a purse?" he asks.

"Nope. Who needs a purse when you have seven bodyguards to patrol your every move and a stalker to make eating and drinking a dangerous activity?"

When Hudson's jaw ticks, I can see how affected he is by the current situation. They were possessive and protective before, but now I have their baby in my womb. I'm anticipating their need to keep me safe will be even stronger.

As we walk down the hallway, my bodyguards fall into step, and at the door, the sight that meets us is ridiculous. Five more bodyguards flank the door, and the other six men who hold my heart in their hands wait behind. Their faces are all marred with worry, eyes searching me over to find any injury or hurt. Hudson's told them about the pregnancy, but we won't get a chance to talk about it now.

I wish we could. I wish they could all wrap their arms around me and confirm what Hudson told me.

Instead, fourteen men escort me from the hospital into the waiting vehicles outside.

Mr. Wright attempts to shoulder Hudson out of the way, but there's no way he's letting me out of his sight. Sliding into the limousine after me, he sits close, throwing his arm around my shoulders so that the other bodyguards who climb in get the picture. His body language is screaming out that I'm his girl.

When we pull up to the hotel, there are fans and photographers waiting. Hudson gets out of the car before me, already flanked by the new bodyguard team. Before I have a chance to panic, he scoops me into his arms, and I bury my face into his neck, using a hand to cover myself as much as possible. He strides into the hotel as though I weigh nothing, his heart beating a steady pace against my skin.

"Are you okay?" he says.

"Yes." I tell him, holding on tighter around his neck.

We're in the elevator in less than a minute, and then I can relax. "You can put me down now."

"No chance." He smiles down at me, his honey-colored eyes so warm that I feel as though I could rest in their attention forever and never need another thing.

"Blueday is going to have a shit fit when they hear that you guys are back."

"Maybe," he says. "Or maybe they'll realize that you need us, with a baby on the way."

"It's hardly on the way. Eight months is a long time. And anyway, not all pregnancies work out."

"You have to be positive, Luna. Imagine the best, and it'll happen."

"I wouldn't have taken you to be a believer in manifestation."

He bends to kiss me, not caring that the bodyguards are standing around us, watching and listening to everything. "When we left you at the airport, I kept imagining us all back together. Even when the others were telling me it was impossible, I kept thinking that there must be a way. Something will happen, an event that will put us back in the same place and look what happened."

"You think you manifested a baby," I snort. "The baby was very physically put in there before those photos leaked."

"Maybe," Hudson says. "Or maybe I just wanted you so much that the universe gave in."

"Maybe it was me," I say. "Maybe I wanted you all so much that the universe gave in."

"Maybe y'all should just stop talking about it. Haven't you ever heard of tempting fate?" Mr. Wright says.

"Fuck fate." Hudson sounds so fierce that I touch his face to try and calm him. "You think fate ever has anything good in store for us? No, we make our own destinies."

"Well, maybe you can make your own destinies in private from now on." He nods in Luna's direction. "We'll have to report into our contact at Blueday that you're going against their guidance."

"Their orders," Luna spits. "Report away. I'm done worrying about the opinions of some sweaty balding corporate executives."

"I won't pass on that feedback," Mr. Wright says, but somehow, I don't believe him.

We're only in my suite for five minutes before there's a knock at the door. I say knock, but really, it's an impatient thump. Mr. Wright uses the spy hole and mutters something under his breath before opening the door.

And there they are.

My gorgeous men of steel. The loves of my life. The men who want to give me the only thing I've ever really truly wanted.

A family.

They stream into the room, ignoring the suited men who've replaced them in an official capacity. When Mr. Wright puts a hand up, I tell him to stand down. This is my life. They are my men. No one is going to stop them from being with me ever again. Hudson leads me by the hand into my room, and when they've all passed through the door, Jax closes it for privacy.

I don't even get a chance to speak before they're on me, hugging the breath out of my lungs and kissing the words from my lips. "Luna," they say over and over as I'm passed between the men whose touch warms my heart. Jax is the first to place his hand over my stomach, gazing down at my still normal-looking belly as though it contains the secrets of the universe. "Is it real?" he asks.

Nodding, I put my hand over his. "It doesn't feel like it's real, but it is. The doctor was very definite about the result."

"And you're happy about it?" His soft brown eyes widen with hope.

"Happy doesn't even come close to how I feel about it," I say. "But what about you guys? This isn't exactly what we set out to achieve."

"It's better than that," Connor says. "So much better." He rubs the spot on his arm where his tattoo is hidden beneath his shirt. *Nothing without effort*, it reads. I guess, when you think about it, we did put in a lot of effort to make this baby. Maybe not intentionally, but I still appreciate every moment we were together.

The emptiness I've felt since they left has gone. With my men around me, I feel whole again.

"Does that mean that we're back together?" Ben asks hopefully.

"I think it does," Mo says. He winks one of his dark eyes at me, and I immediately remember what it was like to hold onto his body and feel him easing inside me. I remember what it was like with each of these men, and even though I can't put my finger on the exact moment our baby was conceived, it doesn't take away anything from it.

"I'm going to tell Blueday the truth. That I'm having a baby and that we're together…all of us. If that's what you want." I add the last bit because I'm still in disbelief that this is all happening. I'm still struggling to comprehend that even one of these men would want to step up in these circumstances, let alone seven.

"Of course it's what we want," Connor says with absolute conviction.

"You should do it soon before those goons out there have a chance to get in there first, and the press has time to report it," Mo says.

"It's probably out there already," Elijah says. "News

doesn't publish overnight these days. It's uploaded in seconds."

"Even more reason to pick up the phone now."

So that's what I do. I call my agent and ask him to link in someone at Blueday – whoever he can get hold of – and I tell them everything.

It would be an understatement to say that their response isn't happy.

But I don't care.

When I hang up the phone, I feel the happiest I've ever been in my life. Who knows what's coming next? All I care about is that I'll have seven men by my side as we walk a new path.

And I couldn't be more excited.

33

CONNOR

We can't all stay with Luna. There's not enough room in the suite, and anyway, she needs to get some rest. Hudson and Asher stay to keep watch over her and make sure she gets everything she needs. There's no way we're trusting the safety of her food and drink to anyone else at this point.

I head over to see Angelica first thing in the morning, with Mo and Ben. We haven't slept at all, but that isn't going to stop us from doing what needs to be done.

We wait in the lobby of her hotel and call up to Angelica's room, hoping she'll want to talk to us. After she tried to keep us away yesterday, I'm not so sure, but at least, if she puts the phone down, we'll be here to intercept her on her way out.

"Tell me what we're doing here?" Ben asks, rubbing his face and slumping into a green velvet bucket chair, immediately resting his leg straight to take the pressure off the prosthetic.

"We're letting Angelica know that this shit with Luna needs to get sorted."

"Because we don't think she's already trying her best? I mean, it's not as if she'd want a stalker interfering with the tour she's running. It's not exactly great for her reputation, any more than it is ours."

"I don't think she's considering all options," I say, but to be honest, I'm not really that sure of what other options she could be taking into consideration. I guess I just want Angelica to know that we've got Luna's back and that we want to see results. If nothing else, a little pressure in the right place can get things moving.

"Before you call her, I want to tell you something," Mo says. He stands and paces a few steps, shoving his hands into the pockets of his jeans. It's not like Mo to have bunched shoulders filled with tension. He's a man who's lived through enough to have become stoical in even the most difficult of situations.

"What is it, Mo?" Shifting forward in my seat, I wave for him to take a seat opposite me.

He glances at me, then at the seat. Once he's sat down, he seems ready to talk. "You know me…I'm not a man who believes in instincts. I always think that going with gut feeling is a recipe for acting with emotion rather than logic. But I have this feeling that I can't shake."

"What feeling?" Ben says, leaning forward.

"A bad feeling about a person." Mo rubs his chin and grips his other hand into a tight fist. "I didn't say anything before because my feeling isn't based on any evidence. I haven't seen this person do anything bad. I don't know anything about them other than they make the hairs on the back of my neck stand on end."

"Someone's giving you the creeps?" I frown, still not quite getting what Mo is saying.

Mo nods. "You know all of the issues that Luna's had

have been close…someone needed to be able to access backstage to get to her things. They've also happened around the world. We know it's the same perpetrator."

"So, some super weirdo fan is following Luna around the world. People do that shit. It's not unheard of."

"No, it isn't," Mo says. "But maybe that isn't what's happening. Maybe it's someone in the crew?"

"The crew?"

"Yes, Connor. The crew."

"You think that someone hired to help Luna's tour is the one scaring the shit out of her?"

"Maybe. As I said, I don't have evidence, just gut-feeling."

I slump back into my chair, resting my hands on the arms and allowing my legs to fall. If Mo's right, we've could have been passing the time with a man capable of hurting our girl. "Who?"

"As I said, I'm pointing the finger at a man who could be innocent. I just…we can't let this go on. Luna's having a baby. Even the worry that something might potentially happen will be stress, and stress is bad for a developing fetus."

"So tell me who it is."

"Marcus, the lighting guy," Mo says.

I glance up at the ceiling, trying to put a face to a name. There are so many people on the crew, and I've spent so much of my mental energy focused on Luna that I haven't paid much attention to the people who I should be able to trust.

Ben nods, gripping the arm of his chair. "I agree that guy is creepy. I've seen him looking at Luna like he wants to eat her liver with a nice glass of wine and some fried onions."

"Fuck. You too?" Mo says.

"You should have said something," I say to both of them. "We're a team. We're stronger together and keeping secrets will only make us weaker. I don't know how many times I have to repeat myself."

"It wasn't a secret," Ben says. "Just a passing thought that I didn't think would be worth sharing.

"Well, in the future, can you share your passing thoughts?"

Ben raises his eyebrows. "If I shared them all, we probably wouldn't still be friends."

Mo chuckles, the joke breaking the tension between us. "I don't think you should tell Angelica that we have a bad feeling about Marcus. She's going to go on the defensive. She brought the guy into work on her team. She'd feel responsible, and it's human nature to try to defend against that possibility."

"So, what should I do?"

"Tell her that we need to rule out everyone in the crew. Tell her that we're going to be fingerprinted and that if the rest of the crew don't come forward, it will look like they have something to hide."

"Okay. That could work." I pull my phone from my pocket and dial Angelica's number. After five minutes of encouragement, she agrees to come to the lobby to meet with us.

When she emerges from the elevator, I can tell she's on the warpath. Her face is pinched, and her head is angled down like a battering ram, and I have to take a deep breath to push down my anger. This is about Luna. It's not a fucking competition to prove who's top dog. If she really cared, she should be willing to take on any ideas about the stalker.

"You have to be quick," she says. "I have a lot to do today."

"I'll be quick," I say, standing so I can be at a height

advantage. Subtle things like body language can make a big difference in getting what you want in a situation. "The issue with the stalker is going to hit the press sooner rather than later."

"Why? Do you know something?"

"I mean that it's inevitable. If they get any closer, Luna could get really hurt, and then everything will be out. All the focus will be on us and what we've done about it."

"It's not our responsibility," she hisses. "This is up to the police to deal with."

"The focus will be on us because whoever has been doing these terrible things has been close. There might be insinuations that it's someone hired by Blueday…one of the crew."

"No one in my crew could do such a thing. How will they know it's not one of you?"

I stand taller, looking down my nose at the woman who's making my life so fucking difficult. "That's why we're going to the police to volunteer our fingerprints. We want to make sure that we're completely out of the frame. It's the only responsible thing to do."

Angelica narrows her eyes, and I can almost see her mind whirring over exactly the route Mo predicted. She fiddles with the beaded necklace at her throat. "I can see what you're saying. Maybe it would be good to get ahead of the game."

"So you'll ask all the crew to volunteer their fingerprints?" I hold my breath waiting for her answer. Inside my guts are in knots. I know if this doesn't happen, I'm going to be fighting to maintain my control. I'm going to want to tear Marcus limb from limb, even without evidence. I just want this all to end.

"Yes," Angelica says. "We'll do it here in London."

"Okay. Great," I say. "Can you let me know if anyone refuses?"

"Nobody will refuse," she spits, already turning to leave. "Now, if you'll excuse me, I have things to do." Angelica stomps off, her sensible heeled shoes clomping against the marble-tiled floor.

"Well, that went well," Ben says.

"The proof will be if anything comes out of this. For all we know, that guy might just have been bought up by strange parents. It happens! And if it's not him, we have exactly zero leads to go on."

"Whatever happens, we're not leaving Luna alone," Mo says softly. "If we have to trail her around the world on our own dime, we will."

"Absolutely," I say. "Now, let's get this shit done. We can head over to the hotel, pick up the rest and get to the nearest police station. Then, two of us will need to relieve Hudson and Asher at Luna's hotel."

As we're leaving the echoing space of the hotel reception, Mo rests his hand on my arm. "We'll figure this out, Connor. I know we will, and when we do, we can concentrate on what's really important."

I hope he's right.

34

JAX

Getting my fingerprints taken in a London police station is not how I expected to spend my vacation time. The process is quick, though, and when we're done, Connor calls Angelica to find out what is happening with the rest of the crew.

As she talks, his eyes narrow, and his mouth draws in, turning his expression to thunder. When he hangs up, Mo immediately asks what's wrong.

"They're all coming to have their fingerprints taken except Marcus. He's saying it's a human rights issue and that they can't coerce him into going."

"What the fuck?" I growl. "Does that mean all of this shit was for nothing?"

"No," Connor says. "Angelica had the talk with everyone over coffee. When Marcus stormed off, she bagged his coffee cup, and she's bringing it with her. He might not want to give his prints willingly, but we'll find out if it's him one way or another."

"Wow," Hudson says. "I wouldn't have taken Angelica for a forensics enthusiast. I didn't think she bought into your plan."

"I guess when she saw Marcus balk at the idea, she started to get suspicious too."

"So we'll find out soon?"

"I guess we will. There are prints on the cards left with the underwear and a partial print left on the water bottle. If they can get enough prints from the coffee cup, they'll have enough evidence to arrest him."

"That's if he sticks around," I say. "Now he knows things are closing in on him, he might get on the next plane."

"If he does, the U.K. police will contact the U.S. He won't get away with it, but it could end up being much more complex to deal with."

"Whatever happens, at least we'll know *who* we're dealing with." Connor rubs his face, the stress of the past few days showing in his gray pallor and the darkness around his eyes.

"What would the charges be?" Mo asks.

"Harassment, maybe? And something to cover the water incident. I don't know what that would be called here? Crime definitions aren't the same world over. We'll just have to wait and see. We don't know it's him yet. His refusal to have his prints taken could just be genuinely about not wanting to have his personal identifiers on record. I get that."

"And then we'd be back to square one."

Connor sighs, glancing around at the rest of us. "Whatever happens, we're keeping Luna under our protection. It might not be official anymore, but we're fathers to her baby. We're family now. No one can stop us from being with our girl."

"Our girl," I say softly, letting the feeling wash over

me.

Smiles form on the mouths of my friends. "Look at Jax getting all sentimental about his feelings," Ben laughs.

"Hey, you're forgetting that this idea was mine in the first place, and you all thought I was crazy."

"To be fair, you only told me about that," Hudson reminds me. "And yes, I did think you were crazy for even hoping that Luna would look in our direction."

"Not so crazy now," I smile.

"So, what are we going to do now?" Elijah asks.

"We're going to go see our girl," Connor says, already striding in the direction of the door.

We find Luna curled up on a chair in her hotel room, reading a book about pregnancy that she must have ordered in. Her long chestnut hair is swept over one shoulder, and her sweet little nose is wrinkled in concentration. When she looks up to find us gathered in the doorway, her smile is one of pure joy.

"Did you know the baby's heart will start to beat soon? They can see it on a scan this early?"

"No, I didn't know that," I say, slumping into the seat next to her. "What else did you find out?"

"That morning sickness can last a long time, but ginger can help to settle my stomach." She points to a steaming mug of yellow-looking liquid and a plate of cookies.

"Sorry about the sickness," Asher says. "But the cookies look good."

"And you'll be pleased to know that there are no problems with having sex either."

"Pleased is an understatement," I say, rolling my eyes theatrically.

"Of course, Jax would be more concerned about his cock than anything else," Connor says. "Don't worry about sex right now, sweetie. Just concentrate on you and the baby."

Luna blinks, her face falling like she's a kid and someone just stole her teddy bear. "But what if I want the sex?" she says softly.

"Then we'll be more than happy to give it to you."

"GENTLY!" Connor shouts, his military training coming out. "Gently, and not all at the same time. We need a schedule."

"I'm not breakable," Luna says. I can see this is really affecting her, and I understand it too. She might be having a baby, but she's still a woman. The part of her that wants to hold onto herself is there, fighting to keep at least something the same.

"No, you're not breakable," I say firmly. "You're the strongest woman I know. What Connor is saying is that we'll take it slowly and see how you feel. Everything's new for all of us, and that's okay. Being with you is what counts. We don't need to swing from the chandeliers for it to feel fucking amazing."

"Thanks, Jax, for that eloquent and touching summary," Elijah says. "Luna, we're yours. You tell us what's good and we'll deliver. That's how it is now…it's how it will always be."

"Now that's profound," Mo says. "But he's right. We'll do everything we can to keep you safe and happy, and if that means sex, then we'll put aside our own feelings and just do it."

There's a rumble of laughter, and even Connor seems to relax a little.

"So, when's the sex happening then?" I ask.

"For fuck's sake," Hudson mumbles, but he's quick to shut up when Luna stands, dropping her soft white robe to the floor and revealing her beautiful – and very naked – body beneath.

"Now, that's what I'm talking about," I say, tugging off my shirt in one fluid move and stalking Luna like prey.

"Jesus," Connor says.

"I don't think this is his scene," Elijah laughs, but he's following me anyway, his trousers already unbuttoned.

"Just remember, to be careful," Connor says, but he's shirtless too, his hand rubbing his tattoo in that way he always does when he's thinking about life.

I'm the first on the bed, crawling up to cover Luna with my body, her frame so tiny in comparison. She reaches for me as though we've been doing this for years, and we kiss as if our life depends on it. Around us, the bed adjusts to the weight of other eager men, taking their places so they can show our girl just how much she means to us. I nuzzle my nose to hers. "You know we love you, right?"

Her pretty green eyes blink slowly, my words taking some time to settle.

"We love you," Elijah says, taking her hand and bringing it to his lips. The kiss is sweet and tender, a reminder of the gentleness she needs right now.

"And we'll love the baby too when it arrives," Ben says, resting a hand on Luna's shoulder.

Luna's eyes well with tears, but she's smiling, so they must be good ones. "You know what's awesome?" she says, running her hands down my spine. "We don't have to use condoms anymore."

"I'm going to be the one to point out that we weren't always great at doing that in the past," I say. "Kind of what got us into this awesome predicament in the first place."

Mo clears his throat. "I know I'm not the only one thinking that things are about to get really messy."

"Messy is good," Luna smiles. "Although, you boys could start cleaning up after yourselves. Just a thought."

"Yes, ma'am," Ben says, with a clipped salute.

"How many washcloths do you get in a penthouse suite bathroom?" Asher asks, sounding genuinely interested. How these guys are maintaining conversation when there is a naked girl in the room is beyond me.

"Can we worry about the clean-up operation after we've made the mess?" I huff, leaning down to tease Luna's pretty pink nipple with my tongue. Her hands slide into my hair, tugging gently, and I cant my hips against her pussy, feeling the heat and driving myself crazy in the process. Luna's hands nudge the top of my head in the cutest, most demanding way. I guess my girl wants to get her pussy licked, and I'm more than happy to indulge her.

The first swipe of my tongue over her clit has Luna flinching. It's already a little swollen, just from the teasing. Glancing up at her, our eyes meet, and she smiles, licking her lips.

"I think Luna needs something to fill her mouth," I say.

Asher is more than happy to oblige, shifting closer and cradling her head, so she doesn't strain her neck. As his cock breaches her lips, I lick her again, the sight of her sucking my friend's cock enough to tighten my balls. I swear that watching Luna fuck my friends is the sexiest thing I've ever seen.

Mo and Elijah lean in to suck her nipples, and Connor takes her hand, wrapping her slender fingers around his straining dick. There might be seven of us, but we're learning how to take our places around one girl.

I let my tongue dip inside her entrance, tasting her arousal. She's wet enough to fuck but not needy enough yet. I want her begging and quivering, and then I'll give her what she needs. I'll fill her sweet pussy with my cum. I'll mark my place in her life.

A few more licks and Luna groans, the vibrations

making Asher swear. A few more licks, and she'll make him come, which seems fitting. He was the first man to share Luna's bed, after all. He was the pioneer and the man who set up this whole situation for the rest of us. I'll never tell him, but I'll forever be grateful that he didn't listen to Connor and resist Luna's advances.

She wriggles her hips, but I pin her down with my arm, licking faster and hard until she's moaning and Asher's pulling back, not wanting to come just yet. And my nuts are fit to burst.

That's it. I can't take anymore. I just have to be inside her. In one fluid movement, I'm over her, spreading her legs and thrusting deep. Luna's legs come up to grip me and around my hips as Connor strokes her face, giving her a minute to catch her breath before she sucks him too. Her body undulates with mine in a way that feels completely synchronized, and I close my eyes, focusing on a pinpoint of light in the darkness behind my eyes, chasing the feeling of release that I know is coming soon. Each roll of my hips grazes her clit, and her pussy grips mine even tighter, making it my turn to groan.

Pulling back from Connor, she stares at me with glazed eyes. "Don't stop," she says. "Don't you fucking stop." And I don't. I keep rolling my hips. I keep the even pace, watching her clutch the sheets as her beautiful breasts bounce with my movements. She's wrecked and desperate, eyes scrunched so tightly it looks painful, and then, like a flash of lightning has passed between our bodies, she comes.

Oh God, the ripples of her cunt around me are just too perfect. I can't hold out anymore.

When I come inside her, it is like sliding drunk into warm water. It's like every part of me that needed release finds peace.

It takes me a minute to return from oblivion, and when I pull out, I watch my cum leak from her little hole, fighting the urge to push it back inside her.

"That's it, Jax. Make some room," Elijah says, clapping me on the back in a friendly-bro kind of way. He pats Luna's hip and tells her to roll over. Once she's on her hands and knees, Connor slides between her lips, and Elijah stretches her pussy around his huge cock, and I'm hard again in a second.

This girl is our moon and stars. She's the sun on the hottest day, warming our weary bones. She's the light in our darkness, and as my friends take turns to give her pleasure, all I can do is watch in awe.

35

LUNA

I think my brain is broken. I think Jax fucked it out of me, and now I'm just a shell of my former self, lost in pleasure.

But then Elijah is inside me, and Connor is easing his cock between my lips, and somehow, I draw back into myself, reforming just enough for them to splinter me into pieces all over again.

Seven men.

I know what Jordy's thinking. How the fuck would any woman manage to physically cope with all of the masculine urges?

What she doesn't know is that I spend half of the time that I'm in bed with them, experiencing another reality. I think it's what the word bliss refers to. I think that's where I go.

"Luna," Connor says, stroking my face. "Baby."

I nod, swirling my tongue around his cock in a way that makes him thrust forward, hitting the back of my throat until I gag. Fuck, that's sexy in a way that I don't quite understand. Who knew that a little bit of dominance would flick my switch? Who knew that soft words and harsh fingers would make my brain melt?

And my body.

Before I can prepare for it, my pussy is clamping down on Elijah's cock in wave after wave of perfect pleasure. I fall onto my elbows, losing all control of my limbs, and somewhere above me, Connor's coming on my shoulders and hands, as Elijah releases inside me.

Messy was an accurate prediction, but there is nothing bad about it. My men are marking me, and a primal part of me that's been buried deep only wants more.

And more I get.

I'm hauled into Asher's lap, sliding down onto his cock so easily that I don't have any time to adjust. He controls the rhythm, partly by thrusting up from beneath and partly by gripping my hips and tugging me against him. "Fuck, baby. Your pussy feels so good," he says.

There are so many things that I want to say to all my men. How awesome they make me feel. How each of them holds a unique and special place in my heart. How grateful I am that they've come into my life. That whatever happens in the future, there will never be a moment of regret about what is happening between us.

But my body is so limp with pleasure, and my mind so addled, that nothing other than moans and puffs of air will come out of my mouth.

"That's it, baby," Mo says, moving behind me so that he can fill his big hands with my breasts. I know, if I wasn't pregnant and Connor hadn't laid down the "gentle" rule with such force, that he might have tried to penetrate me too. But things are different now. Only slightly, but different enough for me to notice.

I kiss Asher's soft lips, my gaze meeting his eyes that

are always the color of the clearest sky on a summer's day. Turning, I seek out Mo's mouth, finding his dark eyes soulful and intense. My men are such a contrasting group, but that just makes this so much more special.

Coming again seems like an impossible feat, but when Mo's fingers slide between my body and Asher's to seek out my clit, it's like an instantaneous reaction. Whip fast, the pleasure shoots up my spine, arching my back until I'm leaning against Mo, and Asher is speeding, speeding, chasing his release.

Maybe I black out for a moment because I don't remember being lifted from Asher and placed onto Ben. I don't remember my hands being wrapped around Mo's and Hudson's cocks. And when I finally come back to reality, Ben's thumb on my clit is already threatening to send me away again.

My hips feel tender and stretched, my pussy is swollen beyond anything I've ever experienced, and every muscle in my legs aches, but I can do this. I can bring it home for all my men as they bring it home for me.

I have to hold Ben's hand and shake my head because I can't take anymore. I want to watch him enjoy the friction that our bodies make together. I want to see the furrow between his brows ease away, knowing that I've made him happy enough to forget all of the troubles he's carrying on his broad shoulders. And when I see the moment that he lets everything go, I stroke his face and bend to kiss his lips.

Five down. Two to go.

And I have an idea.

"Mo, will you lay down on your back with your legs spread open?"

He eyes me cautiously, his obsidian pupils reflecting only the light coming from the nightstand fixture. Even though he's wary of what I'm asking him for, he does it.

That trust and submission settles over me like a warm blanket.

"And Hudson, will you kneel between Mo's legs?"

Jax snorts from where he's reclining on the bed, watching everything with a quirk of a smile on his face. "You know we're not down with fucking each other, right?" he says. "This is purely a one-way agreement between you and us."

"I know," I huff, shuffling closer to where my men are staring at me expectantly. "Although that would be hot." When I wiggle my eyebrows, there are a few muttered expletives. I guess any man-on-man action is off the table for now. A girl can hope.

I sit astride Mo, facing away from him in the reverse cowgirl position that hits all the right spots. If I pull this off, it's going to be a fucking triumph. Sinking down onto him is like pushing a chocolate-covered finger into my mouth. Sweet and yet intrusive. His big hand rests against the skin of my ass, squeezing my cheeks together for maximum tightness, and it feels amazing.

"Luna, are you trying to kill me dead?" he says. I glance over my shoulder at him, smiling at the way he has thrown back his head in ecstasy. Hudson comes closer, still not quite sure what his role is in this, his hands finding my breasts and squeezing first gently and then harder, in the same punishing rhythm as my hips. Our mouths meet, tongues tangling, breath mingling, and when I can feel Mo starting to swell inside me, I rise up high, gripping Hudson's shoulders to propel me into his lap. In a second, he's inside me, his mouth opening into a surprised O. So now he understands the assignment!

Behind me, I can hear Mo using his hand on his slippery cock, and I twist to watch as he watches Hudson and me. There's a fierceness in his gaze, demandingness that flickers over my clit like a hot tongue. When Hudson is gritting his teeth and gripping my hips, I push back until

STEEL 7

I'm sliding from his lap and back onto Mo.

Their cocks are both big but different. Mo's is slightly thicker, and Hudson's slightly longer with a bigger ridge at the top. Switching between them hits different spots inside me, but it's not only that. It's the sheer naughtiness of fucking two men at the same time, teasing them until they're gasping and playing with themselves, getting more and more flushed with each switch.

I want to come again so badly. My body is primed, my thighs are wet and sticky, and as I look between my legs at the sight of my pussy stretched open around Mo's cock, and my clit so swollen, I get even closer.

"Come," I tell Mo. "Let it all go inside me."

He groans, the muscles on his thighs and calves flexing with the pressure. When he comes, it's like an exorcism, the groan he makes so loud that I look to the door, wondering if my stupid bodyguards will come barging in.

They don't.

I guess the sound of a man yelling out isn't enough to worry them.

Hudson's impatient now, grabbing me under the ass and hauling me onto his cock. Throwing my arms around his neck, I hold on for dear life, feeling very much like a rodeo rider on an angry stallion.

He's waited for the longest and watched every one of his friends get off. It's not surprising that he's as coiled as a bull elephant in musth. "Fuck, Luna. You drive me crazy," he hisses through gritted teeth. "Fucking come on my cock. Give me that sweet pussy."

His words come out like the delirious ramblings of a drunken man, but that's okay. I'm delirious too. Delirious and happy and bubbling with contentment. I'm pleasure-filled and exhausted, on a high similar to the way I feel after singing.

And as Hudson comes inside me, I come too, hugging

around his sweat-slicked chest and breathing in his masculine scent, knowing that this is it.

I've found my place in the world. I've found my family. And whatever happens in my life from here on out, I'm never letting them go.

36

ASHER

I wake, feeling disorientated, surrounded by my friends in various states of nakedness. Connor is on one sofa by the window and Mo on the other. The bed is big enough to fit the rest of us if you don't mind finding yourself getting inadvertently spooned by your burly friend. We really need to get the bed situation sorted. I'm pretty sure that between us all, we could fashion a bed frame that would be big enough to sleep us all, but what about a mattress?

Google is going to get called upon later to help me find out.

Luna is snuggled between Hudson and Ben, as naked as the day she was born and as pretty as a maiden from a fairy tale. I mentally picture a drawing I could do of her, with ethereal wings and hair so long it could wrap around her calves like tendrils of ivy. I could create a series of Luna-inspired fairy-tale drawings. For a second, Luna with snow-white skin and pouty red lips enters my mind, and then I chuckle, realizing that if Luna was Snow White, then we would be the seven dwarves.

When Connor's phone rings, it disturbs us all from the blissful peace that descended over us after the most awesome sex ever. He has to get out of bed to find it in among his discarded clothes, and his expression when he looks at the screen is enough to tell me that he's not going to relish the conversation.

"Angelica," he barks, impatient before she has a chance to utter a word. If she's in a bad mood, Connor's attitude isn't going to improve it.

Angelica's voice is audible from across the room, but rather than sounding angry, her pitch is high and excited, or maybe it's frantic.

"Fuck," Connor growls. "That asshole. Are they sure?"

Connor shakes his head. "He's gone?"

I'm struggling to my feet at his point, frustrated that I can't hear what Angelica is saying, but by the time I'm across the room, Connor's already hanging up.

"It's him."

"Marcus?"

"Yes. The fucker's been touring with us this whole time and trying to terrorize Luna. He's supposed to be on her team."

"Mo was right." Ben pats Mo on the arm, a gesture that is more awkward than it should be because we're all still naked.

"Marcus. The lighting guy?" Luna's mouth hangs open in shock, and I realize that she had no idea about our suspicions and that this is all news to her.

"Yes. That's how the issues have followed you around on tour. Blueday has been paying the stalker to follow you from city to city."

"And the police have him?" Luna asks Connor, clutching the bedsheets high around her neck as though the very thought of him has her wanting to protect herself. Hudson senses that she's feeling vulnerable and throws his big arm around her shoulder, pulling her closer to his chest.

"No," Connor says. "He refused to give his prints, and he's AWOL."

"But they're looking for him?"

We all focus on Luna, who has watery eyes and a tremble to her chin. Gone is our fierce girl, and when her hand drifts down to her belly, I realize why. She was okay when she was just fighting for herself, but now she's pregnant, things are very different. She needs us to step up and deal with this It might not our professional responsibility anymore but there is no one she trusts more than us.

"We'll find him," I say. "We'll make sure he's put away."

Connor reaches down and tugs on his underwear and pants, leaving his belt undone. "Mo, Hudson, Asher, and Jax, let's go."

He doesn't have to say another word. We're dressed and ready to leave in less than five minutes. In that time, Luna pulls on a robe and perches on the edge of the couch, flanked by Elijah and Ben. Her fingers twist together in her lap as she watches us tying shoelaces and throwing on jackets. "Be careful," she whispers. "This guy…he's not right in the head. Who knows what he might be capable of?"

"Don't worry," Elijah says, resting his hand on her thigh and squeezing. "These guys have dealt with a whole lot worse and lived to tell the tale."

"We'll be fine," I say, crossing the room and dropping down on one knee to kiss her. Even after everything, I don't think she realizes just how much she means to us or how much we will fight to keep her safe. There is no way one psycho fuck is going to interrupt our future happiness.

With a soft kiss to her lips, I stand and give Elijah and Ben a look that conveys that they're responsible for looking after her while we're away, and for the first time, it crosses my mind that this is such a major benefit of a poly relationship. There is never going to be a time when I need to leave Luna alone. With seven of us, she's always going to have someone close who she can rely on.

Once we're out of the suite, the conversation about what to do next starts in earnest. "What did Angelica say exactly?" I ask Connor.

"That Marcus had packed up his bags and left without a backward glance."

"We need to get to the airport."

"You think that's where he's headed?"

"Well, what other option does he have? He doesn't know England. He's not a native here. He won't know where to go to hide, and he'll be worried about the police here arresting him. If he gets back to the U.S., things will get a lot more complicated for the police to deal with. The incidents took place in multiple jurisdictions. It'll be a mess."

"Okay, you guys head to the airport. Me and Jax are going to the hotel where they were staying to see if we can find anything."

We separate into two groups, taking two separate taxis. The main international airport is Heathrow, so that's where we head to. Mo calls Angelica on the way, asking for Marcus's home address. We scan the departing flight lists for possible flights he might be taking and instruct the driver to take us to the appropriate terminal.

"This is such a long shot," Hudson says.

"Maybe," I say, "But we don't really have any other choice than to pursue the most likely angle.

"You know the airport is huge," Mo says. "It will be

like finding a needle in a haystack."

"And he could have gone through security already," I remind them. "If he's passed through to the departure lounges, we're not going to have a chance of apprehending him."

"So, let's pray that he hasn't."

"Well, the next flight he can take isn't for four hours. He won't be able to check in for a while. We might have time to catch him before he does," Hudson says.

We're halfway to the airport when Connor calls. "I've spoken to the concierge," he says. "Marcus ordered a cab an hour and a half ago to take him to Heathrow. They don't know which flight he's taking, but you're heading in the right direction."

I confirm the terminal with Connor, and he agrees to leave with Jax immediately in case we need backup.

"What are we doing when we get there? Making a citizen's arrest?"

"Hell, yeah," I say.

"This guy is going to make a scene," Mo says. "He's going to use every trick in the book."

"Well, it just so happens that I have a trick of my own up my sleeve."

"Oh yeah? And what is that?" Mo and Hudson stare at me with interest.

"This." I pull out my security ID, which is tucked into a black leather sleeve with a white emblem on the inside.

"Nice wallet," Hudson says. "You enjoy playing police dress-up?"

"I enjoy being able to flash my ID and for people to assume that I'm official," I say. "If we need to, just shout FBI, and I'll flash this. Literally, no one is going to intervene."

"It might just work," Mo says, "And I guess, as it's our

only option, we better hope that it does!"

Hudson huffs, his hands clenching into fists in his lap. "This is all a fucking joke. We're running around like headless chickens to find a pathetic asshole who has a crush on a superstar and not enough balls to ask her out like a normal human being and to add insult to injury, we're talking about role-play. I mean, for fuck's sake. I don't feel like this should be my life."

"Don't forget that you're in a relationship with one girl and six dudes," I say.

The cab driver clears his throat, and Mo starts to chuckle. "Maybe you need to choose your words more carefully," he whispers. "We don't want this man veering off the road out of shock."

The rest of the journey continues in the same vein, and by the time we pull into the drop-off area of the airport, we're all wound up and ready for action. "We should split up," Mo says. "Keep your phones on and call if you make a sighting."

"Don't tackle this guy alone. We get one shot at this. We don't want to fuck it up."

"He's built like a twig. My mom could take him," I tell Hudson, but I know where he's coming from. We have one chance to make sure that this guy is locked up and Luna is safe. None of us want to be the one who risks it.

With my phone clutched in my hand, I jog down to the far end of the terminal. Mo takes the center doors and Hudson heads to the other end. As soon as I'm in the building, I'm scanning each and every person, looking for Marcus's hunched shoulders and straight, mid-length hair. I pay particular attention to the banks of seats, as he will most likely be waiting to check in. There are shops along the perimeter, and I take a moment outside each to crane my head and look at all the browsing customers. Where the fuck is this guy?

My phone begins to vibrate in my hand, and Mo's name flashes across the screen. "He's here. Look for the sign for Departure Gate, and you'll spot him."

Already breaking into a jog, I search frantically for the sign Mo referred to. "Is he going through?"

"No," Mo says. "He's sitting with his luggage. Waiting like we thought he'd be."

"Stay back," I say. "Don't let him see you."

"I'm watching from a safe distance," Mo says. "I know I wasn't a soldier like the rest of you guys, but I'm not an idiot."

"I can see you. Call Hudson," I say.

Mo begins to tap away on his phone as I jog around a large family, all dragging extra huge suitcases. I catch the tail end of Mo telling Hudson where Marcus is, and I'm already scanning to find him among all the tourists.

"Can you see him?" Mo says, his arm pointing further than the bank of chairs I'm looking at. When I raise my line of sight, I spot him immediately.

"Fucker," I mutter under my breath, and Mo places a hand on my arm as I go to stride forward.

"Just remember the point of this is getting Marcus out of this airport."

"I know," I say. "I just really want to kick the shit out of him before we hand him over. We're not going to get another chance."

"The man is disturbed," Mo says. "I know you're angry because I am too. I hate what he's done to our girl, but there is obviously something very mentally wrong with him. No sane man goes around stealing and slashing up people's underwear or lacing their water with chemicals."

Hearing Mo's point isn't easy. I'm raging, wanting to tear this man's arms off for scaring Luna and separate his head from his body for hurting her. But that isn't going to help anything. Getting him off the streets is what we need to do.

"I've called Connor to tell him we've found him," Hudson says as he comes to a standstill to the right of Mo. "He said there's a warrant out for Marcus's arrest. We need to find a cop and notify them."

"No way. I want the pleasure of dealing with this asshole myself."

"And what are we going to do? Call a fucking Uber to deliver him to the police station?"

"Look, there's some armed police over there." Mo points to where two armed officers are patrolling, their huge weapons in their hand but pointed safely at the ground. "Asher, you go. If they see me running toward them, I'm likely to get a bullet through my head. Hudson, let's go and grab Marcus. I'm ready to get my arm around this asshole's neck and squeeze until his eyes bulge."

"I'm ready to make him squeal like a pig, but we need to act with reasonable force."

I'm off before they can say anything else, jogging toward the cops, my eyes on Marcus in case he makes a move.

"Officer," I say.

Both cops pause and turn, their hands gripping their weapons. "There is a man in this terminal who has a warrant out for his arrest. He's over there." I point to Marcus, who's currently rooting around in his bag for something, completely unaware of what's going on. "He's responsible for stalking the singer, Luna Evans. I'm one of her bodyguards. I've come here to prevent him from getting on a plane and escaping justice." I hold out my ID card for Steel 7 Security.

"What's his name?" the cop nearest me asks, eyeing me suspiciously. I don't blame him. I'm not dressed like a security guard. My clothes are crumpled from lying scrunched on Luna's carpet. My hair hasn't been brushed, and I have more than a little stubble on my cheeks.

"Marcus Johnson."

The cop begins to speak on his radio, asking for verification of the warrant. When it comes through, he nods at me. "Stay back," he says. "I'm going to call for backup." As the cop radios his colleagues, Marcus begins to glance around. Hudson and Mo have been careful, though. They remain out of sight until they're on top of him, Hudson grabbing him in a headlock that squashes his throat so hard that his attempt to scream ends up a pathetic wheeze.

"My team have got him," I say, just as backup arrives. From then, things move fast. Hudson hauls Marcus toward the cops, getting a few hard digs into his ribs as on the way. Mo's there too, kicking Marcus sharply in the knee when he struggles by flailing his legs.

The cops have Marcus in handcuffs so quickly, confirming his identity with his passport that Mo hands over.

The satisfaction is immense, particularly because Marcus' pathetic attempts at struggle disappear at the sight of so many cops in bulletproof vests holding rifles. Not such a big man now.

Connor and Jax make it just in time to see Marcus being led away to a waiting car. When we're reunited, there is back-slapping and bro hugs as we deal with the relief that it's all over and Luna is safe.

After, when the jubilation has settled, Connor sighs. "You know, while she's in the limelight, there will be others."

"But she'll have us to deal with it," I remind him. "There will never be a time when at least one of us won't be there to protect our girl."

Later, when we've made our way back to the hotel, we find Luna resting safely between Elijah and Ben. With her hair spread across the pillow, she looks so perfect. We decide not to wake them, even though all of us want to get close to our girl. There's no rush now. Just a long future together, and many more nights to look forward to as we walk together as a family.

This relationship might have started in an unconventional way. A scribbled sketch under the Athens sunshine was the catalyst to bring us all together. It might be unconventional in its form too; seven men and one woman isn't the most obvious relationship construction.

But for the first time in a long time, I feel at peace.

Before I leave the room, I search around in my pocket for the gift I bought Luna on the way back. It's a pretty gold necklace with a crescent moon charm. I want her to always remember this day for something positive. And for every day that follows to eclipse the next in perfection.

EPILOGUE

LUNA

"So tell me again what they're going to expect from us?" Connor says, frowning as he pours me a huge glass of milk. I swear, these guys think I'm growing a football team in my uterus, not one single tiny baby girl.

"They want to follow us around, film our day-to-day lives. It'll kind of be like a reality show that has lots of planning beforehand. Obviously, Blueday wants to ensure that everything that gets aired paints us in a favorable light." I take a sip of the cool milk, then reach for the cookie jar. Before I can overstretch, Jax is pushing it across the table toward me.

Not for the first time, I'm thankful that there's no one breathing down my neck about staying in shape and living off avocados and grilled chicken. If anything, my men are happy to see me putting some meat on my bones. They think about my health first, then the health of the baby. My image comes way down the line, which is fine. Every picture of me that gets officially published is airbrushed into a work of fiction anyway.

And they all like me a little juicier than I used to be.

"And you say that there's already been a show like this?"

"Yeah. The production company for ours is the same one that filmed that show about the McGreggors. Don't you remember it? Laura and her harem of ten men? It was called McGreggors Uncovered."

"I never saw that show," Mo says, slumping back in his chair.

"We were probably still overseas when it aired." Hudson rubs his hand over his heart, and I know immediately he's thinking about his brother. Every time he does it, I get a pang for Jake too. When this pregnancy is over, I'm going to get a tattoo tribute to my brother with angel wings too.

"Well, I can see if it's available to stream. I think it would be good for you to watch it and make sure it's something you are comfortable with doing."

"None of us is that comfortable with our lives being exposed for other people's entertainment," Elijah says. "But we understand the benefit to our family, so we'll do it."

I sigh, dunking my cookie into the creamy milk and taking a bite. Damn, it's good to eat comfort food. "I'm sick of seeing my name associated with Marcus's trial. There is too much speculation about our relationship. I just really want to be able to control the narrative. I hate that we even have to consider this shit, but without the positive publicity, I might as well just give up."

"And that's exactly what we don't want to happen," Asher says, reaching across the table to take my free hand. "Singing is important to you. It makes you happy. And just because you've shacked up with seven men and found yourself in the family way doesn't mean you shouldn't be able to carry on doing something you love."

"It's not going to be forever," Ben muses. "It'll just be for one season, right? To change perceptions."

"Exactly," I say. "Just one season. But only if you guys are one hundred percent on board. I love singing, but I love you guys and our future daughter more."

As I say it, I rest my hand protectively over my belly. We decided to find out what we were having so I could better mentally prepare for it. I'd already had enough surprises, and it feels good to be able to plan for her.

My brother's girlfriend Sandy's having a baby girl too, so I'm sure they'll be the best of cousin friends. It couldn't have worked out more perfectly.

"Blueday has sent a list of ideas for what the production company can film." Pulling the folded paper from my pocket, I smooth it out on the table and scan over it. "House hunting, shopping for the crib, a night out…" I pause for a moment and shake my head. "Can you believe they have the audacity to put in brackets that I can only be seen drinking water?"

"I guess they think a mocktail could look like you're pregnant and drinking alcohol," Jax says.

Making a growling sound, I poke the list. "They literally think I can't tie my own shoelaces."

"Don't stress the small stuff," Mo says, rubbing my back. "What else is on the list?"

"A day at the spa with Sandy."

"Do you think she'll go for that?" Connor asks.

"I have absolutely no idea. How about this one? Movie night at home."

"What? They want to film us watching TV?"

I snort, reaching for another cookie. "I guess they think they'll catch some foot rubs and cuddling. Maybe a popcorn fight. We'll have to think of ways of making our ordinary life more interesting."

"Our ordinary life rocks," Jax says. "Don't you worry. I'll make everyone laugh, and it'll be fine."

"Better warn the production company to bring a wide-lens camera," Asher says. "To capture all of Jax's huge head."

There's some good-natured jostling, and while Connor is telling them to grow up, I fold the paper and put it back in my pocket because Jax is right. It doesn't matter what the production company films, it'll be fine because we're awesome together. If they capture nothing but our real relationship, it'll do exactly what we need it to do: show the world that we're normal, despite our unconventional relationship.

"Anyway," I say, trying to interrupt their shenanigans. "I'm meeting up with the Reverse Harem Ladies Club. It's my first time."

"Well, you must be way more qualified than any of the others," Connor laughs. "Aren't they all in smaller groups?"

"It's not the number of men that counts," I say, raising my eyebrows. "It's what they do that counts."

"Then you're definitely the queen of that club." Hudson comes up behind me and wraps his arms around my waist, pressing warm kisses to my neck.

I put my hand up quickly. "Don't start with all of that," I say. "I just spent half an hour washing off the mess you made of me this morning. I don't have time to do it all over again."

"You love our mess," Jax says.

"That is absolutely not the point," I say. "I do not want to be late."

I leave my men at home and am accompanied to the cute café where I'm meeting up with Sandy and her friends by Mr. Wright and three of his team. Since the stalker was captured, Blueday has decreased the number of bodyguards who have to follow me around, but four still draw so much attention. I'm looking forward to a time when maybe one or two will be enough. Mr. Wright actually apologized for not taking Marcus more seriously. Over time, they've actually become more like friends, which is just how it should be. I guess the fact that I have seven huge boyfriends is enough to make them buck up their ideas up too.

The café is as cute as I imagined and I'm the last to arrive, despite aiming to be early.

I'm used to heads turning whenever I go anywhere so it's no surprise to see people staring. I guess my look is so distinctive that even when I'm wearing sunglasses, it's easy to make me out. Thankfully no one asks for an autograph or a selfie, and I make it to the last vacant seat at the table.

"Luna," Sandy says, standing to hug me. "I'm so happy that you made it."

"I've been looking forward to this so much," I say. "It's the only normal thing in my calendar right now."

"Normal?" one of the women at the table snorts. The rest laugh, but it's not in a mocking way. More self-deprecating. "It's been a long time since anyone called us that." She holds out her hand. "I'm Connie, by the way."

"Nice to meet you." The rest of the women introduce themselves. There's Natalie, who's in a harem with three men, Connie, who has four firemen husbands, Melanie, who's shacked up with five cowboys, and Sandy, who's bagged six men. Hudson was right. I am the queen of this club.

"So you hit the jackpot," Natalie says, tucking her blonde bob behind her ears as though she's readying herself to hear some major gossip. "Seven men." Shaking her head, she makes a whistling noise, which I'm not sure is appreciative or overwhelmed.

STEEL 7

"Seven," I say proudly.

"How do you do seven?" Melanie says. "Five is mind-blowing. Like, seriously. I'm so tired right now. They're just on me all the time. A girl needs some personal space sometimes."

"You're only feeling like that because you have a new baby," Connie says knowingly. "Once you're past this stage and feel a little more like yourself, you'll be back to loving all the attention."

"I just feel like there is someone permanently interested in my boobs. They're just always out. I'm like a cow." She hangs her head mournfully, and we all burst out laughing.

"And what about you, Sandy?" Connie says. "How are you getting on being pregnant?"

"The pregnancy has just made me even hornier," Sandy says. "I think they're getting tired of me."

I put my hand up to halt her. "I love you, Sandy, but promise me you won't start talking about Tyler and sex. I just can't deal with hearing about my brother that way."

"I promise," she snorts.

"I'm further ahead than all of you in this," Natalie says, "And I can confirm that it only gets better with time. Things settle down. You get used to each other's needs and wants. You find ways to compromise so that everyone is happy. For example, Miller likes his own space in bed, so we've bought him a separate bed in the same room. Now I get to cuddle up with Max and Mason every night, and Miller gets to have a quality sleep. We still have the intimacy of all being together. You just have to give it time and see how it works. Be adaptable."

"Now, that's a great idea," Connie says. "We invested in this huge bed, but it's not always that comfortable to sleep together all the time. I only have space for two of them to be next to me. It would probably be better if they just rotated into the bed for sleep time. The sexy times are always all of us."

"Really?" I ask. "We tend to mix that up too. I don't think I could always handle them all together. It's nice sometimes, but I guess I'd miss the intimacy of being with just one man."

At that moment, the waitress comes over to present me with a menu. "I miss the intimacy of one man too," she says.

The other girls laugh. "You found your harem yet, Kyla?"

"Nope," she says, sticking her bottom lip out like a disappointed toddler, "But I've got a new job in this tattoo place around the corner. It's owned by eight of the sexiest men you have ever seen. There's more ink on them than the *New York Times*."

"Ooooo," Natalie says, her eyes widening at the news. "That sounds like potential."

"Eight?" Kyla snorts. "I mean, I'm a lot of woman but not enough for eight to share."

"Seven are sharing me just fine," I say proudly.

Kyla looks at me for the first time, and her eyes widen. "Luna Evans? What the fuck?" Her hand flies to her mouth. "Sorry for the cursing. I just never thought I'd see you in this place."

"She's the latest recruit to our very exclusive club," Connie says proudly. "We're just waiting for you to find your harem."

"Just one man would do me fine," Kyla says. "The problem is that finding even one is more taxing than I can bear."

"Elijah has two great brothers," I say. When Kyla's eyes widen like a rabbit's in headlights I smile. "Aim high. Think positive. Manifest your ideal life."

"Is that what you did?" Kyla asks.

"I guess I did," I say, thinking back over everything that has happened in the last few years.

When I was singing on the street corner, I'd envision myself on a stage in front of thousands of people. At the time, I thought it was helping me to look and sound more professional, but maybe it was more than that. When I found out about Tyler's polyamorous relationship with Sandy and his friends, I started to wonder what it would be like to be at the center of so many men. Over time, the men went from faceless to having the faces of the men hired to protect me. And look what happened.

I guess I believe that if you think positively, you take the opportunities that life presents. And maybe you can draw into your life the things that start off as just hopes and dreams.

Pressing my hand to my belly, I think about my child. How many years have I thought about having a family of my own? And now it's becoming a reality.

Mom's out of rehab and sticking to her plan for the time being. Tyler is happily settled with a family who I love. And my own home is filled with men who adore and treasure me.

Life couldn't be better.

"I'll take a chocolate muffin and a chamomile tea," I tell Kyla. "And the name of that tattoo place you work at. I've been meaning to get some ink."

I'll take a leaf out of Hudson's book and carry the name of my brother on my body so that he's always with me.

And when the baby's born, I'll name her Jacqueline so that he's with her always too.

It's time to be thankful for everything I have and look forward to a bright and positive future.

"The world is yours for the taking," I tell Kyla as she notes down my order in her notebook.

My seven men have shown me that it really is.

STEEL 7

ABOUT THE AUTHOR

Stephanie Brother writes scintillating stories with bad boys and step-siblings as their main romantic focus. She's always been curious about the forbidden, and this is her way of exploring such complex relationships that threaten to keep her couples apart. As she writes her way to her dream job, Ms. Brother hopes that her readers will enjoy the full emotional and romantic experience as much as she's enjoyed writing them.